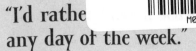

"I'd rathe...
any day of the week."

Did Mark mean her? Was he...flirting?

Laura glanced at the bottle in his hand, hesitating. What would one more round really hurt, anyway? Mark seemed to sense her indecision.

He waggled the beer in front of her. "Come on. How miserable are you, really? Just two beers miserable? Because that's hardly miserable at all."

She had to laugh at that. She was far more than two beers miserable.

"Fine," she said and grabbed the bottle from his hand. "You win."

He chuckled and took another swig of his beer as she started on hers. She'd just stay for one more.

Besides...what was the worst that could happen?

Dear Reader,

I'm excited to share with you my new book, *Island of Second Chances*, a story about how sometimes we have to lose what we hold most dear before we find out what's most important to us.

After an ill-conceived affair with her married coworker, Laura Kelly winds up pregnant. Her lover abandons her, however, and she's left to face the pregnancy all alone, but then a tragic miscarriage sends her into a deep depression. Devastated by the loss, she drops out of her high-profile career and decides to take an extended vacation on St. Anthony's island, where she battles her own guilt and sense of loss.

Mark Tanner used to work building Tanner ships, but after being betrayed by his brother, he moves to the fictional Caribbean island of St. Anthony's determined to build a sailboat fast enough to win the local race. He hopes the prize money will help finance a trip around the world so he can heal from a bitter divorce and the tragic death of his son.

Tanner is skeptical of new neighbor Laura at first, but warms to her when he realizes she's struggling with grief just as he is. He teaches her how to use her hands and quiet her mind, and maybe how to heal her heart. Just when they discover that they might be able to heal each other's guilt, fate intervenes as a looming hurricane threatens the coast and everyone on the island.

I loved the idea of a couple at odds coming together and bonding from their loss. I hope you'll enjoy this book about how love and losses can be intertwined, but ultimately there's no more powerful way to heal than through love.

All my best,

Cara

CARA LOCKWOOD

Island of Second Chances

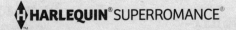
HARLEQUIN® SUPERROMANCE®

Recycling programs
for this product may
not exist in your area.

ISBN-13: 978-1-335-44913-9

Island of Second Chances

Printed in U.S.A.

Cara Lockwood is the *USA TODAY* bestselling author of more than seventeen books, including *I Do (But I Don't)*, which was made into a Lifetime Original movie. She's written the Bard Academy series for young adults and has had her work translated into several languages around the world. Born and raised in Dallas, Cara now lives near Chicago with her two wonderful daughters. Find out more about her at caralockwood.com, friend her on Facebook, Facebook.com/authorcaralockwood, or follow her on Twitter, @caralockwood.

Books by Cara Lockwood

HARLEQUIN SUPERROMANCE

Shelter in the Tropics
The Big Break
Her Hawaiian Homecoming

COSMOPOLITAN RED-HOT READS FROM HARLEQUIN

Boys and Toys
Texting Under the Influence

Dedicated to my love, P.J. Benoit.

CHAPTER ONE

BUZZZZZZT. BUZZZZZZT.

It seemed Laura Kelly had only had her eyes closed for a minute, and suddenly, the air was full of the sound of some ruckus. A chain saw? A swarm of killer bees? What the hell was that?

She sat up in bed, her mouth tasting sour, as she glanced around the unfamiliar bedroom, bewildered. Then, she remembered. St. Anthony's Island. Her escape route. She looked down and saw she wore the same jean shorts and white T-shirt she'd worn through three time zones yesterday to get here. She'd had three flight delays and a taxi cab driver who'd gotten lost twice before she finally reached the island at 3:00 a.m.

There it was again. The horrendous sound. She clearly hadn't dreamed it. Yawning, she reached for her phone, but it was dead. She'd forgotten to plug it in. The little clock on the bedside table blinked 12:00. It had to be early in the morning, though the sun trickled in through the vertical blinds near her kitchenette.

She got up, groggy, and wandered to the patio doors. Her rented condo was on the second story, at the end of the row. She saw that she had two neighbors to her left and three below her, and that was it.

She'd known from the listing that the complex was remote, the way she wanted it, but now, standing on her balcony, looking out at the blue-green water, she realized her little building was the only one for seemingly miles. Pristine beach spread out in both directions, not a single towel or umbrella in sight, just brilliant white sand under a blazing sun.

The loud buzzing caught her attention once more, and she glanced down to find its source: a buzz saw in the hands of a man attacking a piece of wood with a steely determination.

He was shirtless, his back to her, dark hair cut short, and he was wearing cutoff camo shorts and no shoes. The cut muscles of his shoulder and back worked steadily, sweat glistening on them. He was cutting the plank literally steps from the complex.

Beyond that was a sailboat sitting on the beach. It looked to be old, or at least in desperate need of repair. It sat on a scaffold, lacking a working sail and looking worse for the wear on the bottom. Also, most of the deck was missing.

She rubbed her face and tried to yell down at

the man, but the volume of the buzz saw made that impossible.

What was so important that the man needed to saw this early? Noah's ark? She decided she'd have to go tell him kindly to knock it off. Until nine, at least.

She stabbed her feet into flip-flops, found her way to the condo's front door and went down the open stairway to the parking lot. Unsure of the fastest route, she wandered to the side and around the back until she found an opening to the beach and the infernal noise. She found the man, bare back and all, hunched over a solid plank of wood, saw at the ready.

Sawdust flew all over his stone patio and what looked to be a makeshift workshop of sorts—an oversize storage shed with shelves for tools. Beyond, the sailboat in need of TLC sat on its stand.

She wondered how he'd managed to get the condo board to sign off on this. The boards she knew in San Francisco would never allow such a workspace in the condo common area, which she assumed the beach had to be.

Laura shook her head at the whole situation.

The man was taller than he looked from above, and she only barely registered the knot of muscles in his shoulders and biceps as he worked to steady the saw. All she could think about was the horrible noise bouncing through her ears and ricocheting through her skull. What kind of man went on vacation in the Caribbean just to literally saw wood? She glanced at him, and then beyond him, to the rusted-out bow of the boat on risers near the beach.

"Excuse me," she shouted, now that she was just feet from the man. *"Excuse me!"*

The noise was far too loud for him to hear, even though she was less than two feet from him. Laura, losing her patience, reached up and tapped the man hard on his bare shoulder.

The man instantly shut off the saw and glared at her over his shoulder, his eyes barely visible through the work goggles he wore. Seeing her, he put down the saw and raised the goggles, revealing brown eyes that almost looked amber in the morning sunlight. He pushed the goggles up to his short brown hair and studied her.

He had a rugged face, etched a little by the weather, but with that almost ageless quality only middle-aged men have. He could be thirty-five or forty-five. He stayed in shape, clear from the cut of his bare chest. He wasn't sporting six-pack abs, but his stomach was flat and lean.

Laura realized with a shock that the last time she'd seen a man wearing this little clothing, it had been Dean. In a hotel room.

She shook the thought from her mind and

tried to focus on the man's face, trying not to look at the miles of very tanned and very bare skin before her. He was annoyed, that much was clear by the thin slash of his mouth, and the way his brow furrowed.

"Excuse me," Laura began, trying to be polite. "Hi. My name is Laura and I'm staying up there in 2-C, and it's so early, so could you keep it down?"

A smile quirked the corner of his mouth. "Early?"

"Yes, and I've been traveling and could you keep it down…until nine?"

"Well." He looked at his watch. "Considering it's *eleven thirty*, that might be hard." He flashed a winning smile.

Eleven thirty? It was that late? Laura felt a blush creep up her neck.

"Oh, well… I…" But she was so sure it was so early. Her body screamed that it was six in the morning but the sun in the sky told her it was later. She tried to calculate the time zone changes but her brain felt too muddled for the task.

"You're the tourist." The man cocked his head to one side, as if she might be a new exhibit at a museum.

"Well, yes, and—"

"Look, I'm sorry this is loud, but it's the middle of the day. Next time, maybe you should check the time before you..." He glanced down at her ruffled hair and slept-in clothes. His face showed his disapproval. "Get out of bed."

Now, Laura felt her temper flare and she'd all but forgotten her mistake about the time.

"Could you just please try to keep it down? There are such things as city noise ordinances."

The man grinned then, a bit of sweat dropping down his squared-off, tanned face. "City ordinance? Just where are you from?"

"San Francisco."

He studied her with amused, dark eyes. "Well, that explains it."

"What do you mean by that?" Now, Laura felt the anger bubble up in her, hot and fluid. Was he calling her a liberal hippie? An alfalfa-sprout-granola-eating leftist? She'd heard all the insults, mostly from her right-leaning family who lived in downstate Illinois. She was proudly *moderate independent*, thank you very much.

He just shook his head, and the sun glinted off tiny slivers of silver running through his hair, just the right amount of middle-aged gray. Laura wanted to tell him he was clearly old enough to know better. Or old enough to show a little more politeness to strangers.

He chuckled to himself then, as if he'd read

her mind. Nothing about this was funny, so why was he laughing? She felt off balance with this man. Like somehow this entire conversation was one of his inside jokes.

"St. Anthony's doesn't have ordinances like that," he informed her, crossing his thick arms across his chest. "So, you're out of luck."

"What about the other neighbors? This noise pollution is—"

"Noise *pollution*?" The man put his head back and laughed.

"What's your name?" She'd have to report him. To someone. Somewhere.

"Mark."

"Mark what?"

"Tanner." He grinned. "And you are?"

"Laura Kelly." She raised her chin in defiance. She didn't care if he knew who she was. She'd be filing a complaint...with someone, somewhere.

"Well, Ms. Kelly, are you going to call the police? You should know the local chief is a buddy of mine."

This wasn't going well. Not well at all.

"What about the neighbors?"

Mark sighed and shook his head, studying her. "Three of the six condos are empty right now. Hurricane season coming and all. There's you, me and Fred, who's eighty-three and gets up at six to take his daily walk on the beach, so I cleared it with him to work here."

"You didn't clear it with me."

He took her in, glancing at her flip-flops, to her jean shorts and her T-shirt all the way to the top of her head. "No, I didn't, sweetheart. But, seeing as you're just passing through, I don't see a reason."

Sweetheart? She wasn't his *sweetheart.* Now, that really irked.

"I cleared it with the owners of your condo." Mark shook a bit of sawdust from his hair, clearly unconcerned. "So if you've got a problem with the noise, I suggest you take it up with them. They should've warned you in the rental agreement there'd be...what did you call it? Noise trash?"

"Noise pollution."

He chuckled once more, showing even white teeth. "Right. That." He shook his head.

"I'll be talking to the condo board then."

Mark just grinned. "Considering I own the entire first floor, I'm actually the president of the board."

That revelation hit her like a ton of bricks. "You own..." She glanced down the way at the entire first floor. Well, that's how he managed to clear putting a big workshop on the beach in front of the first floor then. He owned it. She couldn't imagine how much that cost, but knew it was a lot.

"I…" Laura had nothing more to say to that. He had the police in his pocket and he had a controlling share of the condo building, so complaining to the board would do no good. Hell, he *was* the board, sounded like.

Then he turned his back on her, fired up his saw again and began work once more.

Conversation done, apparently. At least, he thought so. She turned on her heel, fuming. He might think this was done, but, Laura vowed, this little disagreement was far, far from over. She'd been through hell and back, and she wasn't about to let this man derail her. She was here on this island for a reason—to forget Dean, to find some way to heal—and she wasn't going to let a rude neighbor get in the way of that. This wasn't done. Not by a long shot.

CHAPTER TWO

MARK TANNER TURNED and watched the feisty woman with the disheveled bob bounce out of his view. The woman needed some sunlight. Her bright white legs looked like neon billboards for the mainland as they furiously walked away from him.

But, he had to admit, her curves weren't bad, and if you went for bossy types, she'd probably be a feisty go-getter in bed. She was just his type: small, tight and a handful. He shook his head, figuring that wherever she'd come from, she was used to getting her way.

But, Mark didn't spook. She could rail against him all he wanted, but he had to finish this boat. It was the middle of the day, after all, and he had no patience for tourists who wanted to get their beauty rest at *nearly noon.*

He glanced back at the rusted-out old hunk of a boat that once belonged to his father. He was behind schedule in fixing her up. That wouldn't do. This project was too important. He glanced at the small set of bronzed baby shoes that Timothy once wore that hung on a string above his worktable. Beneath them, he'd tacked up a photo of his boy as a baby, grinning a gummy grin from ear to ear.

He glanced out to the beach beyond. He could almost see his little boy running there, waddling into the water with his chubby, toddler hands outstretched for some shell. When he picked it up, he'd beam with triumph and call for his father's approval.

With a sickening dread, Mark realized he couldn't remember what his boy sounded like. His voice had been sweet and high, but now, in his memory, the voice had faded. The picture of his son stood mute in his brain, like some old-fashioned silent picture reel.

No. Couldn't be. Mark squeezed his eyes shut. He would not let the memory of his boy fade. He worked harder to remember his sweet, high-pitched voice but couldn't bring to mind the exact sound.

He stopped and pulled out his phone. He had a video of his boy there. He pulled it up and set the video to full-screen and saw his boy running through the sand in the wobbly video he'd taken on his phone.

"Daddy! Look!" Timothy cried as he pointed to a starfish that had washed up on the shore.

It was a treasured find. "A star, Daddy! It's a star!"

The sweet voice washed over Mark's ears and he felt a brief peace before the sadness sank in. He'd never hear that voice in life again. He'd never get to hear what Timothy would've sounded like as he grew up, as his voice changed and matured. He put the cell phone back into his pocket, feeling the heavy weight of sadness cling to him once more. But he couldn't let grief stop him. He needed to focus on that emotion and turn it into something that mattered.

He returned his attention to the wooden planks before him. That's why he needed to restore this boat. That's why he couldn't stop working. Not until it was finished and not until it sailed in the warm, blue-green sea.

He cut the power on the saw to double-check the board he'd just cut. He focused again on the hull of the boat he would christen *Timothy* after the little boy who'd once been the light of his life. Before his life had been taken, a bright little candle blown out far too soon.

"Working hard, I see."

Mark froze, recognizing the voice behind him that he'd know anywhere—his older brother, Edward. He felt anger, hot and thick, well up in his belly. Edward, the brother who betrayed him. Edward, his enemy.

Mark slowly put down the buzz saw. Then he flicked up his safety goggles and turned to face his brother. Just two years older, he carried the same dark eyes as Mark, the same lopsided smile, but that's where the similarities ended. Mark was a man of his word. Edward, he knew, was a liar.

"What are you doing here, Edward?"

His brother shrugged one shoulder. "I wanted to see how you were doing."

"Don't bullshit me." *If you cared about how I was doing, you would've never slept with my wife.* Ex-wife now, technically. Wife then, though.

"Language, kid. What would Mom say?" Edward wore expensive loafers and designer sunglasses that caught the Caribbean sun, blinding Mark for a second.

"If she were still alive, she'd be too busy kicking your ass to care."

Edward just shook his head. "For what?"

For screwing my wife. For stealing her away from me. For...being the worst brother on earth at the very time I needed you most.

"For stealing the family company, for starters." Edward and Mark had grown the family boat-building business into an empire, until Edward had the board vote Mark out in a hostile takeover last year, six months after Timothy died.

"I told you to take some time off after…" He swallowed. "Timothy. You needed it, and you didn't listen to me, and so, yes, for the company's sake *and* yours, I forced you out."

Mark nearly choked on a dark laugh. He loved how his brother always managed to twist everything around, make his underhanded dealings sound like the right thing to do. "Don't pretend this is about the company or me. It's about your greed. You've always been greedy. Ever since we were kids and you ate my Halloween candy while I slept. Some things never change."

"You're still on me about Halloween? I was eight. You were six. We were *kids*."

Mark shrugged. "The story just seems relevant, considering you always wanted what I had."

Edward exhaled. "Look, I know you're pissed at me, but—"

"Pissed at you?" He took off his work gloves in jagged, angry movements and tossed them on his workbench. "I'm not pissed at you. I can't stand to look at you. You screwed me out of my business *and* you screwed my wife."

"She's your ex-wife now." Edward sounded stoic, even steely. Not even an inkling of regret. None. "And you know why she made that choice. After what you did to her."

Mark felt a pang of guilt. He knew what he did, and he knew why he did it. *I never meant her any harm, but something had to be done.*

"You know why I did that. And deflecting this back to me is still not an apology. For God's sake. She's pregnant with your baby."

Edward visibly flinched.

"Didn't think I knew?" Mark challenged him. "Did you forget how small this island is? How people talk?"

"I..." Now Edward was on his heels. "I was going to tell you."

"Uh-huh. Sure you were." Mark ground his teeth together. His heart pounded in his chest and he felt hot and cold all over. Mark hated the anger that bubbled up inside him, that threatened to take over, that bleached the already bright sand at his feet a starker white. He wanted to punch his older brother in the face, craved to see the shock and pain flood his features. He wanted to yell until his voice gave out, but he also knew there'd be no point. Edward never listened.

Edward let out a long, weary-sounding sigh. Since when did *he* get to sound exasperated? He wasn't the one betrayed by the only family he had left.

"I came with a peace offering," Edward said, holding up a manila folder. "It's a contract. You should come back to work with Tanner Boating." He nodded at Mark's husk of a boat in the sand. "This isn't good for you. For your head or your bank account. Restoring that old hunk of junk is a waste of time."

Just when Mark thought Edward couldn't tick him off any more, somehow his brother found a way to do it. He felt the fury grow hot inside him.

This was the boat that belonged to their father, and it wasn't much, but it was his. That's why it made it all the more important to restore it. For Timothy. And how dare Edward ask him back, as if he'd ever in a million years work under his brother?

"Not interested." Mark turned his back on his brother, signaling the conversation was over. It had to be over, before Mark really lost it and did punch his brother in the face. He might be friends with the St. Anthony's police chief, but he doubted that even he could worm his way out of an assault charge.

"Mark, look, bud, come on. Come back to work for me. You can help Tanner Boating build the fastest boat on the island. We're going to win the St. Anthony's Race again this year. We're going to break the island record."

Mark clenched his fist. "No, you're not. *I'm* going to win that race. And the prize money." A hundred thousand dollars.

"You don't have enough time to finish this, and you're just one person. Come on, come join our team."

"I'm never going to work for you," Mark ground out between clenched teeth. Why did Edward never realize when he stood on thin ice? "I'm going to build this ship. I'm going to win that prize money and I'm going to sail around the world. For Timothy. That's what I'm going to do."

He left out the part that he might not come back. Why go there? Edward wouldn't care anyway.

Edward just shook his head. "You can't do it by yourself."

"I'm not. I have friends." Mark thought about Dave and Garrett. They'd help him. They promised.

"Are you sure you can count on them?" Edward asked him, making Mark doubt himself for a second. Was that a threat? Had Edward somehow gotten to his friends? No. Dave would stay true. They'd known each other twenty years. When Mark and Elle had been married, Dave and his wife would do everything together with them. That kind of friendship didn't just disappear overnight, did it?

Edward dropped the manila folder down on the worktable. "I'm going to leave this in case you change your mind."

"I won't."

Edward clucked his tongue in disapproval and left. Mark's hands shook with anger as he clenched them into fists. He listened as his brother's steps faded away, and then he knocked the manila folder off the table, papers flying everywhere. The ocean breeze kicked up then, scattered them everywhere.

Mark knew his brother spoke some truth; he was just one person and he could only work so fast. The competition was in two months and he wasn't sure he had enough daylight between now and then to get it done. If he didn't, the *Timothy* would never even leave the beach.

Dave and Garrett would help him finish it. He texted the two of them, asking to meet this week. Plan, strategize and figure out how to make this boat faster than Edward's.

Taking the *Timothy* out to sea on an extended voyage was the only way Mark could think of to keep his boy's memory alive, to make sure he was not truly forgotten, even as his own memories grew dim. That's why it was more important than ever that he focus, that he work harder and longer and that he get this done.

LAURA GLARED OUT her balcony sliding glass door, doubting for a minute whether or not she should've even come to St. Anthony's. *Did I make a mistake?*

She thought about how she'd cashed in her 401(k). *It's done now*, she thought. She'd already be paying the penalty on the money, even if she put it all back tomorrow. Besides, any time she thought about packing up her things and heading back to San Francisco, she just got nauseous.

The entire town reminded her of Dean. She couldn't leave her apartment without being flooded with a hundred unwanted memories. The dark restaurant with the cozy table in the back where they'd met sometimes. The convenience store they'd ducked into when they'd been carrying on a torrid affair and worried about running into people they knew. Laura knew it was wrong. She did. But she'd also never intended for it to happen.

She and Dean had worked on a software launch together, heads bent together for hours over their desks, which sat across from one another in the open floor plan of the company. She'd liked Dean's outrageous, irrever-

ent humor, which always made her laugh. She'd
told herself that theirs was strictly a profes-
sional relationship, even though a part of her
had known the flirting wasn't just in her head.
Now she knew none of that was as harmless as
she'd thought.

She and Dean would go out to lunch, first
with a group of colleagues and then increas-
ingly one on one. Dean would share details
about his unhappy marriage and his aloof, un-
caring wife, and she would admit the loneliness
of being single and her fear that she'd remain
that way forever. She realized now how clichéd
all of it was, how wrong she'd been to let things
go so far with Dean. But she'd never meant for
it to get physical. She really hadn't.

Dean had joked that she was his work wife,
and she'd loved the title, because she loved how
in sync they were. It had felt like they shared
the same brain at times. He completed her sen-
tences in board meetings and she anticipated his
every work need. Then came the office holiday
party at an upscale San Francisco sushi restaurant, where he cornered her near the bathrooms.

"I've fallen in love with you," Dean had told
her and kissed her. She'd been shocked, and yet,
she tentatively had kissed him back, and in that
instant, everything changed.

After that, she became the star in her own

star-crossed lovers tale, fighting valiantly for true love despite all the many obstacles. She knew it was wrong to think so. She knew that, but sometimes love came in surprising ways, a powerful force she couldn't control.

Even now, even after everything Dean had done to betray her…to betray their love…she still felt the itch to contact him. She glanced at her phone, noticing, of course, the lack of new messages. Should she contact him? See how he was doing?

No! What was she thinking? Text Dean? Why should she care how he was? He didn't care about her. Dean had made that abundantly clear the last time she'd seen him.

The worst part was that she felt like the heart-ache, everything she'd lost, was a punishment from God. She'd done the wrong thing, and this pain was what she'd earned.

She lay down on the bed, feeling as if she'd never be whole again, wondering if she could ever heal.

AFTER STARING AT the ceiling for an hour, unable to fall back asleep, Laura decided she wasn't going to waste a beautiful day in the Caribbean and quickly donned her sturdy black one-piece suit and her newly purchased floppy straw hat.

After walking at least a mile to reach a spot

of desolate beach, she couldn't hear Mark's buzz saw anymore, thank goodness. Beside her sat a brand-new cooler she'd found in the condo that she'd filled with drinks and snacks. She'd wanted to get away, and get away she had. Not a single sail dotted the blue-green horizon as the sun blazed down, coating everything in a thick warmth. Down the beach, she saw a figure walking—a woman in a shawl?

Laura tilted her head back on her bamboo mat and let the sunlight warm her cheeks. She inhaled deeply the smell of the ocean breeze and listened to the gentle rustling of palm tree leaves near her. She could almost feel the beach healing her from the outside in. This was why she came. To get away from it all.

She imagined her problems existing far, far away, and now the only thing she'd have to worry about was when high tide might come and wash away her cooler. This is what she needed…the absence of stress, nothing here to remind her of Dean. Just the gentle roll of waves against the beach.

Then came a distant cry.

A seagull? she wondered. She propped herself up on her elbows and glanced down the beach. The sound came from the woman walking along the water. Laura realized now that the woman wasn't wearing a shawl at all. It was a baby sling. She held a baby, probably no older than three months, who was now wailing as the mom adjusted the baby in the fabric against her chest.

Laura felt her stomach tighten.

In her mind, she saw herself that morning she'd taken the pregnancy test. The positive filling her with both dread and excitement all at once. She was going to have Dean's baby.

Then, she remembered Dean's reaction. How he yelled, blamed her for the accident. Then she remembered the sudden cramping, the bright red blood. The trip to the emergency room in the ambulance as she miscarried.

Her sister had been there in the hospital when she woke up. Maddie told her she dodged a bullet, but it didn't feel like it. It felt like the bullet hit her right in the chest.

She felt like she couldn't breathe as she watched the mother and baby coming closer.

Anytime she saw a baby, she thought of her own, who would now never be born, the baby she'd carried inside her for a slight twelve weeks. How could something so small have changed her life forever? She knew it sounded irrational, but to her, the minute she'd found out she was pregnant, everything changed. She became a different woman, her life suddenly veering down a different path. With every baby she saw, she saw her own laughing back up at her.

I lost a baby. I lost my future. I'm thirty-five. I won't have another one. Hell, maybe my body doesn't even know how to make one the right way. The man I thought loved me didn't at all. Of course I'm not fine.

She wished her mother was still alive. She wanted to hug her, wanted to ask her what she should do now.

She couldn't look at a baby without feeling that profound sense of loss, because something deep inside her told her that she'd never be a mother now. She was thirty-five, and she'd had one chance at being a mom, and her body failed her.

She glanced at the happy mother, cooing to her baby. She wouldn't be able to stay here, watch this, see the life she would never have.

Laura knew she couldn't ask the woman to leave. It wouldn't be fair. It wasn't the baby's fault. Or the mother's.

In a rush, Laura packed up her things. She threw on her ankle-length cotton cover-up sundress and began walking. The buzz saw would be better than the baby crying. If she listened to the baby much longer, she knew she'd burst into tears.

After she'd walked a bit, she could hear the

buzz saw again. She gritted her teeth. If it wasn't one thing, it was another.

She thought about marching in there and giving Mark Tanner a piece of her mind, when she suddenly saw a gray tendril of smoke rising up from his workshop. An acrid, unmistakable smell filled the air.

Was that...a fire?

CHAPTER THREE

SOMETHING WAS BURNING. At first, Mark thought it might be just his imagination, just sawdust flying from his saw as he hacked into the planks before him. Then he thought it might be someone grilling, except the fire smelled decidedly closer. He cut the buzz saw and turned around to find that the manila folder his brother brought had landed near his gas generator, and somehow had managed to catch alight. Smoke poured from the folder and heavy bits of sawdust that coated his small workspace.

Mark spun around, looking for something to douse the fire. He tried to kick sand on the flames, but that only seemed to add more sawdust to the fire, fueling it, making the flames grow.

He rushed into his kitchen, looking for a towel or a blanket, anything he could use to suffocate the flames. But before he could, a blur in a dark cover-up rushed past him and dumped a cooler full of ice on the fire, as well as two cans of some soda, and the small flames went out in a sizzling hiss.

She also happened to douse his saw, too, which now had pieces of ice covering the blade. And the flying soda cans knocked over one of the boards on his sawhorse, which clunked against his nearby worktable and sent Timothy's bronze booties flying in the air. They landed with an awkward thump in the sand. The picture of his boy as a baby also came loose, fluttering down to the ground.

"Hey!" he cried, lunging at the photo and the bronze booties. If they were dented, so help him… "What are you doing?" He scooped up the small bronze shoes from the sand, clutching them protectively in his hands.

"*Helping* you," she said, putting a hand on her hip.

She wore a muumuu, that was the only way he could describe it. The ankle-length sundress exposed only her elbows and left absolutely everything to the imagination.

She was too young to be so…dowdy, he thought. He knew she had a good body; he'd seen her legs earlier and knew the woman kept in shape. So why was she wearing a blanket out on the beach? Must be shy. Or timid. Or worse, conservative. Very, very conservative. Strait-laced, clearly. Even her outfit annoyed him.

She thrust her oversize sunglasses upon her head, pushing back her short dark bob and glared at him, her eyes looking greener than the Caribbean in the sunlight.

"Help?" he cried, sweeping his arms wide to encompass the disaster before him, even as he noticed that one of the soda cans opened on impact, sending a spray of sticky liquid onto his bare feet and all over the expensive blade of his saw. Great, just great. "Why don't you just punch me in the face next time? You'll create less damage."

An annoyed wrinkle appeared between her eyebrows. "Don't tempt me," she shot back, clutching the new empty cooler beneath one elbow, her green eyes shining like emeralds with just barely contained anger. "Maybe I should have. You were running around in a panic instead of dealing with the fire."

Oh, good grief. He wasn't panicked. He was calm and collected. He never panicked. What was she talking about?

"I wasn't panicking," he said. "I was going to get something to put the fire out."

"By running around like a chicken with his head cut off." A knowing smirk tugged at her mouth.

"I wasn't."

"You were."

Now she was making him argue like a five-year-old. Unbelievable.

"Glad I was walking by because you clearly needed help. I saved your boat." She nodded toward the husk of his boat. He glanced down and noticed that she'd also splashed one end, which carried the hint of char on one board, where the fire had lapped dangerously close to his baby.

He dropped to his knees to inspect the board and make sure it hadn't been damaged. If he had to start the frame all over again... But, no, the damage was surface only, just a small smudge mark he could all but wipe off with his finger.

"I know you meant well, but I didn't ask for your help." He knew he was being ungrateful, and he didn't like it, but she was like a cow skipping through a china shop, destroying everything in her wake and then demanding he thank her for the damage. He knew the woman was trying to help, but now he had to worry about his saw and whether the soda had damaged it.

But first, he inspected Timothy's shoes, connected by a single string, and thankfully saw no damage. He gently placed them back on the nail, hanging by the particle-board backstop of his worktable. Then he picked up the saw. He unplugged it from the extension cord and wiped it down with a work rag nearby.

If it was damaged, he didn't know how he'd replace it. And without a saw, what would he do? He'd never finish the boat on time.

Then he heard a sound. A high-pitched crying. A baby. His phone! Somehow, in the chaos, it had been flung into the sand. He grabbed it, noticing that the impact had started an old video of Timothy from when he was just a baby. He was crying, fussy for his nap.

Mark clicked off the video and wiped off the screen, which was covered in dots of sticky soda.

That's when he realized she was still standing there. What was she doing? Hadn't he made it clear she wasn't welcome?

He glanced up and saw that she seemed frozen in place. She glanced at Timothy's bronze baby shoes and at the phone he still held in his hand, her face a mixture of grief and pain. He felt all those emotions he saw fighting for control behind her sea green eyes. He knew them all—pain, grief and an aggressive, bottomless loss of hope. But why did hearing a simple video of Timothy make her feel this way? What had happened to her? Or was she just unhinged for some other reason?

"Laura," he said, and then stopped. What was he going to ask her? *Are you okay?*

She turned then, eyes brimming with tears,

and he knew with a certainty that whatever had triggered this grief was still fresh. Before he could say any more, she dropped the cooler and sprinted away from him.

He felt a sudden urge to go after her, but then what? Maybe she wasn't grieving. Maybe she was just a crazy person. Maybe he was projecting his own feelings on her. What did he know?

Still, he felt guilty. Guilty because somehow he'd made her cry. And guilty because he knew she suffered in some deep, damaged way that only someone who'd lost something truly dear to them would know. It didn't sit right with him. He felt the need to make it up to her.

"Well, damn," he muttered beneath his breath as he swiped up the cooler she'd dropped. "Now I'm going to have to do something nice."

It went against his gruff, no-nonsense, let's-not-spend-time-talking-about-our-feelings self. He'd never been a touchy-feely guy, but he couldn't just let her suffer alone. He knew what that felt like.

LAURA FLED TO her condo and flung herself on the bed, angrily swiping the tears from her face. She hated that she'd become so weak, so completely unstable that a simple video of a baby and some bronzed baby shoes could so undo her in the moment.

It wasn't right. She should be getting better, and yet, she just seemed to be getting worse. She was a walking sponge, just oozing tears all the time. She just wanted it to stop, all of it. St. Anthony's was supposed to be the place where she got away from all the things that hurt her, where she could finally heal. After all, the island was named for the patron saint of lost things. And she'd never felt more lost in her whole life.

Why did this happen to her? Why had God seen fit to take her baby away before he could even be born? Why was she the only one mourning him?

But then again, she knew why. She'd been wrong, so very wrong, to be in love with Dean. This was God punishing her, she felt, for the mistake she made: falling in love with a married man.

She squeezed her eyes shut. Dean was a mistake. She knew that. But, the baby wasn't. No matter what anybody said.

Her sister had told her that she'd have other babies. But Laura didn't want another baby. She wanted the baby she lost. She glanced down at her flat belly, hidden beneath her flowing cover-up. Now it might never be full.

She wished she could talk to her mother. Get

some measure of comfort, but her mother had died years ago.

Feeling lost and alone, her willpower crumbling, she grabbed her phone and dialed Dean's work cell.

He answered on the second ring. "Hello?" he sounded harried, his voice low.

"Dean?" She hated how angry he sounded that she'd called, how disappointed. He used to always sound happy when he heard her voice. Now he always sounded like she was calling to deliver bad news.

"What are you doing calling me?" he whispered, his voice a furious, low buzz. Then, she realized that he must be at his house. The house he still shared with his wife.

"Dean. I'm sorry... I'm just..." *Lost. Alone. Hurting. Wishing that you still loved me...or that you'd ever loved me at all.* She hated all the desperate feelings that bubbled up, determined to break the surface. Dean sure had been happy to hear about the miscarriage. Ecstatic, even. Why did she think he'd comfort her now?

Dean sighed, a sound full of patronizing pity, and she felt even worse. "Look," he said, voice softer. "I'll try to call you when I get into work, okay?"

She heard shuffling in the background, and

then a voice. His wife's? She felt her stomach tighten with jealousy.

"I've got to go. I have to take my wife to the doctor," he said, louder this time, in a voice that sounded too businesslike, and she knew that Angela was in the room. He was pretending to talk to someone at work.

"Is she all right?" Laura asked, cautious. After all, she wasn't heartless.

"Well, we were going to tell everyone at the office this week, but she's sixteen weeks pregnant."

The words hit Laura like a ton of bricks. She felt all the wind knocked out of her lungs. Pregnant? His wife was…pregnant? Laura was speechless. Words failed her.

"Oh, yes, thanks," Dean prattled on in a pretend conversation with a coworker who didn't exist. Completely oblivious or not caring that he'd shattered what was left of her world. "I'll check in with you when I'm back in the office. Thanks. Bye."

And then he hung up, the line dead as she clutched her phone in her numb hand. Dean's wife was pregnant. She was going to have a baby.

Sixteen weeks along?

She'd been twelve weeks along just a month ago when she'd lost her baby. That meant…

That meant that he had to have known that

his wife was pregnant at the same time Laura was. That also meant that he had been having sex with Laura *at the same time* he had sex with his wife. The wife he claimed he hadn't touched in two years, the wife who apparently hated sex. But she didn't hate it enough to get pregnant apparently, Laura thought bitterly.

She knew Dean had lied, but this...this was a whole other level.

No wonder he'd been so relieved when she'd lost the baby. There was no way he'd leave his pregnant wife. Besides, there was no reason he'd leave his wife, period, not if Angela was actually a loving partner rather than the cold, distant monster he'd described.

Suddenly, she felt a searing rush of rage. She ought to pick up that phone and call his home landline to try to talk to his wife. Or message her on Facebook. Shouldn't she know she was married to the worst kind of liar?

But then the rage drained out of her and all she felt was pain. She'd been so incredibly stupid. Why had she ever believed a word he said?

And when, oh, when would God stop punishing her? She knew she'd made a mistake, but when would she be forgiven? She'd asked so many times, in church, on the plane here and once again now. *Please. I'm sorry. I was wrong.*

She didn't know how long she lay there, but

eventually the daylight faded outside and dark shadows covered the length of the condo. She ought to try to get up, find something to eat for dinner, but she couldn't muster the strength or the will to do it. Why bother?

She heard a soft knock on her door distantly and wondered if she'd imagined it. She lay quietly, listening.

Another knock sounded, followed by silence.

Nope, definitely someone at the door. But she couldn't muster the energy to get to her feet. She didn't think she'd ever be able to leave the bed again. She lay motionless, anticipating another knock, but it never came.

Good, she thought. Whoever it was went away.

She felt a sudden urge to move, to get out of the condo. She hated wallowing in self-pity. It just wasn't her. Maybe going to the beach would clear her head? After all, she'd traveled all this way, paid to be here. What was the use of being on an amazing tropical island if she was just going to stay cooped up inside?

She sniffed, pulled on a pair of jean cutoffs over her bathing suit and stuffed a wad of tissues in her pocket. Then she flung open the front door and found her cooler waiting for her there. The cooler she'd dropped downstairs at Mark's workshop.

She reached down to pick it up and found it heavier than an empty cooler should be. Laura set it down once more and lifted the hinged lid. Inside, she found her Cokes and four bottles of beer. Along with that was a hastily scribbled note that read:

Sorry about earlier.
Mark
P.S. If you want company while you drink these, you know where to find me.

CHAPTER FOUR

AT FIRST, LAURA laughed out loud. Mark expected her to come over for a drink? After how rude he'd been? After he'd practically shouted at her when she'd put out a fire?

Then, after the laughter faded, she reconsidered. It *was* a nice gesture. Surprisingly nice from a man she could best describe as gruff, and at worst, surly.

The exact opposite of Dean in his heyday. Dean, who used sweet words and bright promises to charm everybody he met. It was why he'd been the director of sales at her former company. He could sell anything to anybody. Mark wasn't like that. He could barely sell an apology, she reasoned. *Sorry about earlier?* About when? When she'd saved his workshop from fire and he'd told her he didn't need her help? Or when he'd implied her thoughts about noise pollution were completely moot?

But, given how Dean turned out, maybe she should give gruff a try. Besides, what was one beer? Part of her didn't want to be alone right now. She didn't want to stew in her own misery, to turn over all the ways Dean had betrayed her in his mind, to face the yawning black chasm of her own sadness. Dean would have a baby, all right. Just not hers.

Then again, smooth-talking Dean had turned out to be a liar. Maybe the opposite of Dean was just what she needed right now.

Honestly, she wanted a distraction. Any distraction.

She grabbed the cooler and headed downstairs.

As she stood in front of his metal door, she knocked, the tin plunking sound reverberating in her stomach. The door swung open and Mark greeted her with a neutral expression.

He'd put on a shirt and taken a shower, she saw, as his hair was still wet. The faded T-shirt stuck to his very muscular chest, leaving little to her imagination. This was better than a frown, and yet still she felt like she might be intruding.

"Uh. Just wanted to thank you for this." She lifted the cooler. He glanced at it, mute. Did he not write the note that invited her to come over for a drink? Was he not going to invite her inside?

She hesitated on his welcome mat, wondering if she'd read the entire note wrong. It certainly *seemed* like an invitation. "Well, then."

She hated awkward silences. Why was he just staring and not saying anything? "I guess I'll go."

She was halfway turned around when his voice stopped her. "Did you want to come in?"

"Uh…sure?" she said, glancing at him over her shoulder. "I mean. If you're not busy."

He slowly shook his head, dark eyes watching her. "Not busy." Then he retreated from the door, leaving it open, and she stepped into his condo.

The place smelled like the open air of the beach and ocean because his patio doors were flung wide open. His workshop and the partially restored boat obscured some of the dark, rolling sea, but she could hear the waves gently lapping against the beach. Outside, the moon rose above the ocean, casting a silver light on the water.

The layout of his place was largely the same as hers, although his kitchen was slightly bigger and newer. Instead of touristy bamboo furniture, his was entirely dark, simple wood and modern lines. Also, his place was twice the size of hers; he'd knocked down a wall and made two condos into one. Somehow his place seemed more masculine, too, yet tastefully decorated. A large photograph of a sailboat hung on one large wall near the kitchen, drawing her eye. The matting said *Tanner*.

"Your boat?" she asked. She set the cooler on his kitchen counter and walked up to the over-size photo of the impressive sailboat to study it.

"My brother's now. But used to be, yeah." He fell silent once more as he whipped the bottles of beer out of the cooler and popped open the caps with an opener. Laura suspected there might be a story there but didn't push it. Mark was a hard man to read, and she was still feeling him out.

"Is the one you're building going to be like that?" she asked.

"Kind of," he said, handing her a bottle.

She took it gratefully, wondering if a little beer would make conversation less like pulling teeth. They clinked bottles and Laura took a deep swig of the cold, fizzy beverage, letting the lager slip down her throat. She'd only just starting drinking her first beer and already she wanted her second.

"Want to sit outside?" he asked.

"Yes," she answered a little too quickly. She took another deep swig of the beer.

"You need another one of those?" he asked her, and Laura realized she'd drank nearly half the beer already.

"Probably." She sighed, thinking about how

lately every day just screamed for strong drinks and lots of them. "It's been that kind of day."

"For you, too, huh?"

She glanced at his dark eyes and thought she saw a flicker of pity there. Or maybe understanding. She nodded. "I plan to drown my sorrows in alcohol."

"Well, then, we're going to get along just fine, after all." Mark reached back in his fridge and grabbed a few more bottles, loading up her small cooler so full that the lid wouldn't close. "I was going to finish up this beer alone, which probably means I'm an alcoholic. If we do it together, then we're both just being social."

He laughed and she joined him.

He lifted the cooler and headed outside. Laura followed, the warm ocean breeze ruffling her short hair as she followed him past his workshop. The full moon hung in the sky and shed a gray light on the beach. He'd set up two beach chairs not far from his shop, facing out to the ocean.

"Beautiful," she said, staring at the moon, amazed at how many stars she could see here, far away from the lights of the city.

"Yeah," he agreed. They both sat in the chairs and he laid the cooler between them. "You never really get used to it."

Laura finished her first beer and Mark handed

her a second. He whistled, sounding impressed. "Boy, you weren't kidding about the alcohol."

"I don't know if you have enough beer to make me forget about my day." Dean was going to be a father. She might never be a mother. "It's the worst ever."

"Can't be, because mine *definitely* was," Mark said as he took a sip of beer. "Started with this pretty lady yelling at me for working in the morning, except that it was practically lunchtime and…"

Pretty lady? The compliment didn't slip past Laura. He thought she was good-looking?

"Okay, okay, okay." Laura raised her beer bottle like a shield. "Sorry about that. I was jet-lagged. I thought it was early."

"Uh-huh." Mark grinned, flashing a teasing smile that somehow looked even brighter in the moonlight. Laura couldn't help but think how handsome he was when he wasn't solemn or grumpy. "Well, apology accepted."

"And what about you, Mr. Grumpy Guy With a Saw, who might also be a pyromaniac?"

"I'm not a…" Mark frowned, but then he pointed his beer bottle at Laura. "You're teasing me."

"Maybe. For all I know, you set that fire on purpose so I'd come running and save you."

"Why would I do that?"

She took a sip of beer, savoring the cold, crispness as it slid down her throat. Already, she began to feel the tightness in her stomach relax as the second beer hit her stomach, and she glanced out across the dark ocean waves. Above the water, thousands of stars glistened. "Maybe you like pretty ladies who also put out fires."

He laughed. "Maybe," he agreed.

Were they flirting? Laura wondered. It had been so long since she'd even been interested in flirting, she couldn't say. Surely not.

She studied him. He *was* attractive—if you went for lean, muscled guys. With just a hint of gray at the temples and dark eyes that never missed a move. She would've put herself in that category, before Dean. Before losing her baby.

He took a swig of beer and glanced up at the star-filled sky. Then, he glanced back at her. "So? Go on. Tell me about your day. It had to be bad for you to suck down that beer so fast. What's driven you to drink?"

"Oh. You don't want to hear about my problems." She couldn't imagine he'd be the least bit interested.

"Actually, I would," he said, leaning back in his deck chair and getting comfortable as he stretched his long, tanned legs out in front of him. "I'm bored to death of my own problems. I need a change of pace."

"Well…" Laura hesitated. Was she really going to pour her heart out to a stranger she barely knew? Tell him secrets she'd not even told her closest friends in San Francisco who had no idea about the baby or Dean? "I don't know. Most of my friends don't even know what's been going on. It's not the kind of thing I can really share."

"Okay," he said, setting his beer down by the leg of his chair. "Let's break this down. So you're here for how long?"

"A month. I don't know. I haven't exactly made a plan." She shrugged. She'd never imagine she'd be on such an open-ended trip before. But then again, she'd never imagined she'd have an affair, either. Life was full of surprises.

He raised his eyebrows. "Miss Noise Pollution doesn't have a plan? I have to say, I'm surprised."

"Why?"

"I thought you'd have your whole life planned out in one of those—what do they call them? Day riders? Runners? Calendar whatevers?"

"I like calendar whatevers, and no, I don't." Actually, she used to. Not that she had a physical calendar she carried around, but her online calendar was extensive. She even used to put major milestones in it, like *ask for a raise*, or *look for a new job with more responsibilities*. She'd been that odd job candidate who relished answering the question, *what's your five-year plan?* She always had an answer.

Now? Not so much.

"I used to be a planner," she admitted. "But that was before I learned that the old joke, 'how do you make God laugh? Make a plan,' was actually no joke."

Mark nodded, agreeing. "Amen, sister," he said and they clinked beer bottles.

Laura realized she was having a good time. Amazing, but true.

"So back to how horrible your day was," Mark said.

"I thought we'd let that go."

"Oh, no. I don't let anything go." Mark flashed another grin. "So you don't know how long you're staying, but I'm guessing you aren't moving here for good."

"Probably not."

"Okay, then. A month. Maybe two at most you'll be here, living above me. Then, you're probably never going to see me again. So what's the harm in telling me something? I don't know any of your friends. I won't tell any of them."

He had a point there. She sighed. "Where do you want me to start?"

"Wherever you'd like. The workday is done. I've got a beer in my hand and I don't have anywhere to be, except out here, enjoying this." He lifted his beer bottle to the scenic view before them of the dark waves glistening in the moonlight. He had a point.

The beer helped her shed her inhibitions, and she forgot why she shouldn't tell this man everything. He seemed like he really wanted to know. And he was right—he was a captive audience. Might as well see if he was a genuinely sympathetic ear.

"Well," she said. "It all started with me making the mistake of falling in love with the wrong person."

Mark laughed. "What did you go and do that for?"

"He was charming. And persistent. And he said he loved me."

"Oldest tricks in the book," Mark said and Laura had to laugh a little. She watched his profile in the moonlight. He turned to study her and she felt the weight of his attention.

"So what made him the wrong man?"

"For starters?" Laura took a big swig of beer for courage. *Here goes nothing*, she thought. "He was married."

Mark coughed, and for a second, Laura feared he was judging her, like she knew her sister did, like she knew everyone would who ever found out. Only two people actually even knew about the affair: her sister and Dean. She realized she had no idea how a stranger would react. Derision? Probably.

She deserved it, too, she thought. She could feel the heavy weight of guilt pressing against her shoulder blades. Why had she shared this information? With a man she barely knew?

She could see his shoulders shaking a little in the moonlight. Was he angry?

Then he broke the silence with a laugh, and she realized with a start he'd been laughing at her.

"You?" he managed to sputter. "You had a torrid affair? Miss Noise Pollution?" He laughed a little harder and slapped his own knee.

Well, this wasn't the reaction she'd been expecting. A lecture, disapproval, maybe. But laughter? "What's so funny?"

"It's just… I can't imagine you… You're so buttoned up. So prim and proper. You, breaking one of the Ten Commandments? I just can't imagine it." Mark swiped at his eyes. The man laughed so hard, he actually started to tear up.

Laura felt a prickle of indignation run down her spine. She wasn't that straitlaced. Was she?

"It's not funny."

"It is, though. Have you met you?" He shook

his head. "Today, you were wearing a muumuu to the beach, like head-to-toe *covered*. Not exactly the type to have an affair."

"Well, I did. I mean, I didn't plan on it exactly, but it happened, and I take responsibility for it, but...I mean, it's not something anybody I know would ever think I'd do, probably." Laura thought about her small circle of girlfriends, most of whom were married and none of whom she could ever confide in about this. None of them would understand, she knew that for certain.

"Well, then, you *are* full of surprises. Here's to bold women who aren't afraid to break the rules." He offered up his beer bottle for a toast. Reluctantly, she clinked the neck of her bottle against his.

"It's not something I'm proud of. I don't even think I should be toasting." Now, Laura felt weird about it. Was he mocking her? "I mean, have you cheated?"

"Nope," he said, taking a big drink. "Was cheated on, actually. My wife slept with my brother. They're together now. They're even..." He bit off the last of his sentence, as if regretting even bringing it up.

Laura felt the blood drain from her face. Now he'd hate her. He'd have to.

"Oh... I am so sorry. You must...must hate

me. I've got to be the kind of person you hate the most. A cheater."

"Why? *You're* not my brother. Or my wife." He shrugged one shoulder and took another long drag of beer. "They're the ones who betrayed me."

"But—"

"Look, your sins aren't against everybody. I'm sure, Miss Noise Pollution, you had a very good reason for cheating."

That was kind of him, she thought, not to plunk her in the category of *horrible person* automatically. She knew many people who would.

Laura thought about Dean's silky words, about his gentle hands. "Not really. I mean, I thought… I guess I thought it was true love. I thought we were going to be together. But in the end, I'm not going to make excuses. I just wanted to, I guess."

"I'm liking you more already," Mark said, turning his head and grinning. "That's more than my wife ever admitted."

Still, Laura felt rotten. She felt as if she'd wronged him, too, somehow, just being in the camp of women who wore scarlet *As* on their chests.

"Come on. I don't hate you. So what? You had an affair. I mean, I don't think cheating is right, but at the same time, you've got a little bit of an edge to you. One I didn't expect.

I kind of like it." Mark studied her in the dark and she felt a little unnerved by his gaze. Was he flirting with her? Surely not. Mr. Surly Boat Building Guy? "So did he leave his wife? What happened with Mr. Wrong?"

"No, he didn't leave his wife. The opposite, actually." She squeezed her eyes shut, remembering the sound of Dean's harried voice on the phone, the almost casual way he'd delivered the earthshattering news. "He got her pregnant."

Mark whistled low. "Well, that sucks."

"Yeah. I just found out today." She took a long swig of the bottle and found that she'd downed half of this one, too. At this rate, she was going to be drunk very soon. Somehow that thought didn't seem to bother her in the least. On a day like today, she almost welcomed oblivion. Anything to make her mind stop looking backward.

"So he's going to stay with his wife?" Mark leaned over his chair, moving closer to her. "Make a happy little family? Or at least happy until his wife figures out he's been dipping his wick in other places."

She nodded.

"Well." Mark slapped his knee. "Can't say that sounds too good for you."

She remembered how Dean had been so disappointed to find out she was pregnant. She wasn't sorry to lose Dean. He'd proven himself a liar and unworthy of her affection. She knew that on a base level. It wasn't losing Dean that hurt so much.

"Well, I don't want Dean. Dean was a prick."

"*Dean?* His name is Dean? Well, with a name like that, of course he was a prick." Mark chuckled low and Laura joined him.

It felt good to hear someone else bash Dean. Hell, it felt good to talk to someone other than her sister. How long had it been since she'd had a real conversation with someone? Ages. The secret of her affair with Dean had driven a wedge between her and all her friends, and she hadn't been able to talk about it openly, not even the miscarriage. Her friends didn't even know she'd been pregnant. But she wasn't ready to tell Mark that. Not that. Not yet. Talking about losing her baby somehow made it even more real.

He leaned forward. "There's something more, though, isn't there?"

"What do you mean?" Laura suddenly felt defensive. Could he see right through her? How did he know there was more?

"I mean, there's more to this story. You've lost more than Dean." He seemed so certain, and yet, how did he know? Did he have ESP?

"I…" she began, alcohol swirling in her brain. "I don't know if I want to talk about it. Besides, what about you? I can't be the only one to spill my guts. If I'm talking about my no-good, horrible day, then you have to tell me why yours was so bad, too."

Mark cocked his head to one side. "Fair enough."

"What made your day so bad?"

"My older brother, the one who slept with my wife *and* stole our company from me, came back and asked me if I'd work for him."

Laura coughed, nearly choking on her beer. That sounded like one winner of a sibling. "What did you say?"

Mark paused and studied the label on his beer. He began picking off the edges. "I said hell no."

Laura laughed and offered her bottle up for another toast. "Here's to the power of no." They clinked their mostly empty bottles once more and she giggled. "I'm actually having more fun than I'd thought."

He glanced at her and grinned. "Me, too."

"You're not as grumpy as I first thought, either." She gave his bicep a playful shove. She felt the compact muscle there, the solidness of it.

"What? Me? Grumpy?" Mark laughed as he absorbed her jab. "I'm Mr. Sunshine over here."

Now it was Laura's turn to cackle. "You?

Have you met you?" She relished quoting him now that the tables were turned. She reached out and put her hand on his shoulder, a gesture she'd meant to be purely platonic, but as her laughter died down, she realized she'd kept her hand there a beat too long.

Suddenly aware of the heat of his skin, the strength of the muscle beneath, she wondered what his arms might feel like around her, and she remembered the glisten of his muscles in the sunlight just that morning. She wondered what it would feel like to run her hands down his bare arm.

As soon as the thought popped into her head, she squashed it. What was she doing? She hadn't thought of a man like that…well, since Dean. And look where that got her. Was she really so eager to jump back into the fray? Was she even ready to have a man touch her again? She had lousy instincts about men. Dean had just proved that.

She pulled her hand away a bit too quickly, heat creeping up her neck. She glanced quickly at him, but he seemed not to notice, or at least not to register her touch.

Not that she should be surprised. As if he'd ever in a million years be interested in her. *Miss Noise Pollution*, he'd called her. Here she was, worried about sleeping with a man who probably had no intention of ever sleeping with her. Her head swam with alcohol and she knew she ought to stop before she truly made a fool of herself.

"Well." She put down her now-empty beer bottle. "It's late. I probably should be going."

"Are you serious?" Mark asked, spinning in his chair and gawking at her. "This is what you call drowning your sorrows in alcohol? Honey, you're a lightweight."

"I am not." Laura lifted her chin in defiance. She wasn't exactly a heavyweight drinker, but she could hold her own.

"Then prove it." He handed her another beer bottle.

What was this? College? Would he ask her to do a beer bong next? Please. "Come on. Don't be silly. We're not twenty."

"Nope. We're not. Thank God." He grinned. "And I'm glad, because twenty-year-olds know nothing about the world. I'd rather have a seasoned woman any day of the week."

Did he mean her? Was he…flirting? She glanced at the bottle in his hand, hesitating. What would one more round really hurt anyway? Mark seemed to sense her indecision. He waggled the beer in front of her.

"Come on. How miserable are you, really?

Just two beers miserable? Because that's hardly miserable at all."

She had to laugh at that. She was far more than two beers miserable.

"Fine," she said and grabbed the bottle from his hand. "You win."

He chuckled and took another swig of his beer as she started on hers. She'd just stay for one more. Besides, what's the worst that could happen?

CHAPTER FIVE

LAURA WOKE UP feeling like an elephant had stomped on her head and someone had filled her mouth with sand. Searing white light bashed her closed eyelids, and a pulsing, distant thud of pain thumped in her temples. She feared opening her eyes. The light would no doubt make her hangover ten times worse. All she wanted to do was lie here, very still, and hope to fall back asleep.

Flashes of the night before came to her. Beer, Mark, laughing…then more beer. She'd drunk her misery away, yes, she had, but she'd also brought more misery to her brain, which right now wanted to crawl out of her skull to get away from this crushing migraine. Her stomach roiled, too, and she felt a wave of nausea overcome her. Not good.

She'd have to open her eyes sometime. She cracked one eye open, expecting to see the palm-tree-decorated comforter on her rental condo bed, but instead found herself lying beneath a gray-striped blanket on a large king-size bed in a room she didn't recognize.

Laura sat up in alarm, the sheets falling from her body, and then realized she was wearing nothing but her bra and underwear. Laura covered her chest with her arms and realized with alarm she was *sitting in Mark's bed*. In her underwear.

But where was Mark?

She listened frantically but heard nothing. Was she alone? What the hell had happened last night?

Frantically, she searched her memory of the night before. Beers on his deck. Lots of beers. Then… Oh, no. Tequila shots. Did that happen? Yes, she had a fuzzy memory of Mark slicing limes. Tequila was never good. She might as well just hit herself in the head with a rock. Why did she think tequila was a good idea? But then, nothing after that. Oh, Lord. What had she done? She couldn't recall anything more.

God, she'd only ever blacked out once in her life in college. That was fourteen years ago. What the hell was wrong with her?

She heard the front door of the condo rattle open and swing shut. Mark? Was that Mark? Frantically she glanced around the room for her clothes. Where were they? And, more important, did Mark…take them off?

She heard a soft knock on the bedroom door. "Hello?" Mark called.

"Uh…yes?" Laura scrambled to pull the covers up to her chin. Granted, she was wearing a sturdy pair of cotton boy shorts and matching bra with more coverage than most bikinis, but still, she felt vulnerable and exposed.

"Morning, Drinking Beauty," Mark teased. "I've got your clothes here. All laundered." He backed into the room, not looking at the bed. Did he keep his head turned because he was being a gentleman?

He dropped them on the edge of the bed.

"Why did you wash my clothes?" she asked, stunned.

"You don't remember?" he asked, back still turned.

"Remember what?"

Mark chuckled low. "Get dressed and come get coffee. Have I got a story to tell you." He shut the bedroom door behind him, and Laura scrambled to get her clothes. What had she done? Had he…? Had they…? Did they have sex? Why couldn't she remember?

She felt red flames of embarrassment lick her face. She wasn't that kind of girl. But she had admitted to an affair. Had he thought she was easy? That she just jumped into bed with anybody? She didn't, for the record.

Laura pulled on her shorts and her T-shirt, her head still throbbing and her tongue feeling like she'd spent the night sucking on sandpaper. She managed a quick glance in the mirror above his dresser and saw her hair in complete disarray. Her short dark bob stuck out in all directions and yet was completely flat on one side. Plus, a smudge of old mascara ringed her left eye. She looked awful.

Laura tried her best to tidy herself up, but she needed more than just water from the sink to really make a dent. She gave up easily, too hungover to do much about her frightening hair. The effort of putting on clothes exhausted her. Her stomach protested at every move, threatening to empty itself at every turn.

She opened the door, cautiously at first, and saw Mark, his back to her, making coffee in the kitchen. She shuffled out, unable to move faster, her head still in a vice.

"Hello?" Her voice came out as a croak, and Mark turned, a knowing grin on his face.

"Well, hello." He wiggled his eyebrows, and she worried then and there that they'd done it. And she had no memory. Not one single memory of them having sex. She tried to focus on what she did remember, but it all just felt like one white-hot headache.

"Uh, what, uh…happened last night?"

The coffee machine hummed, and the strong smell of some dark brew wafted through the air. Morning sunlight filtered in through the vertical blinds of his patio, striking her head like laser beams.

"You had a lot to drink." Mark wore cargo shorts, flip-flops and a tight T-shirt over his muscled chest. He looked amazingly put together, not a hair out of place and freshly shaved. He leaned back against the counter, crossing his muscled forearms across his chest, dark hair slightly ruffled and that cocksure smile on his face. How could he roll out of bed looking so… sexy?

"I know that." Laura's head pounded. She pressed her hands against her temples, almost hoping to squeeze the headache out of her head. Also, oddly, her nose felt sore, she realized. "But…what else?"

"Well. You at one point yelped, ran down the beach and shouted at the ocean, 'I don't need you, Dean!'"

"Oh, I didn't." She suddenly wished the ground would open up and swallow her.

"You did. Then you started throwing handfuls of sand into the ocean." Mark's grin got bigger. He uncrossed his arms. "And cursing. A lot."

A dark memory tried to wiggle its way to the

forefront of her brain. Yes, that sounded actually right. The feel of the wet sand in her hands. The rush of anger. The release of her fury. Yep. That seemed about right.

"Then you face-planted." Mark hit the counter for emphasis, showing her how she'd landed as his palm smacked on the granite.

Oh, no. Well, that explains the sore nose.

"Right in the sand." Mark was having trouble not laughing at this point. The corners of his mouth twitched, and his dark eyes never left her. "I mean *monumental* face-plant. And you just lay there for a minute. Groaning."

"I didn't." Could this get any worse?

"You did. I tried to help you up, but you told me you were just going to lie there. Let the sea take you somewhere. That maybe it was all better this way."

Laura flinched. "That sounds dramatic."

"You were very determined to lie there in the sand."

"I'm…I'm *so* embarrassed." She smacked her own forehead, but that just made her headache worse. She peeked at Mark between two fingers. "Then what?" She almost didn't want to know.

"Then you tried swimming out to the ocean, even though you were on sand, so it was really less like a butterfly stroke and more like a belly crawl." Mark did his best imitation with just his arms as he struggled against air. If she'd done that, she must've looked ridiculous. "You did make it to the water, though, and got yourself good and drenched."

"My clothes… That's why you washed them."

Mark crossed his beefy arms once more. He was still grinning. The coffee machine beeped, signaling its ready brew, and Mark poured two cups. He handed her one, which she reluctantly took. She didn't know how much her uneasy stomach could stand, but the coffee smelled good so she decided to give it a try.

"I didn't think you had it in you, Miss Noise Pollution, but let me tell you, you created a whole lot of noise last night," he said. "You better be glad I'm president of the condo board."

"Ugh. No."

"Yes. Lots of shouting and squealing. And cursing. Lots of cursing about Dean." Mark seemed to be enjoying this a little too much.

Laura slumped into a nearby armchair and he followed her, taking a seat kitty-corner from her on the couch. He set his coffee mug on the glass table by his knees.

"And I haven't even told you the best part," he said.

"Do I want to hear it?" she groaned. She held

the coffee cup in both hands and took a sip. It tasted remarkably good. She took another.

"When I finally dragged you out of the surf, I told you we needed to go back to my house and get you into something dry and put you to bed, but you just stripped right on out of your clothes, threw them at me and then went running down the beach shouting, 'I don't wanna go to bed!'"

"Ugh," Laura groaned. "Really?"

Mark chuckled and reached into his own back pocket, pulling out his smartphone. "'Fraid so. I got proof." He drew up a video he'd taken on the moonlit beach the night before. Sure enough, there she was, running away from him and shouting, arms flailing in the air and dark hair bouncing. Laura almost couldn't watch it, yet she couldn't look away, either.

"I want to die right now."

"That's also what you said about a half beat later, when you ran out of steam and threw up all over the sand."

"No!" Laura smacked her face again, forgetting about her bruised nose. "Ow."

Mark chuckled as he leaned forward, tapping her knee. "You, Miss Straitlaced, are one helluva interesting time when you drink."

"I'm not usually. But tequila does weird things to me," she admitted. She brought the coffee cup to her mouth and sipped at the strong brew. "In fact, now that I think about it, tequila was what I was drinking the last time I got in trouble…in college."

"Well, whatever it was, you put on quite a show." Mark grabbed his own mug from the coffee table and took a sip.

"So you didn't take my clothes off?"

Mark chuckled, nearly spitting out his coffee. "No, no. You were more than happy to take them off yourself. I had to encourage you *not* to take off your bra. You really, really wanted to."

She shook her head.

"I finally persuaded you to come home with me, but only after you ran around for a good twenty minutes more, shouting at the top of your lungs. I'm surprised the other neighbors didn't call the police. But then I got you into bed."

"So…uh…we didn't…I mean…I don't remember if we…" This might be the most embarrassing thing she'd ever asked a man in her life. "Did we have sex?"

Mark burst out laughing. "No, we didn't, Miss Noise Pollution. Which I'm going to continue to call you but for entirely different reasons now." He glanced at her. "I don't take advantage of women who can't consent."

"Oh." That was good then.

"And you were in no condition to consent."

Laura felt searing humiliation. Why had she let herself go like that? She knew why. Because of Dean. Because of everything that happened. She'd wished for oblivion, and she'd gotten it all right.

"I'm sorry," she said. "I don't usually act like that. I swear. It's not…me."

Mark shrugged. "Well, all I can say is running after your half-naked ass on the beach beats the hell out of sitting by myself on the couch."

Laura got a flash of a memory, but couldn't quite bring it into focus. She strained to recollect it as she stared at him sitting across from her. The dark shadow of a memory formed. What was it? She couldn't quite remember.

"You're sure we didn't… I mean, nothing happened?"

"We didn't have sex, if that's what you're asking," Mark said. "But I didn't say *nothing* happened."

Oh, God. Something did happen! *Ack.*

"What did I do?" It had something to do with that couch. She had an inkling of a memory she couldn't quite pull into the light.

"Well, wouldn't you like to know?"

MARK LOVED TEASING LAURA. It just might be his new favorite pastime. He watched as all the color drained from her face as she imagined the worst-case scenarios from the night before.

The girl knew how to let loose, something he never would've expected from her. She also had an amazing body, one that he'd appreciated in the silver light of the moon as she'd jogged down the beach in her underwear. All firm thighs, small waist and jiggling in all the right places.

"Tell me," she pleaded with him now, her face streaked with old mascara. She looked like a complete mess, but she also looked adorable.

"No," he teased.

"Mark!" She playfully slapped his arm and he liked the contact.

"What? A gentleman never tells." He couldn't help but laugh as she growled, baring her teeth.

"That is *not* what that saying is supposed to mean." She slapped at his arm again.

"Fair enough." He grinned. Now she was getting mad, and her green eyes flashed with growing frustration even as her cheeks grew pinker. God, he loved seeing the passion in her. It reminded him of the woman from last night, the one who'd laid herself bare…emotionally and pretty much literally.

In truth, nothing happened, and yet, everything had at the same time. He'd finally caught her at the edge of the beach, corralling her back to his condo and wrapping her up in a towel as best he could. By then, she was hardly keeping her eyes open, and the fire had drained out of her. He'd been worried about her getting sick again, and that had been his main focus as he steered her to his bed. But before he could even get her to the bedroom, she'd resisted him.

"I wanna go back outshide," she'd slurred and tried to change course. He'd resisted, and yet she'd forced him to stagger backward a little. Somehow he'd caught his foot on the rug and tripped back into the couch. She fell on top of him, the towel falling away. He still remembered the soft feel of her full, heavy breasts against his chest, the thin cotton fabric of her bra hardly putting up much of a barrier between them. The way he'd wanted her in that moment in a way he hadn't wanted a woman in a long, long time.

Then she'd leaned in and he'd thought for sure she was going to kiss him.

But instead, she'd collapsed on his chest and begun snoring. Loudly.

"Nothing happened," he said now. "I promise. Just lots of you yelling. And then you passed out."

"Really?" she asked, looking uncertain.

"Really," he confirmed. "By the way, you snore."

Laura chuckled a little.

"Oh…my head." Laura cradled her head in her hands.

"Want a little hair of the dog?" He offered her an unopened beer.

"No. Please no." Laura held up her hands together as if trying to ward off any more alcohol. "That sounds like a terrible breakfast."

"How about I cook you a real one then? I don't know about you, but bacon always cures what ails me."

She looked up at him and managed a weak grin.

"Bacon it is," he said and got to work on whipping up something for them both.

It had been a long time since Mark had felt this relaxed in his own kitchen. Hell, in his own skin, for that matter. His world had been turned upside down since his boy had died.

God, that awful day. He wanted to shake it from his memory. He glanced outside, past his patio and to the shell of his father's boat. He hadn't even thought about the boat in more than twelve hours! The boat was usually the last thing he thought about when he went to sleep and the first thing he thought about when he woke up. Of course, he'd been busy chasing Laura down the beach half the night. Still. He needed to stay focused. He'd need to get to work soon if he wanted to have any hope of finishing it before the race.

"So, the boat? Want to tell me about it?" Laura asked, catching him staring.

"Oh. Well, I want to restore it and race. Every year, there's a big sailboat race on the island. And the prize is a hundred thousand dollars."

"Whoa." She looked suitably impressed. "That's a lot of money."

He nodded. "Yep, and when I win it, I'm going to go sail around the world. I've got a team who will help me finish the boat and help me race it. And after that, I'm just going out to sea. It's the only place I feel…okay."

Laura frowned. "Why is that? I mean, why on the boat?"

Mark swallowed, wondering how he was going to explain this. "I've always loved to sail. But now…it's really because it was my son's favorite place to be. Before he died."

Laura's face went pale. "Oh, I'm so sorry. I didn't mean to—"

"I know," Mark said, waving his hand as if it was a dismissable foul. He was so tired of people apologizing all the time if he ever brought up Timothy. It wasn't her fault he'd died. And frankly, talking about him meant no one would forget him. "I'm naming the boat *Timothy*… after him. He wasn't quite three when he died."

"Mark." Laura clutched her chest as if her own heart were breaking. "That's just so awful. What happened?"

"Accident," he said, curt, cutting off the word before it even left his mouth. Accident. That's what they called that horrible day Timothy walked into the ocean and never came back. "My ex-wife was watching him on the beach one morning when I was away at work. She fell asleep. Timothy wandered into the water and never came out."

It was the other reason Mark wanted to be out on the sea. That's where his boy was.

"She fell asleep?" Laura sounded shocked. "But that's horrible. The boy in her care and…"

Mark nodded. It was horrible. All of it.

"I don't know what to say." Laura's eyes brimmed with tears. Was she going to cry? He was momentarily baffled by the response. Why did she feel the loss so acutely? He was used to looks of pity. But hers was something else. Like she'd experienced loss herself.

He was about to ask her about it when a hard knock came on Mark's door. Laura looked a little startled but recovered as Mark checked his phone. Only then did he realize he'd forgotten to plug it in. He guessed it must've died shortly after he'd shown Laura the video of her dancing on the beach. Mark walked to the door, praying it wasn't his brother, or this morning was about to get a lot more hostile.

He swung open the front door to find Dave standing there, tall and blond, looking his usual tanned, thirtysomething self. Dave was one of the best sailors on the island. He'd won the race three years in a row, and he'd be helping Mark do it for a fourth time.

"Do you answer your phone?" Dave accused as he swept into Mark's condo.

"Phone died," Mark said and then added sarcastically, "Well, come on in. Make yourself at home."

Dave saw Laura and stopped in his tracks. "Oh. Uh… I didn't realize you had company. I can come back."

"No, come on in. She's my upstairs neighbor. Laura, meet Dave, the best skipper on the island."

Dave extended his hand and Laura took it, though Dave barely acknowledged her. He seemed distracted, worried even. "I'll come back, man."

"No. Stay. I've got a few ideas I want to go over with you about the boat, and we're way behind, really, so I need extra hands today if you can spare them…"

Dave was really starting to look uncomfortable as he shifted uncertainly from one foot to the other. He glanced anxiously at Laura, who managed a weak grin, her hangover still haunting her.

"No, why don't I let you... I mean... I'll come back."

"Dave. Come on. You're here. Let's go over a few things."

"I can go," Laura said, standing up for a wobbly second, holding her head. Poor thing looked like she might topple over. That hangover was a doozy.

"No, stay," Mark said, and Laura gratefully slumped into the couch once more. Mark returned to the kitchen where he finished cracking eggs in a bowl, added a bit of milk and then put them in the melting butter in the pan on the stove.

"You haven't had breakfast yet. Dave? You want something?"

Dave reluctantly followed Mark to his kitchen. "Uh, no, man. I've eaten, and anyway I can't stay long. The wife wants me to help shop for strollers today."

Dave and his wife were expecting their first child in a few months.

Mark was happy for his friend. He and Katie had been trying for years and the pregnancy came after they'd both thought neither one would ever be a parent. Dave was a stand-up guy, a good guy, and Mark knew he'd make a wonderful father. Katie would also make an excellent mother. But the news still caused a pang in his heart.

"Any names yet?"

"A few." Dave relaxed a little bit but still didn't sit down. "Katie wants to name her Madison, after her mother's maiden name. I prefer Penelope, after my mom."

"How about Penelope Madison?" Mark offered.

"Could work," Dave said, but then sank into a moody silence. He glanced at Laura once and then back at Mark.

"What is it? You look like you just found out your dog died." Mark dropped his spatula on the kitchen counter. "Come on. Spit it out."

Dave laughed, a nervous little bark. "Why do you say that?"

"Because you always were a lousy actor," Mark said. He turned the stove off, the smell of freshly cooked scrambled eggs filling the air.

Dave looked like he was about to face a firing squad. He glanced once more at Laura.

"Look, she can hear whatever it is you have to say," Mark said, suddenly not caring. "We decided we don't have secrets." He winked at her and she smiled shyly.

"I don't know how to say this." Dave glanced down, looking ashamed.

Fear and apprehension rose in Mark's chest. He remembered what his brother had told him about trusting his friends. Had Edward gotten to him? Had Dave been bought?

But they'd been good friends for years, worked side by side on winning boats for the last three years. Sure, Edward had been part of that, but Mark always thought of Dave as his friend first. After all, Mark had been the one to find him in Florida and recruit him to come sail the Tanner boat in the race.

Dave had helped the Tanner brothers win prize money that they ultimately put into Tanner Boating. Dave, of course, had his own money, after inheriting a multimillion-dollar corporation from his dad. He largely lived off a trust fund, using his free time to sail, which had become his life's passion. Edward couldn't bribe Dave. It's one reason Mark had been so certain Dave would be on his side.

"I can't race with you."

"What do you mean, 'can't'?" Mark felt the panic rise in his throat. Why couldn't Dave race?

"You know Katie and Elle are friends."

Elle, Mark's ex-wife. Yes, he knew Elle and Katie were friends—good friends. Best of friends, actually. The four of them had been nearly inseparable when they'd been a couple. But since the separation and then divorce, Dave and Katie had worked hard to befriend them both. "Yes," Mark said carefully. "But so are we." He paused, suddenly wondering if that were still true. "Aren't we, Dave?"

"Of course, we are. You know that. It's just…"

Mark wasn't sure he wanted to hear what came next.

"Listen, you know that I'm on your side," Dave said. "But Katie is pregnant, and so is—"

"I know," Mark interrupted, holding up his hand. He didn't want to talk about how Elle was expecting his brother's baby. Dave suddenly couldn't look Mark in the eye. "She feels that she's got to take Elle's side, and she's asked me—" Dave swallowed hard "—not to race with you."

"What?" Mark felt the betrayal like a sharp jab to the gut. He felt irrational anger flare up in his chest. Why would she ask him to do that? And where were Dave's balls? Was he just going to roll over because his wife said so? Mark had done a lot of good things for Elle and Dave, and he'd been good friends with both of them.

In the living room, Laura sat stock-still, just listening, eyes wide. But he had more important things to worry about than what she thought of this mess. The eggs he'd just cooked were getting cold, but he didn't care. Breakfast hardly seemed important. "But what about the boat for Timothy? What about sailing around the world?"

He felt his plan slipping away. He needed that plan. He'd been counting on it.

"I'm sorry, Mark. But I won't be able to help you finish it or race with you. If it were just up to me, then I'd be with you, man. But I'm in a tough spot here." Dave's eyes begged for mercy. "If I don't do this," Dave added. "I think Katie might seriously leave me."

"After all Elle did to me? She ran off with Edward!" *She's having his baby.*

"You know she wasn't the only one who made mistakes." Dave let the accusation hang there. Sure, throw that in his face, now that he was down.

"That's not fair." Mark felt the need to defend himself. He knew they all took her side, even though she'd done the unthinkable with Edward. But his son had *died*. How else was a father supposed to act?

"What about your brother? Is Garrett with you?"

Dave shrugged. "I don't know, man. You'll have to ask him." He paused. "I'm sorry. I am, but this is my wife. Maybe after the baby

comes, she'll calm down a little about all this."
Dave sounded more hopeful than Mark felt. He
also looked miserable, caught between his wife
and best friend.

Mark knew then that it went deeper than just
keeping peace at home. This was about prior-
itizing your wife above your friends, and on
some level, Mark had to respect that. He didn't
have to like it, but he'd have to live with it.

"Look, I don't want to come between you.
I know how much you love each other." Mark
did. But he couldn't look his friend in the face
now, either. He knew their friendship was irrevocably damaged. He also knew he couldn't
ask his friend to give up his wife for him.

"Thanks, man." Dave clapped his friend on
the shoulder, but Mark only felt the sting of the
slap. He knew he was doing the right thing,
but it still felt rotten. He was losing one of his
closest friends. And he just assumed Garrett
would be a lost cause. The two were brothers,
and blood was thicker than water.

"I won't ask Garrett to choose, either," Mark
said. They'd lost one crew member, so what
was one more? The two of them couldn't race
alone anyway. "So that leaves me on my own."
Mark couldn't help but state the obvious. The
words left a bitter taste in his mouth, but then
why should he be surprised?

He was always on his own. Nobody but him. Since Timothy had died. Since even before then. If there was one thing this world had taught him, it was don't rely on anybody else. "It'll be a shame, two of the best sailors on the island sitting this race out." Mark meant it as a statement of fact, but it came out sounding bitter.

"Listen, Mark. I…" Dave stopped. There was nothing more he could say. Not really. "I guess I'll go."

"I think that's best," Mark agreed, feeling bitter disappointment settle in his stomach.

Dave didn't offer his hand and Mark didn't either as Dave slowly walked to the door. Mark felt like the last hope for his boat, for his promise to Timothy, walked straight out the door.

CHAPTER SIX

"WELL, THAT WASN'T very neighborly," declared Laura, at a loss for what else to say. She'd heard of friends taking sides in a divorce, but she'd never seen a guy bail out of a friendship faster than that before. And especially not when his friend lost his son. What kind of friend did that?

"No, it wasn't," Mark agreed, but the dark cloud was back at him again, the lighthearted banter gone.

"Was he going to help you restore the boat, too?"

Mark nodded. "Not that I'll even be able to finish it now." He turned abruptly then and stalked out onto the back patio.

Now would probably be a good time for Laura to leave. After all, she'd already intruded too much, and her head still felt like it was in a vice. Yet, she wasn't about to leave him like Dave had. She knew what it felt like to be abandoned.

She followed him as he walked out to his

workshop. He crossed his arms and glared at the boat's hull.

"What if I help?" she asked, not even sure if she could. Her head still distantly throbbed from her hangover. Still, what was a headache compared to losing a child?

She knew the boat was his way of dealing with losing his son, and well, she couldn't just stand by and do nothing.

He scoffed, keeping his back to her. "Why would you do that?"

"Because I know what it feels like to lose hope," she said. "If this boat can bring back yours, then we need to do this." Laura never felt more certain of anything in her life. Yes, Mark was prickly and sometimes hard to deal with and teased her relentlessly, but if she could help him overcome his grief for his son, then she'd do it. She'd want the same for herself.

He paused, and his shoulders shrank a little.

"But what about racing it? I need at least three more sailors."

Laura frowned as she glanced at him and then the boat. "But you're going to sail the world by yourself?"

"Racing is a different animal, because everything is about speed. That's why you need more hands—literally—on deck."

Laura nodded, still in problem-solving mode. "Do you know other sailors on the island?"

Mark seemed to consider this. "Maybe. Not as good as Dave."

"But, can't we find other sailors? There have to be some on the island."

Mark shook his head. He put his hand on the hull of the boat. "Look, Laura, I appreciate you trying to help. But this isn't your problem."

"Mark." Laura wanted to help. She needed to help. She felt it in her bones. This was the first time since her miscarriage she'd actually *cared* about something.

"No. Laura. Just…" Mark waved a frustrated hand. "Just go. Please."

"But—"

Mark let out an exasperated sigh. *"Go,"* he growled. The force in his voice surprised her. She was on her feet, her heart thudding in her chest. Why was he turning her away?

He stomped away to the beach, leaving her staring after him, wondering why he was so angry and why he didn't want her help.

WHY WAS THIS so hard? Mark kicked the sand in front of him with his bare toes, watching it go scattering across the beach the very next morning. He'd spent the night tossing and turning, unable to think of a way to replace Dave, not knowing how he could even restore the boat by himself.

His dreams were dashed. He couldn't even be mad at Dave, exactly. He got that he had to stand by his wife, but why was Katie taking Elle's side? She'd slept with his own brother, hell, *run* off with him, and Mark was the bad guy?

But then again, he knew why. He blamed her for Timothy's death. There'd been the accusation of neglect. Of why she'd let him walk into the ocean that day.

The words bubbled up in him still, a seething indictment of his ex-wife's careless mistake. Anger still burned in him. If he'd been on the beach that day, maybe things would've been different.

But he hadn't been.

And they weren't.

And now, the one thing he'd been clinging to for months, this race and this boat, weren't even an option anymore.

He got about halfway down the stretch of beach near the condo and then slumped into the sand, suddenly drained of all energy. He watched the blue-green waves wash up on the shore, the sea foam bubbling against the wet sand, and wondered if he ought to just walk out to sea himself.

The waves rolled in endlessly to shore, and Mark let his mind wander once more to that dark place. Why wait until his trip around the world to get closer to Timothy? He could just get up on his feet and walk right into the ocean. Then all of this pain, all of this grief and loss, would end.

He pulled himself to his feet, not bothering to dust the sand from his shorts. Why bother? He whipped off his shirt and dropped it listlessly to the sand. Would someone find it? Would anyone even notice he was gone? Who would come looking for him?

Edward?

Laura?

The thought of Laura's bright green eyes stopped him a second. He didn't know why. He'd just met the woman. Yet something made him pause.

Her loud laugh? The way she'd run, drunk, down the beach away from him, her white, pale legs pumping hard as she sprinted away from her troubles?

But even she wasn't enough. No boat. No race. No Timothy. It all felt so overwhelming and hopeless.

This time, he'd do it, he thought as he took a step forward into the warm Caribbean, the water lapping at his tanned toes. He took another step and he found himself ankle deep. Another two steps and the water lapped above his knees, warm, inviting. The solution to all his problems. If he couldn't sail on the ocean to be closer to Timothy, then he'd get closer this way.

Did his boy walk out from this very spot? he wondered. He could have, midway between the condo and the natural, sloping dunes ahead of him.

Mark heard the seagulls calling and looked up, seeing the birds circling above him in the clear blue sky. Had that been the last thing Timothy had seen before he'd gotten swept under the waves?

Another step and he was waist deep. He could feel the sandy bottom with his toes, knew the drop off was coming soon, where it went from three feet to eight in a matter of inches. Tiny little silver fish swam around him in the ocean, glinting in the sun. Had Timothy gone after one of them? Delighted by their shine? Completely unaware of how dangerous the ocean could be, the water that would keep coming. The boy was too young to float. His life jacket had been abandoned on the beach, on the towel where his mother lay, eyes closed, drifting off to sleep.

Mark was about twenty feet out now. He took another step and the sandy bottom of the ocean

floor fell away from him, and he sank, his head
dipping below the water, his body buoyed by
the cool salty waves. Water rushed into his ears
and his nose, though he clamped his mouth shut
on reflex, holding his breath. He slipped down-
ward, below the sparkling surface, below the
sunlight that beamed through the top of the
water.

He reached the sandy bottom, still holding
his breath, the surface just a few feet above his
head. He held his breath until his lungs ached,
and then he released it, the bubbles floating upward to the surface and the sunlight. He looked
up, his lungs burning, as each second increased
his need to draw air, his lungs angrily protest-
ing the lack of oxygen.

He tried to keep himself still, but his arms
and legs defied him, and eventually he kicked
frantically to the surface, exploding upward and
drawing in a huge breath.

He was alive.

And he was a coward.

I can't even do this, he thought. Even his own
body defied him. He simply wasn't able to keep
himself below the surface. How unfair, when
Timothy would've fought against the waves
uselessly, his arms not strong enough to keep
himself afloat without his life preserver. Mark
turned back to the shore.

He saw Laura standing there, waving. This day she wore a gauzy, flowered sundress that just hit her knees. Her legs were still pale, almost as white as the small white flowers in the print.

Was she shouting something at him? Impossible to tell with the waves in his ears, the sound of water rushing all around him. He swam away from the deep, and eventually hit soft sand again as he walked toward her. What did she want?

Had she seen him try to kill himself? Had she seen him fail?

"Are you all right?" she asked him, green eyes concerned as she looked him up and down.

"Why wouldn't I be?" he snapped, defensive.

"I saw you walk out there, and then you just…disappeared." She pointed to the roiling waves. "It's like you…I don't know…like you sank on purpose." She shook her head, her dark bob shaking back and forth. She bit her lip, clearly not ready to call him suicidal. Did she suspect?

"Just cooling off," he lied, not wanting to get into it, not wanting to burden Laura, or to open up the door to a million questions he couldn't answer. "What are you doing here?"

"Looking for you," she said, meeting his gaze with determination. She looked like she was about to give him a lecture. What had he done now?

"You found me." He grabbed his shirt from the sand and shook it off, then he used it as a makeshift towel, wiping the stinging salt water from his face.

"You need my help."

Did she mean to prevent him from killing himself? His heart rate ticked up. "With what?"

"Your boat. Restoring it. Sailing it." She swept her arms wide.

He scoffed. "Do you know how to sail? How to restore a boat?"

"No. But you can teach me." She crossed her arms across her chest, determination in the bent of her brow.

"Look, Laura, I appreciate the help, but…" How could she help him? It would take longer for him to teach her how to restore the boat than to just do it himself.

"No." She shook her head, lips pressed into a thin line. "You don't understand. You're not going to put me off or tell me thanks but no thanks. I'm not going away."

"I'm not even sure we can restore the boat in time, and even if we did, we'd need three more people to help race it."

"We can find them." She was so stubbornly hopeful. Why?

Mark let out a long breath. "Why are you so determined? This isn't even your project."

"I need this," she said. "You don't know why I'm really here."

"Because your affair with Dean the Prick ended badly," Mark said, remembering her drunken tirade from the other night.

"That's not it. Not really." She took a deep breath and hugged herself tighter. "I'm here because I got pregnant. By Dean. I lost—" Laura sucked in a deep breath, the emotions seeming to overwhelm her "—the baby. I don't even know if I can have another one, or if I ever will."

Mark stood stock-still. He recognized the grief in her face, in the tremble of her voice. He'd known all along she suffered a loss. Maybe not like his, maybe different, but loss all the same. The pieces all fell together then. That's why she fell apart when she saw Timothy's baby video. Grief.

"And, I *need* something, like you *need* something," she continued, swiping angrily at the tears that sprang to her eyes. "I thought cashing in my 401(k) and coming here would be enough but it isn't. It isn't enough. I need something. I need to put my hands to work, like you. I need to find something to take my mind off this… god-awful loss. Or I'm going to lose it."

Mark knew the feeling. It's why he began restoring his father's old boat; it's why he hatched this plan. Putting his hands to work was a defense against the grief, against the black hole of darkness that threatened to suck him in and never let him out.

"But Dave leaving," he began. "I mean, I don't even know if it's a good plan anymore."

"You're going to give up this easily?" she challenged him. "The very first bump in the road and you're throwing in the towel?"

He hadn't thought of it like that before. Was he capitulating too soon?

"Look, you need this. I need this. And I'm going to make your life a holy hell until you agree to at least let me try. You saw me the other night. You know I can."

Mark suddenly had an image of her running drunk down the beach shouting, "Build that boat!" and knew she was right. The woman was stubborn, he'd give her that. She might be small, but she was unbreakable. An unbreakable pebble, the kind that got in your shoe and bugged the heck out of you.

"You really want to get your hands dirty?" he challenged her.

"Just try me," she said, raising her chin in the spirit of defiance.

CHAPTER SEVEN

OVER THE NEXT WEEK, Laura learned that while she might know a thing or two about software development, she had no idea how to build anything with her hands. She bungled the nail gun, she sawed off the wrong edge of a plank of wood and she nearly botched the sail she was trying to sew together. It was one mistake after another.

To his credit, Mark never lost his cool. He just kept moving her from one project to another, hoping she could find her stride.

That morning, Mark sat her down on top of the new wooden deck with several sanding blocks.

"I'm a disaster," she admitted, feeling despondent. "You really trust me with something new?"

"I think you can do this. I really do. There's no cords, no on-off switch, just this and elbow grease," he said. He sanded a bit of board and then slid his hand across it. "There? You feel how that new part feels?"

She ran her hands down the now-smooth wood, nodding.

"That's what the entire deck needs to feel like."

She glanced up at the twenty feet of deck and suddenly felt the monumental nature of the task. "Every board?" she asked, swallowing hard. That was going to take forever.

"Every board," he told her. Then, studying her a bit, he quirked an eyebrow in challenge. "We could always quit."

Laura shook her head fiercely. "No, we won't," she said. She wouldn't. Even if she had to sand this boat and ten others. This project had become too important. And she feared what would happen if her hands weren't busy anymore.

"I can handle this," she said, meaning it, even as a flicker of doubt crossed his face. She couldn't blame him. He climbed down the ladder at the side of the boat and busied himself repairing the huge white sail that would go on the rigging, while she, on hands and knees, got to work sanding the deck.

"Wax on, wax off," she joked to herself, as she began sanding tiny circles on the massive new deck.

After just a little while, her arms began to ache, then her shoulders and finally even her hands, as she scrubbed the deck endlessly, smoothing out the unfinished wood. She worked so hard that sweat dripped from her nose to the boards she was sanding. She simply swept over the wet marks.

The Caribbean sun beat down on her shoulders. She took off the sweatshirt she'd worn for the cooler morning breeze and let the warmth blanket her skin laid bare in a simple tank top. She'd slathered her normally alabaster skin in sunscreen, but already her shoulders looked pink with bits of tan emerging from the burn.

Time passed and her mind went blank. Thankfully, wonderfully blank, as she focused on leveling the splinters and smoothing the surface. She was in the present, feeling the tired muscles of her arms and back, moving to the rhythm of the gentle scratching of the sandpaper on wood.

"Missed a spot," Mark said behind her as he studied the sanded wood. "Here…and here."

She rocked back on her heels, adjusting the blue bandanna she wore tied over her hair, her dark bob curled around the edges. She glanced back, a little alarmed, but then Mark gently took the sanding square from her hand and bent down, scrubbing a little at an angle. "See? Try it this way."

She turned, positioned herself on hands and

knees and took the sanding sponge he offered, trying his new technique. Laura felt suddenly very aware of the proximity of Mark's body next to hers. "Like that?"

"Perfect," he declared, and she felt a little warm glow inside. She'd gotten it! She *was* getting it. She wasn't all thumbs, after all. Laura felt a little bubble of pride grow in her chest.

"You're picking this up pretty fast," he said, nodding his head in approval.

She grinned. "Thanks."

Mark took a swig of the water bottle in his hand. She felt a little streak of warmth flit through her belly as she watched his lips meet the bottle's opening. Full, determined. Then he offered it to her.

"Water?" he asked, and she suddenly felt the intimacy of the moment, sharing a bottle, putting her lips where his had been.

She took it and gulped it down, feeling the delicious simplicity of quenching her thirst. This is what she needed from this little sabbatical. Getting back to the simple things. Refocusing herself. Living in the moment.

"Thank you," she said, glancing at Mark's tall frame. He'd long since lost his shirt in the midafternoon heat, and sweat glistened on his shoulders. She tried not to stare at his bare chest, but it was hard not to notice the tanned muscles working as he lifted the last board to be laid on the deck.

"Can't have you dehydrated," he said and shrugged.

"Not for the water," she said quickly. "I mean, for letting me help you. This is…perfect. Just what I needed."

Mark barked a laugh as he plunked down the board and straightened. The sunlight hit his dark, short hair, glinting on gold highlights. "It's slave labor, you mean. You've been working hard all week. And for no pay."

"I'm just glad to keep my hands busy. To take my mind off everything that happened." And, she realized, as long as she kept her hands busy, she didn't think about what to do next or when she might need to start thinking about heading home. She had the boat and the race to think about, and that's all that mattered.

Mark nodded. "I know what you mean." He sat down near her cross-legged as he took another swig of water. "I'm sorry about your baby. Really sorry."

Tears rushed to her eyes. She swallowed hard. He was the first person she realized who'd been sorry, truly sorry, about her loss. He was the first not try to tell her this was all a good thing. That her baby's death was something she should celebrate, not mourn. "Thank you."

"It can't be easy to explain to people," he said, as he glanced up at the blue sky above them, dotted with wispy white clouds. "When you lose a child, it's not just the loss of your baby. It's the death of your dreams for them, the death of your hopes for the future. A little part of you dies with them."

A single tear slipped down Laura's cheek and she angrily swiped it away. "You're so right," she said, realizing that he'd put into words what she'd been feeling for so long but couldn't articulate. "It's so true. So many people kept trying to tell me I should be grateful. Dean and even my sister said I should be thankful I lost the baby."

"No," Mark said, shaking his head vehemently. "Don't ever let anybody tell you to be grateful for losing a baby. Babies are wonderful. They're miracles, and the loss of a baby should never be a relief. Never."

"But, the father was married. I'd..." *I'd broken one of the Ten Commandments. I'd sinned and committed adultery and brought this all on myself.*

"It doesn't matter. None of that matters. You lost a baby, for goodness' sake. It doesn't matter how you got that baby." Mark shook his head. He glanced at her. "Want to talk about it? What happened? I mean, I'm a great listener when I'm not being grumpy."

Laura smiled. "You are grumpy a lot."

"Hey." He gave her a playful shove. "Listen, it's good to talk about it, though. Get it out. Don't hold it inside."

Mark seemed so sincere, so open. Laura decided to give it a chance.

"Dean hated the idea of me being pregnant. He wanted…" She almost couldn't say it. "He wanted me to get rid of the baby."

"An abortion." Mark's tone lacked judgment.

Laura nodded. "I couldn't do it. I mean, I thought about it. I did. Being a single mom and Dean not wanting the baby and not even wanting to admit his paternity, but…I just couldn't do it. For me. I get that other people make different decisions and I am not judging them, but for me, this is what I decided."

"I get it. Nothing about that decision is easy."

Laura shook her head. "No. It's not." She glanced upward at the clear blue sky above them. A seagull swept by overhead. "At the twelfth week mark, the end of my first trimester, I went in for my regular checkup with my ob-gyn. She couldn't find a heartbeat, and so she sent me to the hospital next door so they could run an ultrasound. She told me everything was probably fine. Not to worry. Not yet."

Laura remembered that day. She'd felt concerned but not overly so. Miscarriage hadn't even entered her mind. But when she got the ultrasound in the very quiet, dark place where she'd been taken, where the technician didn't say a word, then she'd known something was wrong. Something was very wrong.

"They didn't find a heartbeat. It was awful." So much more than awful. "My doctor told me the baby had died a week before, maybe even longer. The worst part was that I went all that time and I didn't even know."

Mark leaned into her and wrapped his arm around her shoulders. He said nothing, but she could feel the comfort in his embrace.

"The bleeding began a few days after that, but then it didn't stop and I had to go to the hospital. I have this disorder, something or other, that the doctors said meant that they had trouble stopping the bleeding once the baby…well, detached." She looked at him. "I nearly died. I got two blood transfusions."

"That's horrible. I didn't even know that could happen," he said.

"Neither did I."

"I'm glad you didn't die." He squeezed her shoulders.

"Me, too." She leaned into him.

"You know, it just proves my theory. Mothers are strong."

Mother. The very word made her want to cry

harder. "But I was never a…" She swallowed, not trusting herself to actually say the word out loud. "My baby was never born."

Mark took a deep drag of water and then wiped the back of his mouth. "Doesn't mean you weren't a mother. Did you care for that baby inside your body while it was alive? Did you give up alcohol? Did you think about your baby?"

Laura nodded. She remembered how careful she'd been after she knew she was pregnant. No alcohol, not even a drop of caffeine—and she loved coffee. She'd eaten more green leafy vegetables and taken her prenatal vitamins religiously. She'd already been picking out names and trying to figure out where she'd put the crib in her cramped San Francisco apartment.

"Yes, but—"

"No buts. You were a mother. For that time. You cared about your baby. You put the baby first. That's what mothers do." He glanced at her with knowing, dark eyes. "That means you were a mother."

"I never thought about it like that."

"You should," Mark said. He said it so simply, so definitively, as if there could be no other truth.

The thought felt like a revelation. Mothers were supposed to be people who carried to term, who had something to prove for their efforts.

"But I don't have a baby. I mean, to show for it. I never had one."

"You had one. Inside you," he said. "And am I less of a father because my son isn't alive anymore?"

"No! Of course not." She wasn't about to take that away from him. "You'll always be a father. No matter what."

"Well, then, you're a mom. Simple as that."

More tears flowed, and she couldn't stop them even as she tried to wipe them away with the back of her hand. He took a clean work cloth from his back pocket and scooted closer. Their knees touched as he handed it to her. She wiped her eyes and blew her nose.

Laura blew her nose once more and the trumpeting sound made both her and Mark laugh a little. "I guess you're right."

"I know I am." Mark glanced at her. She felt transfixed by his dark, knowing eyes, by the way they saw her and seemed to understand everything about her. She could feel the current of electricity running between them and wondered if he could feel it, too. If he leaned forward right now and kissed her, Laura would welcome it, she realized with a start. The current intensified between them. *Intimacy*, she realized. They'd bonded over their losses, and in some way, she felt like he'd offered her a way forward.

It's not that she'd never be a mother. She'd already been one. She always would be one.

The understanding dawned and all she wanted to do was kiss Mark. He understood, but more than that, he'd shown her an escape route from her depression. *She was a mother.*

"Mark..." She put her hand on his forearm, his strong, tanned arm, and leaned closer. She wanted to kiss him now, to show him how amazing he was, how he'd changed her life in this very moment. He seemed transfixed by her, too, sitting very still next to her. Would he let her kiss him? Should she try? She wanted to.

Her body made the decision for her as she inched ever closer. All she could think about was what his lips might feel like against hers. She was just inches away from him, when abruptly he pulled away, whipping his arm away from her touch, standing up suddenly.

The movement seemed so jarring, so out of the blue, that all Laura could do was sit there, a bit stunned. She craned her neck up at him and watched him awkwardly fidget.

"Got to get back to work," Mark said, uneasily, refusing to look her in the eye. "Sunlight won't last much longer."

She felt white-hot embarrassment flush her

cheeks. She'd misread him. He wasn't interested, not in that way. He was just being kind. Nothing more, nothing less. She watched him as he scuttled off the deck of the boat and shimmied down the ladder away from her. He couldn't get away fast enough.

At least she hadn't actually kissed him. What a nightmare that would've been. She felt herself squirm at the very idea that he'd push her away or look disgusted. Then she would've really been horrified. Now at least, she could just pretend she'd never intended to kiss him. Not at all.

I'm never going to try again, either, she thought. *He's made his feelings clear.*

With nothing else left to do, she bent her head and went back to work, trying to ignore the sting of rejection.

CHAPTER EIGHT

MARK SPENT THE rest of the day and night kicking himself. He knew he'd made a mistake the minute he'd turned away from Laura and seen how she'd stiffened. But he just wasn't ready for…a connection.

Not that the fear stopped him from wanting to taste her. Hell, every inch of his body screamed for him to take the delicate little woman into his arms and kiss the life out of her, *right now*, but that shouldn't happen. It couldn't happen.

Not when she was leaving in a couple of weeks.

Not when he wasn't ready to get involved with someone; not when his heart was still broken.

When he'd seen the intent look on her face, the desire as she'd moved closer to him the day before, he'd panicked. Actually, he could still feel the panic deep inside him, the anxiety that rose up any time he thought about getting involved with another woman. Because he knew women didn't do things halfway. Not any woman he'd ever known.

Hell, he'd only slept with one woman since Elle, and after just a single night of sex, the girl had been practically picking out curtains for his condo. No, he didn't need that right now. Didn't need the drama women inevitably brought with them. The emotional roller coasters, the hurt feelings that he never seemed to understand, the endless emotional need.

Elle had been beautiful but stormy, always mad at him for something, but he had no idea what. She'd kept a running tally of all the things he'd bungled. Her not-quite-perfect birthday gift, him forgetting their first-date anniversary—the woman had a calendar laid out of the first time they'd even gotten ice cream together, which he didn't even know was a thing you were supposed to track. Her moods shifted quicker than the weather on the ocean, except even the storms out there could be forecast. Her moods were 100 percent unpredictable.

At first, it excited him, but then, after they lost Timothy, all he could see in her was a child who refused to take responsibility—for her feelings or her mistakes.

That morning, Mark realized he was in for a different kind of storm when Laura arrived, acting a little more businesslike, a bit colder to him as she went about finishing the sanding of his deck. Mark worried Laura was too much like Elle. She burst into tears when he just mentioned the word *mother*. She was a walking bundle of pain and emotion, wild and volatile.

He kept his emotions bottled up, but just because he didn't rant and rave didn't mean he lacked emotion. His feelings ran deep, like still water.

Mark wanted to kiss Laura. He wanted to do more. But he knew the minute he did, she'd begin to demand things from him and he had nothing to give. He was still in mourning, and the only way he knew how to deal with it was to go off sailing around the world—alone. Sailing was dangerous, and he already knew that if the trip killed him, that would take care of two birds with one stone. Maybe even part of him hoped he didn't come back. He couldn't ask Laura to accompany him on a trip that he half hoped ended with his boat at the bottom of the sea, him joined with his boy forever.

He wouldn't ask her along. And he didn't want her to want to go with him, either. Not what he needed right now.

He watched her quietly take up her post on the deck with her sanding blocks and noticed she took special care not to look his way. She'd only given him a curt "morning" before getting to work. Businesslike was better—for both of them, but he didn't like the idea of her feelings being hurt. It showed he was already starting to care about her, a dangerous place to be.

Maybe letting her in on this project had been his first mistake. He should've just stood his ground. Told her to buzz off. Then he remembered the determined fire in her green eyes and the stubborn jut of her chin and realized he probably couldn't have talked her out of this project, no matter what he said.

He sighed as she furiously scrubbed the deck, looking as if she was working out her disappointment and anger on the boards. Well, at least she has an outlet, he thought. Still, he felt bad.

"You need some water?" he asked her, offering up his bottle in a kind of truce as he stood on the ladder.

"No, thanks," she said, curt, not looking back at him as she worked. "Brought my own today."

So that's how it was going to be?

Don't make it your problem, he told himself. He had enough to worry about. Probably best she just stay mad at him. It was one way to make sure she didn't get too close.

THE MORE LAURA WORKED, the angrier she seemed to get. She didn't know why. Sure, Mark had rejected her, but he'd not been the first man who wasn't all that crazy about the thought of her kissing him. There'd been Jack Aubrey all the way back in fourth grade.

She admitted freely to herself that ever since the miscarriage, she'd been a buddle of unpredictable emotions. She hated it, really. They seemed to overtake her when she least expected it. Laura always prided herself on being a rational woman, a thoughtful, sane, practical person. But the miscarriage had turned her life upside down. Grief, she supposed, did that. Grief wasn't just sadness bubbling to the surface. It was anger and regret and guilt, too.

She scrubbed harder at the boards in front of her, building up a thin layer of sawdust on her hands and arms all the way up to her elbows. Laura hardly cared. She took out her emotions on the wood, still surprised about how deeply she felt rejected by Mark, how somehow she'd built up a great fantasy in her head after just a few days, that maybe they were really connecting, that maybe someone finally understood her.

Why would he be interested in an adulterer? No one wanted a cheater. How could anyone trust her again?

Of course, technically, Dean had been the one cheating. Still. Laura had known he had a wife. She was just as guilty as he was. Chalk it up to one more reason she'd be single for the rest of her life. One more reason why she'd probably never have kids.

Not that my body can do that anyway.

Laura knew she was wallowing in self-pity and hated it. She scrubbed harder as she worked her way into the corner of the deck. She realized with a start that much time had passed, and the sun hung high overhead. She was also nearly done with the sanding portion of her responsibilities. Her shirt was covered in sawdust, as were her hands and arms. Sawdust clung to her knees and her face. It probably was sprinkled in her hair, too.

Laura stretched, feeling the stiffness in her back. She wasn't twenty anymore, and she'd been using muscles she never thought she even had. Her shorts also felt looser. She wondered if that was the pregnancy weight she'd lost or if that were just all the work she'd been doing with her hands.

The warm Caribbean sun bore down on her head as she reached the end of the deck. She dropped her sanding sponges and sat back on her heels. That was a job well done, she thought as she looked across the huge expanse of brand-new decking, newly sanded. She stood, grabbed the broom that was leaning against the mast and began sweeping off the dust, feeling the solid boards beneath her feet. She wondered what the boat would feel like out at sea, moved by waves, surrounded by blue-green water. Laura realized she might never know. She was helping Mark get the boat ready, but it was no guarantee he'd take her out on it. Or that he'd want to.

On her perch, up on deck, she saw a couple walking hand in hand on the beach. She glanced back and saw Mark, shirtless again, moving cans of resin and wood stain around in the workshop. She noticed the way his back muscles worked as he sorted through the cans. She still felt a twinge of attraction, despite the fact that he clearly didn't feel the same way.

Laura wondered if this would be Dean all over again. Dean, who pretended after the end of the affair that he'd never wanted her at all. He sat in boardrooms staring at her blankly, without a hint of warmth. Of course, now she understood why. He'd been busy taking care of his newly pregnant wife. She wondered how he'd reacted when his wife had told him the news. Had he celebrated? Been truly happy. The thought sliced through her like a sharp knife. He'd never truly cared for her at all, that much she knew now.

Laura decided she did need a break. Being here with Mark, working on his boat, suddenly didn't feel therapeutic.

She put the broom back where she'd found it and then climbed down the ladder resting against the side of the boat. Once on the ground, she cleared her throat, but Mark, busy inventorying the cans, didn't turn around.

"Mark," she said.

He turned slightly, almost fearfully. As if he worried she'd start yelling at him. "Yes?"

"I'm going to stop for the day," she said, suddenly feeling relieved to have the words out. Now she didn't have to pretend yesterday didn't hurt, that it never happened. She could just get away from Mark and then she'd feel better.

"But it's just four," he exclaimed, surprised. Usually she worked till sundown. *Well, not today, buddy.*

"I just need a break." She rubbed her wrist, hoping to use muscle aches as her excuse but honestly not really caring if he picked up on the cue or not.

"Uh…sure." Mark rubbed his bare neck, still looking confused.

Laura turned.

"See you tomorrow then?"

She paused, hand on the side of the boat. "Uh. Probably." It sounded weak even in her own ears, but somehow she couldn't quite muster the enthusiasm for tomorrow. She'd just have to wait and see how she felt.

Mark didn't reply, and when she glanced back, she saw he'd already busied himself opening a can of wood stain. He didn't seem to care that her answer was iffy or that she might walk out of his life for good. What did she expect? A grand gesture? An apology?

Right now, all she wanted to do was take a hot shower, throw on some clothes and head to the nearest tourist bar. She was pretty sure a sweet drink with an umbrella would make her feel better. At least, it couldn't make her feel worse.

MARK SPENT THE next few hours carefully painting wood stain on his newly sanded deck. Even he had to admit Laura had done a wonderful job. Better than he'd hoped. And having her working on it had sped up the timeline quite a bit. She was an efficient worker, and now he was not only back on schedule with the boat, but ahead of schedule. He might finish by the race, after all.

Even though you don't have a crew.

He'd deal with that later. First, the boat. Then the crew.

The sun began to dip below the horizon and Mark worked hard to finish up the stain before it did. He tried to focus entirely on the wood stain and the back-and-forth of his paint brush, but part of him couldn't help thinking about how Laura had left. Mysterious and moody.

Like all women, he thought. He'd never figure them out. He knew from her "probably" that there was a chance she might not return to help him now that her little venture in this project was done. *Probably for the best. I don't need the drama.*

But when he thought of her bright green eyes, he realized he missed them already. He missed having her company, her petite frame working so diligently next to him, eager and always prodding him to do better. And he'd offended her, like he did nearly all the women in his life, and now she'd left. Same as all the others.

Even worse, for the last hour, some upbeat dance music blared from the balcony of her condo. It abruptly stopped, and a few minutes later, he heard her footsteps on the metal stairs. He glanced up and from his vantage point on the boat, he could see through a break in the condo buildings to the parking lot. Laura was dressed up in wedge sandals, a short sundress showing off her newly tanned legs, a red flower in her dark bobbed hair and red lipstick. Definitely stark red lipstick.

He felt his groin tighten in appreciation. The

woman was gorgeous, her short cotton dress clinging perfectly to her seductive curves.

She climbed into a waiting cab, one he recognized as belonging to Reggie, the cab driver who'd been the first person he'd ever met on St. Anthony's. Reggie had a wife and three kids, whom he supported by taking tourists around the island. Mark wondered where Laura was off to wearing red lipstick and what she would do when she got there.

The sky turned a deep crimson with the setting sun and he knew the tourist bars would still be in full swing. He knew when Laura got there, she'd have to fight off the men. They'd be on her like bears on honey. He tried not to let that bother him as he finished the last swipe of wood stain. *Not my problem.* Then why did it feel like his problem?

What if she met someone? Went back to his hotel room or took him to hers? Worse, what if she got into trouble? Women looking that pretty nearly always got into trouble, especially when there were drunk tourists around.

He climbed down the ladder from the boat and wiped his hands on a damp rag, mind working. He could shower and call up Reggie. With a little prodding, he figured, Reggie would tell him where she'd gone. And even if he didn't, there was only one main tourist strip in Smuggler's Cove with just three bars.

He could find her easily. And find her he would.

CHAPTER NINE

LAURA SKIPPED OVER the two glaring bars with neon signs and college kids crowding the open patios until she landed at the one bar in Smuggler's Cove with the least amount of neon lights. It was called the Rusted Anchor, which Laura thought ironic and perfect.

The Rusted Anchor felt like a bar for the serious sailor or the serious drinker. She saw both in the place. What she didn't see were umbrellas in drinks or neon party shirts or college spring-breakers. The well-worn bar was bustling, though. A wooden ship's wheel hung above it, draped in fishing netting and buoys, but that's where the kitsch ended. The rest of the place was crowded with worn wooden booths and a few round tables, with an entire wall of windows facing the marina. Rows of perfect sailboats bobbed in their moorings, lined up and ready to set sail.

Laura glanced at them and felt a little pang. She might never see Mark's boat sail now. She might never even help him finish it. Would he give up? Would he continue on without her? Either option seemed painful. She realized she'd hung on to this thought of him taking her sailing, of feeling the deck she'd sanded move beneath her feet as it cut through the waves.

Not that Mark had ever promised her that. She'd been filling in the blanks again with her expectations, without any real evidence to support them. It was just like what she'd done with Dean. He'd told her he loved her and she ran with it, filling her mind with dreams of her future with him and their baby.

She walked past a casual Seat Yourself Anywhere sign near the front and chose an open bar stool. A bartender wearing a simple T-shirt with an anchor on it was drying a glass.

"What can I get you?" he asked her, his face friendly and open and probably at least ten years younger than she was. Still, he was cute, with his blond hair and ice-blue eyes.

"Gin and tonic? You have Hendricks?"

"Yes, ma'am," he said, and she cringed a little. *Ma'am.* That's what she was becoming. More and more.

Feeling alone, she pulled out her phone. No new messages.

Would she be able to work on the boat tomorrow? She didn't know. The boat had been the perfect distraction, to help put her mind on a problem that had a solution: board, meet nail. Brush meet paint. Easy. Simple. Doable. With no such distractions now, all her old thoughts rushed back, and they were all of Dean.

What was he doing right now? Feeding his beautiful, pregnant wife pickles and ice cream? Rubbing her feet? Painting the nursery?

All the thoughts felt like daggers in her brain. Why did she do this to herself? Why did she torture herself like this?

Still, she couldn't help it. She had to silence the morbid curiosity in her mind. She pulled up Dean's Facebook page. Instantly, she wished she hadn't. He had taken a selfie with his beaming wife, his own hand over her belly. The caption read, "And baby makes three!"

The post had dozens and dozens of comments, all gushing, all happy for the couple. Dean looked happy, grinning from ear to ear, the epitome of a proud papa. If she had any doubt about everything he told her being a lie, then his photo confirmed it. He was happy with his wife. She'd just been a distraction.

A text popped up from her older sister, Maddie. How's Margaritaville?

Fine, Laura texted back. Even though it wasn't fine. She'd traveled thousands of miles away and she was just starting to realize there wasn't anywhere far enough she could run to get away from her problems. The last thing she needed was for Maddie, who wasn't afraid to let Laura know in detail all the ways she was mucking up in her life, to tell her how this was all a huge waste of time. Maddie had been trying to fill their mother's shoes ever since she'd passed away. Laura wanted to tell her that wasn't her job.

You going to come back soon? Think of your retirement! You might be able to put money back in your 401(k) without a penalty if you work fast.

Laura sighed and put the phone facedown on the bar. Leave it to her older sister to harp on her about responsibility. She just didn't understand. Nobody seemed to understand.

Mark understood, a small voice whispered in her head. And instantly she remembered the embarrassment of trying to kiss the man. Mark was a nonstarter.

The bartender placed the tumbler of the clear cocktail with lime in front of her.

"Would you like to pay now or start a tab?"

"Tab," she said and slid her credit card over the bar, figuring this was a more-than-one-drink kind of night.

"I've got it, Greg," came a smooth voice to her right. She turned, slipping her phone in her pocket, to see a man who looked…a little like Mark. But wasn't Mark. Older, a bit grayer in the temples, but the same dark eyes, the same strong jawline. "And get me a St. Anthony's IPA, would you?" The bartender nodded and hurried off to get the man's beer.

"Oh, you don't have to do that," she exclaimed, squirming on her bar stool. Sure, she'd dressed up and come out to the bar in the vain hope she might be able to flirt a little, but now, with this age-appropriate man in the linen shorts and button-down light blue shirt, she suddenly felt shy. Not ready. Thrown by Dean's picture of domestic bliss. Now she wasn't sure she had the courage to flirt, exactly.

"I know I don't," he said smoothly. "But I want to." He grinned, and she could feel the charm oozing from him. She wondered if her imagination was playing tricks on her with how much he looked like Mark. She could get used to this, though. His smile and his eyes were so much like Mark's, except friendly.

She nodded, and he slipped onto the stool next to her, his knee casually brushing hers. She liked the contact. He smiled once more and she felt like maybe she did have the courage to flirt. Isn't that why she'd come? To forget…Mark. Just have a little fun. Be a tourist for once. She smiled back at the stranger.

"You have a beautiful smile," he said.

"Well, then, you'll have to make me smile more often." She laughed a little at her obvious attempt to flirt. He joined her.

"Well, I will. Consider the challenge accepted."

The bartender returned with his beer and set it on the bar.

The man held up his glass. "To new acquaintances and many more smiles," he said.

She grinned. "I'll drink to that." They clinked glasses and she took a sip of her gin and tonic, the tart crispness hitting her tongue in just the right way. Now her evening was starting to look up.

"So what's a gorgeous woman like you doing in a dive like this?" he asked.

"That's a terrible line. Does that work?"

"Nope. But I'm hoping to break the losing streak." He grinned.

"I'm a tourist. In from San Francisco."

"Love California!" he exclaimed.

"I'm Laura," she said, holding out her hand. He took it gently and squeezed, his eyes never leaving hers. "Laura, pleasure to meet you. I'm Edward. Edward Tanner."

Laura froze on her bar stool.

"Tanner? Are you related to Mark Tanner?"

Edward frowned. "My brother. Why?"

Then it all hit her at once. The resemblance

was no accident. This was the brother who'd slept with Mark's wife. Who'd stolen the boat company and now he'd bought her a drink. She felt trapped suddenly, as if the walls of the bar were closing in.

Laura felt anger bubble up in her.

"Look, I'm *friends* with Mark," she said and let that sit there, hoping he took the cue and left. She didn't really want to have to spell it out for him, but their flirting was over and so was the drink.

Edward frowned.

"Oh, so he's told you about me, has he?"

"He has." She tried to lace the sentence with as much meaning as she could muster. *I know all about you, buddy. I know what you did. What kind of brother you are. I want nothing to do with you.*

"Well, that's a shame because there are two sides to every story. Don't suppose you want to hear mine?" Edward asked, quirking a hopeful eyebrow.

"I don't see how that would change things. You... I mean, what you did." Laura lowered her voice, as if somehow the other people in the bar would overhear. She glanced at a waitress who scurried by them carrying a tray loaded with fish and chips and hamburgers and fries.

"You mean you've never done something

wrong, something that everyone would think was terrible, but no one ever gave you the chance to explain?" Edward asked, as if he could see into her very heart. She had done something wrong. Something very wrong.

"What if I had?" she asked, daring Edward to come up with a reason to justify taking Mark's wife and the company.

"Then you understand there are two sides to every story."

Laura watched him, waiting.

"Did Mark tell you he lost his son?" Laura nodded once. "Did he tell you what he was like after that? What he did?"

"He was grieving," she assumed.

"Yes, he was. But he lashed out. At everyone. At me, at his friends, at his wife. That day was a tragic accident, but he blamed his wife," he said.

"Yes, but she fell asleep. I get it was an accident, but how irresponsible," she said.

"I know it sounds bad. But Timothy had trouble sleeping at night. She was up with him most nights, and she was just tired. And it's a mistake she has to live with for the rest of her life." Edward glared at his amber-colored beer in his glass. "But Mark, he called his buddy, the police chief on the island. He came, put handcuffs on her. Took her to jail for neglect. She spent two nights there before I hired a lawyer and got the charges dropped. She might still be there if I hadn't intervened."

Laura wasn't sure how she felt about that. If it was truly an accident, did she deserve jail? Then again, her fiercely protective mothering instincts took over, as she thought of Timothy, left unsupervised. Maybe she should be punished.

Laura didn't know. The situation seemed so hard. Before she could say more, she heard someone clearing his throat behind her. When she spun on her stool, she saw Mark standing there, freshly showered and wearing a button-down white linen shirt and khaki shorts. His face seemed flushed beneath his tan, as his dark eyes flashed with anger.

"Am I interrupting something?" he asked, glaring first at her and then his brother.

CHAPTER TEN

MARK FELT THE heat rise up his neck as anger, thick and hot, flowed through him. And jealousy, too. Laura had her legs crossed at the knee, revealing the bare skin of her newly tanned legs, and she was sitting entirely too close to *Edward*, the man he trusted least on the entire island. They practically sprang apart when he approached, as if he'd interrupted a secret rendezvous.

Or was that just his history talking?

Laura didn't belong to him. She couldn't cheat on him. Yet part of him wanted her to be at least enough on his side not to have a drink with the one man he disliked most in the world.

"We just met," Laura said quickly, green eyes wide, pleading. Her red, red lips parted and he couldn't be mad at her. She was too damn pretty. He focused all his rage on Edward instead.

"Yes, I was just about to tell her about how you got me all wrong," Edward said, taking a calm sip of his beer.

"I didn't get you wrong." *I know you all too well.* "Besides, don't you have Elle at home? Where's she?" Mark wanted to remind Edward *and* let Laura know that this little snake wasn't free. He had a woman at home, after all. One he'd stolen, but still.

"She's fine. Tired, that's all." Edward kept his voice even. Laura's head swiveled back and forth as she looked from one brother to the other, clearly uncomfortable. "When are you going to learn, brother, that you're the only one who thinks I'm the bad guy?"

Edward nodded around the Rusted Anchor, and that's when Mark noticed that more than a few of the patrons were glancing at them. He knew almost all of them. The sailing community was a small one on St. Anthony's and even those who came from other islands tended to be regulars. Most of them had money, or at least enough of it so they could live a life like a nomad, hopping from place to place.

Mark glanced up and noticed Dave and his wife dining in a nearby booth. Dave nodded at him, but his wife barely glanced in his direction. At least Elle wasn't here. That would make this ten times worse.

"Is that so?" Mark challenged him. "Laura, what do you think? Did I get him wrong?"

Laura flushed red beneath her new tan. "Look,

I don't want to get drawn into this," she said, holding up one newly calloused hand. Her hands had been working on *his* boat all week, he reminded himself. She was supposed to be on *his* side.

Until you messed it up by pushing her away, an inner voice scolded. *Just like you pushed Elle away.*

"You're already in it," Mark pressed.

"Mark, I…"

"Stop bullying the lady," Edward said, a steely warning in his voice. Laura once more glanced from one man to the other, looking like she wished to be anywhere but here.

Mark, for his part, was one more insulant line away from clocking Edward, right here in front of all his friends and all of St. Anthony's regulars. He was tired of everyone taking Edward's side, even when he was clearly in the wrong. It had been that way since the two of them were little. Edward could do no wrong, and Mark got blamed for everything.

Their father had raced sailboats in his spare time in Florida, where they grew up, and he'd worked as a lawyer by day. Edward was his father's favorite, the one who learned how to sail first, the one who went racing first. Mark had been an afterthought, always having to work harder to prove that he belonged on the sea, too.

Edward took credit for building Tanner Boating, when it was Mark's blood, sweat and tears that had made that business what it was. Hell, it hadn't even been Edward's idea in the first place.

Now all of that was gone. He felt the throbbing unfairness of it, the way nothing in life was fair when it came to Edward. The way he never had to work for anything. Ever. Life handed him things. Their father's approval, his ex-wife's affection and now…Laura. Mark couldn't let that happen. Not this time.

He glared at his brother, mute, words failing him. Edward stared back and the tension between the two men grew so thick the general buzz at the bar lowered as patrons took notice.

"Everything okay here?" Suddenly, Mark felt a heavy hand clamp down on his shoulder. Dave's. Mark felt the sudden urge to shrug off his old friend's touch. He still felt the sting of the betrayal of Dave leaving, even if it was to keep the peace in his own home.

"No, Dave. It's not." Hadn't been for a while. *And you only made it worse.*

"Did Dave tell you the good news?" Edward said.

Dave suddenly looked uncertain. "Edward, maybe…"

"He's racing my boat. For Tanner."

"What?" Mark glared at Dave, looking for some kind of explanation. He knew his friend wasn't sailing with him, but he had no idea he'd *defected*.

"No sense in letting his sailing talents go to waste."

Mark felt like he'd been sucker punched. "Really?" he managed. Dave had the decency to turn red.

"Mark, man, I'm sorry..." He glanced back at his wife, sitting in the far booth and sending Mark death glares. At this point, Mark didn't care about Dave's wife. She could go take a long walk off a short pier.

"Unbelievable." Mark shook his head. Now he didn't know who to hit, Edward or Dave. Or both.

"Even if you do finish that rust bucket of yours, brother, I don't think you'll be able to find a sailor as good as Dave."

"I'm as good as Dave."

"Then you'll need to clone yourself to fill out your crew," Edward said.

Mark's hand twitched, itching to do something. Clock Edward like he'd done when they were kids. Only Mark was never the one to strike first. Maybe that would change tonight. Maybe that would finally change.

"Mark." Laura's voice cut through his anger.

She slipped quietly off her stool and put her own body between him and his brother. "Mark, take me home."

He didn't want to take her home. He wanted to finally teach his brother a lesson. The kind of lesson he never got growing up.

"Mark." She put her hand on his arm. "Please."

The tone of her *please* made him break eye contact with his brother. He glanced down at her sad green eyes. And in that second, he realized he couldn't fight his brother. Not with her there. She'd already been through too much.

"Okay," he said, softening. He took a step back and she followed. He was hyperaware of her and his brother, the adrenaline and emotion pumping hard through his veins. It took every bit of his self-control not to throw a punch.

"See you around, Laura," Edward called to their backs.

Both he and Laura stiffened. He curled his hand into a fist but Laura wrapped her arms around him. "Let's go," she reiterated, and within her tight hug, he knew he couldn't throw the punch he'd been planning.

He simply nodded, as he put his arm around her and they walked out, side by side. Outside, in the warm night air, Laura's explanations came fast and furious, as Mark led her to his pickup truck.

"I didn't know he was your brother until after he introduced himself," she proclaimed. "And I hadn't even been talking to him that long. He only bought me one drink and that was before I knew who he was."

"He bought you a drink?" Jealousy flared in his chest as he flicked the key fob and unlocked the doors, the taillights flaring.

"I didn't know who he was," she protested as she stopped by the passenger side door, palms up, almost pleading.

"But you were fine with having a stranger buy you a drink?" Mark boxed her in between his body and his truck. She was so small, so tiny, she had to crane her neck to look at him, her green eyes defiant in the moonlight.

In an instant, her apologetic demeanor disappeared.

"Why are you so mad about it?" She put one hand on her hip.

It was a good question. Why was he so mad about it? He had no official claim on her, and he'd refused to kiss her yesterday.

But part of him already knew why. Because he wanted her and because he'd lost everything else in his life and just couldn't—wouldn't lose her. No matter how he tried to convince himself otherwise, the truth was staring him in the face. He glanced at her full, red lips and wanted nothing more than to taste them.

"I don't want you hanging around Edward."

She put her back against the door of his pickup. "Why?"

It seemed like she was baiting him on purpose.

"You know why. He's bad news." He barely gritted out the words.

"Is that all?" She tapped her foot, and he was aware they were standing in the parking lot, beneath a full Caribbean moon and in full view of the windows of the Rusted Anchor. Was Edward watching them fight? Was he waiting to come pounce?

When he didn't have an answer at the ready, she barreled on. "You sound jealous."

"I'm not," he lied.

"You don't have any right to be jealous." She poked him in the chest with one finger. The ocean breeze ruffled her short dark hair, so smooth and silky. He wanted to put his hands in it. "You had your chance. You—"

She was going to tell him that he'd missed his chance to kiss her, and he knew he'd blown that moment. If he could take it back now, he would. Instead, he did something rash. Before he even knew what he was doing, he grabbed her by the arms, pulled her to him and kissed her on her full, red lips.

He deserved a slap, he supposed, but instead, she kissed him back. Hard. All the adrenaline and emotion of the last few minutes bubbled up between them, as she opened her mouth for him, and he tasted her.

Their tongues met, crashing together in a sudden animalistic burst of passion. She pressed her body into his, and he felt the soft brush of her breasts against him as he wrapped his arms around her tiny waist. She was running her hands through his hair, driving him wild as her fingers wrapped around the back of his neck. He didn't know how long the kiss lasted. Ten seconds? Ten years? His body was alive again for the first time in a long time with want and need and desire.

Why had he been fighting this, he wondered. He loved her mouth. The way her tongue danced with his. All he wanted to do was take her into his bed and find out all the other ways he could love her.

He cupped her from behind and she moaned in his mouth as he found her firm butt and pressed her closer to him. His own body stirred in ways she couldn't miss. He released her and pressed her against the side of his truck. She raised up one leg, wrapping it seductively around the side of his thigh, and he pressed into her.

He could feel her warmth beneath the thin layer of her dress and he slid his hand up the soft silkiness of her outer thigh to discover she wore only a skinny thong beneath her dress. His fingers teased the elastic band, and he was so out of his mind, he didn't think about where they were, about who could see them, about how they were acting like two impulsive kids.

"Wait," Laura breathed, pulling back, her hand on his. He released his grip on her underwear, slowly coming to his senses. Was he going to take her right here in the Rusted Anchor parking lot? In full view of everyone? He glanced back at the bar, but only saw shadows in the window.

He let her go with a shaky breath as he backed off.

"Sorry... I...I don't know what happened." He was breathing hard. "I shouldn't have... I mean, I'm sorry."

"Don't be sorry." Even in the moonlight, he could see her pupils, dilated with want. "I liked it."

"You did?"

She nodded back toward the windows of the bar. "Even if you were doing it for his benefit and not mine."

"Laura," he began to protest. How could he explain that it wasn't just about one-upping his brother? He *wanted* her. Yet, she opened the passenger side of the pickup truck and shut the door on him before he could even explain.

He shook his head.

This was why he didn't get involved with women. He'd never understand them. They were always angry for crazy reasons that made no sense to him. He sighed. Kissing Laura had been a mistake, he thought. One he shouldn't make again.

CHAPTER ELEVEN

THE CAR RIDE back was tense, but neither one said a word. What was there to say? Laura thought. She knew why suddenly Mark had found an interest in her. He'd seen her talking to the brother who betrayed him and it was just good old sibling rivalry at work.

She glanced at his profile, his handsome, tanned face staring out the window, intent on not looking at her. What more proof did she need? At this point, she wanted to protest even him driving her, but then she remembered they lived at the same address. That was going to be awkward, she thought, seeing him around the condo now. Maybe she ought to just cut her lease short. She had three more weeks reserved, but surely she could find other accommodations on the island.

But was that really the end of the world? Or was Laura just so desperate to get her mind off her problems that making new ones was the only way out?

The small island road ahead of them was lit

only by the headlights of his truck, as all of the streetlights on St. Anthony's seemed to be either in Smuggler's Cove or on major parts of the seaside highway. Outside her window, Laura saw the huge full moon hanging in a sky full of stars. Away from all the lights of San Francisco, she saw some of the constellations her mother, an astronomer, had pointed out to her when she was little.

Her mother had been such a larger-than-life figure. An astronomer doing research at Berkeley, a woman who seemed to have it all, except for the will to live. She'd battled depression all her life.

Did Laura have the same condition? she wondered. Had some life event set off the chemical imbalance for her mother? Maybe her mother had suffered a loss, like a miscarriage, and then just never recovered. Now Laura would never be able to ask her. She might never know.

She still felt angry at her mother, though, an anger that never quite went away. Sure, life was hard. Laura knew it was, but her mother had had two daughters to think about. Laura might have been an adult at twenty-five, but she still felt on some basic level her mother had abandoned her.

They'd been so close, talked every day on the phone and not a day went by that Laura didn't miss her mother. Not a day went by that she didn't wonder why her mother had done it or feel a flare of anger at her choice.

If I ever do have a baby, I'd never leave her, not ever, not even when she's twenty-five. Motherhood was supposed to be a lifetime appointment.

They arrived back at the condo and Laura stepped out, looking up at the dark night sky filled with bright stars.

"There's Orion," she said aloud, pointing toward the constellation's three-star belt. She didn't know why she'd said it. Maybe hearing the words brought the memory of her mother just a little bit closer. She didn't expect an answer from Mark. But he gave her one.

"You know the stars?" he asked, surprised as he shut his driver's-side door with a thump.

"My mom was an astronomer," she said, craning her neck up. "And see? The Big Dipper...and the North Star there."

"You sound almost like a sailor."

Laura looked at him sharply, worried he was poking fun at her. "I'm not."

"It's a compliment," Mark explained as he slowly moved around the side of the truck, hesitating to move closer to her. "Most people don't know as much as they should about the sky."

"My mother taught me all about the sky," Laura said. "Before she killed herself."

Even in the moonlight, Laura could tell Mark's face went pale. "I'm sorry. I didn't…"

"Know. You didn't know. It's okay. I mean, it's not okay, but she was very unhappy for a very long time. One night, she took a bottle of sleeping pills…and she just never woke up." Laura hugged herself, feeling suddenly chilled in the island night air.

"I get it. Some days, death seems like a blessing." His tone was morose and she snapped to attention.

"What do you mean?" Laura asked, voice sharper than she intended.

"Not waking up." Mark sighed.

"Don't say that." Laura felt her temper rise.

"Why not?" Mark looked at her from across the hood of his pickup.

"Because killing yourself is a very selfish thing to do."

"Who would miss me?"

I would, Laura almost said but stopped herself just in time. Why was she so determined to fall for men who didn't truly love her back?

"Just don't do it," Laura said, and then she tucked her purse under her arm and stalked off to the stairs, heading to her own condo and not looking back. Still, she could feel Mark's gaze on her the entire way.

MARK WOKE TO the sound of a hard knock on his condo door. He'd decided not to bother with the alarm that morning. What was the point? Laura probably was done helping him after last night, and what hope did he have of finding someone to sail anyway?

The boat only needed a good coat of waterproof resin and then it should be seaworthy, but why even bother when Dave and Garrett would make sure he'd lose, even if he got his boat in the water?

The hard knock came again.

He dragged himself from bed and yawned, scraping over to the front door. He opened it and saw Laura there, dressed for work, hair tied back with a red bandanna.

"It's already daylight out," she said, almost with an accusing tone. "Why aren't you ready to work?"

"Why aren't..." he began, dumbfounded. What was she doing here? They hadn't made plans for her to come this morning, and yet, here she was.

"Come on, sleepyhead. Let's get to work. The sooner I finish your boat, the sooner I can get back to my vacation." She seemed chipper, even happy.

"I didn't expect you to come this morning," he said, rubbing his head.

"And give you a chance to give up?" She cracked her own knuckles. "No way."

"I thought you were—"

"Hung up on you? Hardly. I'm a big girl." Laura lifted her chin. "Besides, I'm turning over a new leaf. No more falling for unavailable men."

"Oh." He was so confused. When had she decided all this? And what was she even talking about?

"Come on. Let's get this rust bucket done so you can give your brother a run for his money."

"Well." Mark still wasn't sure what was happening. "Even if we do fix the boat, there's still the crew and—"

She ignored him entirely. "Do you have anything better to do today?" she asked.

He had to admit he didn't.

"Then put me to work."

WITH THE WOOD stain dry, all they needed to do was apply a coat of waterproof resin to the bottom of the boat with a thick-bristled brush. Laura spent the day working nearly shoulder to shoulder with Mark and prided herself that she only let a romantic thought or two into her head once or twice. *I'm being so grown-up. Finally. Maddie would be proud.*

So what if things weren't going to work out

with Mark? He was still in trouble, and she'd see her promise through to help him. Then she'd get on with finding whatever it was she was looking for so she could figure out what the hell she was going to do with the rest of her life.

And she could do that without being a walking emotional wound. Yes, she was grieving, and she realized she'd been looking to Mark to save her. Well, he couldn't. Only she could do that. Laura knew that the only way to really make a change in her life was to *decide* to do it, just like she'd decided to leave San Francisco.

She wasn't about to let Mark wallow in failure. After his throwaway line last night about knowing what it felt like to not want to wake up, she knew she had to see this project through. Even if Mark was…well, Mark.

He did go and get them sandwiches for lunch, but he hardly said a word as Laura continued to work.

Finally, after a long day of applying resin, Laura leaned back and paused to admire her handiwork, even as the sun began to sink behind the horizon. The sky blazed a fiery red, but she barely noticed as she once again threw herself into her work. She needed to finish this coat before the sun went down.

"You've got a natural talent with that," Mark

told her as he studied her handiwork, voice full of pride.

She swiped the last of the resin on the side of the hull and let out a bitter laugh. "I can't believe I have a natural talent with any of this. I work on software. I'm basically a computer geek."

"You don't look so geeky to me." Mark flashed his white, even smile, his eyes crinkling up around the edges in a way that made Laura's stomach tighten. Why did he have to be so gorgeous? She wasn't supposed to be attracted to him. He was a mess, and he ran hot and cold.

Still, she hadn't failed to notice he was a good-looking man. Rugged, outdoorsy, tan. Kept in shape and looked downright handsome when he smiled, which wasn't too often. She couldn't help but remember the feel of his lips against hers. He'd been so passionate, so raw. It was hard to believe that it had all been a show for Edward. But how else to explain why he never made a move on her in private?

Mark stood unusually close to her, and she felt his presence, his broad shoulders and the muscled, tanned arms that hung at his sides.

"What next?"

"We're done," he announced, much to Laura's surprise.

"Done? Really?" She couldn't quite keep the disbelief out of her voice.

"Yep. She looks great, doesn't she?" Mark glanced at the boat with a new coat of waterproof resin, the air still thick with the chemical smell, and put his arm around her shoulders, pulling her to his side. Laura liked the feel of his strong arm around her. She didn't wiggle away.

"I couldn't have done this without you, Laura."

"I know. You only wanted to quit about a bazillion times." She laughed a little, and he did, too. It was true. She felt the sudden urge to lean into his touch and then shook herself. No. She wasn't going to do that. She wasn't going there. "So we're really done? With the boat, I mean?" she asked, pulling herself away from his touch and rubbing her own arms.

Mark sighed. "I think so," he said. "Now all I have to do is get her in the water. Want to join me? Tomorrow?"

"Me?" *On a boat with you alone on the water?*

"Yes! Why not? You helped restore her. Why not take her out for a spin?"

"Sure," Laura said before she could even think about what all that time with him on the water might mean. Still, she decided, she could keep her resolve. No more unavailable men. It was a promise she'd made to herself—a promise she planned to keep.

CHAPTER TWELVE

WITH THE CRYSTAL blue sky overhead and the hull of their sailboat slicing through the blue-green water, Laura felt the exhilarating rush of being on the boat, driven by wind and what seemed like magic.

"Here, hold this," he told her, and she grabbed the wheel as he rushed forward to make adjustments to the sail. He wore no shirt and no shoes, and she couldn't help but watch his muscles working as he adjusted the rope. God, the man was gorgeous. Even more gorgeous than this beautiful weather and the sea.

Suddenly, the wind caught the rigging and they were headed swiftly in a new direction.

"Amazing," she breathed, taking in a huge gulp of sea air as the boat cut through the relatively calm waves. He was by her side again, though his eyes were covered by mirrored glasses. She could only see a tiny reflection of herself—oversize shirt, bikini bottom and dark bob tucked into a baseball cap. She, too, had abandoned her flip-flops. It was easier to grip the deck and its endless rocking with bare feet. Now she knew why ancient sailors never wore shoes.

"You like it?" he asked her, and she grabbed the wheel tighter.

"Like it? I love it!" she shouted into the wind. Mark laughed at her enthusiasm, but she couldn't help it. She felt like she was flying, except on water. There was no other way to explain it.

"It's not so fun on stormy days," he cautioned her. "The waves aren't even three feet high today."

"Then I'm going to enjoy them," Laura declared and grinned. Her heart lifted with each rise and dip of the boat's stern. She felt amazed that something as simple as sailing could make her feel so alive, so whole. It was as if sad thoughts weren't allowed here out at sea. Even Mark couldn't help smiling, she noticed.

"You're taking to this like a fish," he remarked as he squeezed in next to her.

"I could do this forever," she said, lifting her face up to the sun and closing her eyes. The warmth against her skin felt right, even as she felt the cool spray of seawater on her face. Nothing could be more perfect than this.

"I should teach you," he said. "How to sail."

"Could you?" she asked, nearly tripping over herself in excitement.

"If you want." He grinned and she smiled back, feeling as if the goofy smile might just bubble over into laughter. She couldn't remember feeling this happy.

Mark went through a quick rundown of the lines and worked on teaching her a few basic skills. She took everything in, studying every detail. She wanted to know this more than anything.

"Just remember," he warned. "Conditions can change like that." He snapped his fingers. "We have calm winds right now, but when they pick up, they take us with them." Mark nodded up at the huge mast towering above them, and the bright white triangle of a sail.

As he taught her how to lower and then raise the mast, he held her hands tightly, and she felt the heat of contact. The sudden tingling in her belly had nothing to do with the dip of the bow beneath a wave, either.

Being so close to Mark, feeling his touch, she couldn't deny that she did have feelings for him. She was already attached, whether she liked it or not. She had to work harder at pulling back. *He might be single, but he's not available*, she told herself. *And no more unavailable men.* She didn't want someone who ran hot and cold like

Dean. She wanted a man who *wanted* her as much as she wanted him. Period. She was done being an afterthought.

Besides, did she really want a man who put his wife in jail? She was still not sure about that. Part of her wanted to ask him about it and then part of her didn't.

During a lull in the lesson, she grabbed her cell phone from her pocket and took a few quick shots.

"Let me take your picture," Mark offered as he secured the rigging. She handed him her phone. She posed at the ship's wheel and he snapped a few.

"Why don't we take one together?" Laura asked. As soon as the question popped out of her mouth, she regretted asking. What was she doing? She expected him to turn her down flat, but Mark, seemingly lightened by the wind and sea, just shrugged and loped over. He put his arm around her and clicked a shot.

"Here you go," he said, handing her the phone. They were nearly nose to nose.

"Uh…thanks," she said, feeling a bit awkward suddenly. His dark eyes were so very close to hers. All she had to do was lean a bit forward and she'd be kissing him. She expected him to scurry away, but he didn't. He lingered, his dark eyes meeting hers in a way that told her maybe he wasn't running very cold today.

Hot. Cold. Hot. Cold. He needs to make up his mind.

"I didn't kiss you because my brother was watching," Mark declared out of the blue.

"W-what?"

"It's what you were thinking. It's what you said that night. It's not true."

Laura swallowed. "It's not?"

"No. You're gorgeous. I…I wanted to kiss you because *I* wanted to."

Did he just call her gorgeous? Laura felt her heart skip a beat.

The wind whipped up and teased his dark hair. She wanted to run her hands through it. She wanted to touch him. *No. He's not who you need. Not right now.*

"But you—"

"Look, Laura. I don't get women." Mark shrugged. The sun hit his bare chest and the bits of sweat on it glistened. "I'm always doing the wrong thing. I'm always pissing them off. Ask my ex-wife." He rubbed his tanned neck sheepishly. "I just… I don't have anything to offer you right now. I'm only here until the race and then—"

"I'm only here for three more weeks," she pointed out, wondering why he was jumping so far ahead. She didn't know what she wanted to be doing next week, much less next year. "What did you think I wanted? An engagement?"

"Well." Now Mark looked a little embarrassed as his cheeks turned pink. "No, but. I mean women fall in love—"

"Slower than men, actually." Laura crossed her arms. "It's science. Look it up. Men fall in love faster than women. Fall out of love faster, too." She couldn't quite help but sound bitter at the last part, remembering how quickly Dean had lost affection for her. She knew all about how quickly men could change their minds.

Mark laughed. Even with his sunglasses on, Laura could tell he was doubtful about the claim. "That's not true. Is it?"

"There's been loads of psychological studies. Men say 'I love you' first and faster than women. It all has to do with biology. Women have to protect their resources. We have one egg a month, and when we're pregnant, that's it for nine months. That's why they can fall in love faster. It's less of a commitment for them, physically at least. Men can afford to… well…" The heat rose in her face as she thought of how Mark's body had felt pressed against hers. "Well, spread their *love* around."

Mark threw his head back and let out a loud cackle. "No way. Seriously?"

"It's actual science." Laura had spent many hours trolling psychology websites trying to figure out if Dean really loved her. Or if he ever had. Turns out, she didn't need Google for the answer to that question at all.

"Well, then, I'm sorry for assuming you wanted to fall in love with me."

Now, it was Laura's turn to laugh. She punched him in the shoulder. "You're so vain."

"I guess I am." He grinned. "Watch your head." She ducked out of the way as the sail swung past and caught the wind, carrying the boat back toward the shore.

"Besides, *you* should be apologizing to me. Because you're the one who's going to get all emotional on me. Men are so clingy."

They shared a giggle, and suddenly everything seemed fine. Laura felt relaxed for the first time in a long time. She was glad he'd brought up that night—the kiss. Now there'd be no need to pretend it didn't happen. They'd talked about it like adults and survived. Now it could even be a joke.

The wind shifted, and suddenly the sail started to luff.

"Okay, now it's your turn to adjust our course and get the wind back in our sails," Mark said as he showed her how to move the boat through a smooth tack. "Don't go too quickly," he admonished, placing his hand beside hers on the wheel.

The day just felt perfect. The sun, the ocean, the wind. This is exactly what she needed, Laura thought. She basked in the sunlight and the amazing beauty around her. She put her hands on top of the hat on her head and looked up, closing her eyes as the sun beat down on her face.

"Laura. Pay attention—" Before Mark could finish his sentence, finish directing her to some line on the boat, the wind kicked up without warning. It was so strong it blew her hat straight off her head.

She flailed for it too late, and it shot up into the air and off the back of the boat. Instinctively, she let go of the line, a rookie mistake. The sail flew out and suddenly, caught by the wind, the boat shot to the right, knocking Mark back on his butt.

In a panic, Laura grabbed for the line that was already pulling away from her at high speed and yanked on it but then yelped in pain as it burned her palm.

"Laura!" Mark cried, trying to get to his feet. Laura glanced at the red slash across her palm. She'd be fine, but she'd lost control of the line, and now she didn't know how to get it back. The white sail above them snapped taut as it caught the sudden burst of energy.

Then, tending to her burned hand, she realized she was losing her footing against the lurch of the boat's deck beneath her feet. She reached out for a line to steady herself but missed. A gasp escaped Laura's lips as she struggled to find a handhold but clutched air. There was no doubt about it. She was going overboard.

CHAPTER THIRTEEN

JUST WHEN LAURA was sure she'd be tossed overboard, Mark's arm snaked out and snatched her around the waist. He'd managed to scramble to his feet and catch her at the same time. He held her tight, her back against his chest, as he used his free hand to clutch the wheel.

"Hang on," he commanded, his voice a rough growl in her ear as he squeezed her close, carefully riding out the wind. She didn't know how long she stayed pressed against Mark. A minute? Five?

The strong wind kept the boat nearly perpendicular to the water. Would the boat capsize? It seemed to be defying gravity as they cut through the waves. She clung to Mark's arm desperately, sending up a little prayer that the wind would die down soon. Then suddenly, the boated righted itself a bit, just enough that Laura felt like she wouldn't be flung into the ocean.

"That was close," she breathed, even as she felt Mark's arm stay snug around her waist.

"It happens," he said. "You've got to keep on your toes." Mark released her, and reluctantly, she stepped from his secure and warm embrace.

"I had...no idea." She let out a breath, turning to face him. "I'm so sorry, I let go." She couldn't believe she'd done something so dumb, and it had nearly capsized the boat. "I mean one second we were..." She put her hand flat out to symbolize the boat upright on the water. "And the next..." She flipped the flat of her hand to one side.

"You okay?" he asked, mouth in a thin line, eyes hidden by sunglasses.

"Yeah," she said, taking in a shaky breath. Was she? It all happened so fast.

"Let me see your hand." Mark pushed his sunglasses up on his head and she could see his dark eyes, strained with worry. She almost didn't want to show him her palm, which still smarted from the rope burn. Eventually, she did, and he stared at it as if trying to read her future.

"Does it hurt?" He traced the mark on unhurt skin, and his gentle touch made her feel a bit light-headed.

"I'll be fine," she said.

Mark frowned. "I think we should go in," he declared and released her hand. "I've got some salve at home that will help that."

"No. Really, it's barely a scratch. I'll be fine."

Mark shook his head. One thing was for sure, his jovial mood had disappeared. "No. We're going in," he said, his sunglasses hiding his true feelings. Was he angry at her? Disappointed?

"I'll do better next time. I'll—"

"No." Mark shook his head. "That's enough for today."

"But…" She felt a sharp jab of disappointment jolt her stomach.

"You won't be much good out here with that injury. We should go back."

"No, I'm fine," she said, but was she? Life on the sea changed so suddenly, and the boat had lurched so quickly, she just wasn't sure she was ready for more excitement. Besides, she could almost feel her sunscreen losing its potency as the warm sun beat down on her bare shoulders. Still, she didn't want to be the one to call the day. She'd be a trooper.

"We're going back in." Mark glanced at the horizon and then back at land.

"Don't go for my sake," she said. "I'm fine." She rubbed her shoulders and clung a little tighter to the railing. She would be fine, too, in a minute, when she could catch her breath and if her palm stopped throbbing. Besides, she wasn't even sure what had affected her more, the near capsizing or his strong embrace.

Mark studied her, his dark eyes missing nothing.

"No, we should head in."

"I'm fine."

"You're not."

Laura let out a frustrated breath. No talking sense into Mark when he'd decided a course of action. The two fell into a more somber kind of silence. Laura didn't know why with Mark the mood always changed so swiftly. Maybe it was better they'd be going in.

MARK DIDN'T LIKE seeing Laura hurt, and he definitely didn't like the fact that he'd nearly lost her overboard. What was he doing, taking out a total novice out to sail when he knew how unpredictable the wind could be?

He spent the entire ride back to the marina beating himself up. He should've waited until he could find an experienced crew hand to help him. Laura should've been a passenger, not someone he relied on. He'd put too much on her for a first sail, and he knew it. If he was on speaking terms with his brother, Edward would've said the same thing.

He glanced at Laura, who stood on the bow

of the boat. She looked unsure, clutching the railing with her good hand while she cradled the injured one in front of her. It was his fault she was hurt, and he couldn't risk her being hurt any more. Not by him. Not out here on the ocean where bad things could happen. She needed to be safe. On shore. Where she belonged.

After they pulled into the marina, Mark jumped off the boat with the line to lash it to the dock. He worked on securing it as Laura watched from the boat.

"You still need a crew," she said, eyeing him.

"Edward's got all the best people," he answered, not looking up as he gave the knot a hard tug.

"I could be on it. Your crew. You could teach me."

He froze as she made the suggestion. And watch her almost get swept overboard again? She wasn't ready. Hell, he might never be ready to nearly lose her like that again.

Mark shook his head.

"It would take too long for me to teach you the ins and outs of racing," he said, straightening. She stood at the ladder, hands on her hips.

"You don't think I can do it." Her voice was all challenge. He glanced up and met her fierce green eyes. The sun brought out red highlights in her dark bob.

"No," he lied. He didn't think she could do it. Some people took to the sea, and others didn't. "It's just not feasible for me to get you where you need to be by race time. And it's dangerous. You saw how it can be, and that's not under pressure, trying to go fast."

"I can do it."

"Even if you could, we still need three more people." Mark stood near the ladder of the boat and held out his hand. There was only about a six-inch gap between the boat and the dock, but he wasn't taking any more chances with her safety.

She glanced at his open palm for a second and frowned. For a minute, he thought she might not even take it, but then she finally slipped her hand into his. He helped her down and kept his hand on hers a beat longer than necessary. He didn't want to let her go, not really, but he did once she was safely on the dock.

Her hair was windblown since her cap was long gone. He noticed the glow of a budding sunburn on her cheeks.

"Edward has the best racers sewn up. People who've been sailing for years, and you…" He glanced at her wounded hand. She looked at it, sheepish. "Well, you'll need a little while to heal from that."

"I'm fine."

"You're not."

"Then maybe I could talk to your brother. Maybe he'd agree to let a racer go."

"No." Mark whirled. "Don't you talk to him." His voice came out angrier than he wanted, but he couldn't help it. The thought of her with his brother made his skin crawl. He didn't want her anywhere near that man.

"Hey. Okay. I just thought maybe you need a peace broker." She held up her hands like a shield.

"No, I don't." That's the last thing on earth he wanted. Not talking to his brother was working out just fine for him. He didn't need to break that habit.

They walked to his pickup truck, and he opened the door. She glared at him, peeved. Of course, she was peeved. Women were always getting the wrong idea. He just wanted to protect her, so why wouldn't she let him?

He shut the door, feeling exasperated as he strode over to his side of the truck, slipped into the cab and revved the engine. Soon, they were on the five-minute drive to the condo. After that, she could easily head upstairs and away from him.

Maybe that was best. Maybe it was foolish to think she could understand. She couldn't help him, not now. The whole race was a hopeless pipe dream anyway. He shouldn't have even set his heart on it. Besides, deep down, he knew all he really wanted to do was go out on the water and never come back. He didn't need the prize money to do that, exactly. If he wanted to end his life, he could do it, prize money be damned.

But her helping him do it...he just...he didn't feel right about it. That's what he really wanted to tell her. *Don't get involved in this. Don't.* He imagined what she'd think if he sailed off into the deep blue and never came back.

He glanced sidelong at her as they drove and saw the hurt look on her face. She was already invested in him. How would she feel if all the work she'd done just led to him being lost at sea?

He didn't want that for her. He didn't want that guilt.

They sat in stony silence for most of the drive home. As they pulled into the condo parking lot, he put the truck in Park and turned off the engine.

"Maybe I could help you look for people," she said, not looking at him, as if the conversation were still going. Clearly, she hadn't let the subject drop. "If you can't train me, or won't," she murmured under her breath, "maybe—"

Frustration welled in him. He swung open his truck door and jumped out. She followed him, even as he grabbed the cooler and some other gear from the back and began loading it into the workshop.

"Laura," he cautioned.

"I want to help."

He took his duffel bag full of gear and headed to his condo's front door. She followed him. The woman just wasn't going to let it go. "Look, I know you mean well, but it's not all that easy."

She stepped up in his space, and now she was so close to him he could smell the salty sea air in her hair. "Why don't you tell me why it's not so easy? I want to help. And you keep trying to shut me out."

"I…" *I don't want to let you in. It would be too dangerous if I did.*

He pushed his key into the lock and swung open the door. She followed him inside.

"What is it?" she asked, the accusation clear in her voice. "Why do you dislike me so much?"

He dropped his duffel bag on the kitchen floor in frustration. Dislike her? He felt the opposite.

"You run hot and cold, like a teenager," she went on. "I can't get a handle on you. Sometimes I think you must really hate me if you keep running so cold."

Cold? Every time she was near him, he could feel the heat in his blood, the base attraction that made him itch to touch her. Cold was the last thing he was feeling.

"You've got it wrong," he said, staring down at her bright green eyes. She glared at him, crossing her hands across her chest. Why did she always get it so wrong?

"Oh, really? I don't think so. I'm just trying to help you. That's all I've been trying to do, and you just want to scare me off."

Because if you stay, I'll really start to care about you. I might already care about you, actually, and it might be too late.

He opened his mouth, but no words came out. Why didn't the words come out?

She glared at him, hurt clear in her eyes. She cared for him, too. That much was obvious by the look on her face.

"You don't like me." The hurt there in her voice was so real. The anger and frustration seeped out of him. All he wanted to do was comfort her. Take her heart away.

"No, that's not true." He took a deep breath. "I do like you. More than like you." He ran a frustrated hand through his windswept hair. "I want you. I want you all the time. Even right now, I want to take you in my arms and kiss the holy life out of you."

"You…" Now, she just looked dumbfounded and doubtful.

There was only one way to prove what he said was true. He put his arm around the small of her back and pulled her to him. She didn't resist. Then he laid his lips on hers.

CHAPTER FOURTEEN

LAURA HADN'T BEEN expecting that. His passionate kiss took her by surprise, and she was suddenly once again in his arms and feeling the
rush of blood in her ears as the thrill of kissing
this man took over. She kissed him back, unable to help herself.

Anger still pulsed in her temples, but it soon
turned to unadulterated passion as he pulled
her to him. She pressed her body against his,
feeling his flat stomach and hard chest against
her. His hands roamed her body, sending a little
thrill down her back even as his tongue gently
explored her mouth. She could taste sea spray
on his lips, and all she wanted to do was dive
deeper into him, get lost in the moment.

She didn't understand how this had happened
so fast. One second, she was angry and hurt,
and the next minute, passion overran every logical thought in her brain.

She wrapped her arms around his neck, and
as the kiss deepened, the flame of desire inside
her burned even brighter. She hiked one leg up

on his hip, and he grabbed her leg, keeping it there, squeezing her knee in a way that made her moan. All she wanted to do was get horizontal somehow, as her knee dropped down and he walked her back to the couch. They flopped down, and he pressed down on top of her, his body weight on her deliciously heavy.

His hand explored up the opening of her shorts and she welcomed his touch, experienced, knowing, gentle.

Even as her brain warned her that he was emotionally unavailable, that she ought not to let this happen, her body screamed out, *who cares?* It wanted satisfaction in the moment, and a desperate need for physical intimacy took over. She wanted to touch someone and be touched, to be seen after feeling invisible for the last month. Invisible to Dean, invisible to the world, even invisible to her very self.

Mark had been the first one to truly see her, she realized, since the miscarriage, to see *all* of her and know her flaws and still want to get this close.

Mark pulled away, breath ragged, as his gaze found hers. "Are you sure?" he asked, a quiver of doubt in his voice, shaky with want.

This was what she wanted. It was what she'd always wanted since their first kiss.

"I'm sure," she breathed with a hefty amount of enthusiasm.

Mark laughed and she did, too. She tugged at his shirt, and then it was off over his head, and she was running her hands down his muscular, tanned chest. He closed his eyes as she explored him and dipped her hands into the waistband of his pants. He came to life beneath her touch, and her eyes widened in surprise.

"Amazing," she murmured, and he gave her a cocksure grin.

"I aim to please," he teased and then dipped down once more and kissed her with a passion that surprised her. He took a break once more as he tugged at her tankini top. In seconds, she'd wiggled out of it, and he trailed kisses down one breast, ending with a gentle tug of her nipple between his teeth.

She moaned in ecstasy, arching her back as he twirled his tongue, flicking against the tender skin. He moved to the other side, repeating the gesture, almost sending her tumbling over the edge with just that gentle touch.

Their eyes met, and she saw the want in them, as he followed the line of his hand down the front of her body. He stopped at her shorts and gave a hard tug. She helped him, lifting her butt, as her shorts and her bikini bottom slid off. Now she was completely bare, lying beneath him on his couch.

She felt no shame. This was right. She wanted this connection more than she wanted anything. She wanted him to save her from the island of isolation she'd been stranded on since the miscarriage. Somehow, in this moment, she was convinced his touch would do that. Would make it all better.

She could feel her bare back pressed against the soft fabric of his sofa. He straightened and moved away from her long enough to get his own shorts off, and then she saw him, fully naked before her. She reached out to touch him with both hands and he leaned into her touch, groaning with want.

Now would be the time she ought to ask for a condom. The most logical parts of her brain knew she ought to. She wasn't on the pill, after all. And there were STDs to consider, but in that moment, she just…didn't care. None of that mattered, nothing mattered expect the feel of her hands on his body and how badly she wanted him inside her.

He seemed equally in the same trance, as he lay back on top of her, as she opened her legs, welcoming him there.

"Are you…sure?" he asked her, hesitating. She'd never been surer of anything as she nodded once. He entered her with a rush. She gasped.

"Oh, God, you feel…so amazing," he murmured, keeping eye contact, and she felt like she'd drown in his dark brown eyes. Staring at him, as he looked at her with such intensity, such amazement, made her feel like molten lava on the inside. "You're the most amazing woman, Laura."

In that instant, she believed him. She rocked her hips to meet each of his thrusts, and soon she felt herself close to the edge as she moaned in pleasure. He kept eye contact, and she felt *seen* for the first time in her life. Dean never looked at her during intercourse, never engaged on that level. But the eye contact, in this most intimate of moments, made her feel connected to Mark in a way she didn't think was possible.

"Come for me," he encouraged her, eyes bright. "Come for me, beautiful."

Beneath the intensity of his stare, she did just that, reaching the climax of her life as pleasure exploded through her body and raced through her brain. She never lost eye contact, and the moment was amazing and real and so intimate. Her breath came in ragged gasps as she fought for control once more, her heart hammering in her chest as if it might break its way out.

"Your turn," she murmured, still knocked

breathless by the hormones rushing through her veins.

"I'll…" Mark made a move to withdraw from her, but she didn't want that. She didn't want him coming outside. She wanted him deeper. She wrapped her legs around him.

"No. Please." She pressed her body against his, tilting her pelvis to him.

"Oh, God. You're going to make me…" And then he came, deep inside her with a guttural shout, a defiant surrender. He collapsed on top of her, shuddering, as the two lay holding each other with shaking arms.

Laura knew it had been reckless. Dangerous, even, but she didn't care in that moment. She craved the intimacy, the connection, and she'd gotten it.

Mark lifted his weary head. "I'm sorry." He glanced down. "I shouldn't have come—" he swallowed "—inside you."

"I wanted you to," she murmured, pushing his head down against her shoulder once more.

"But—"

"Shhh. Let's just stay like this," she said, not wanting to ruin the moment, this blissful, perfect moment of being connected. Of belonging. It's what she'd craved all this time.

He fell silent, his head on her shoulder, his fingers trailing the length of her arm.

"You're amazing," he told her, and she soaked up the words like a flower blooming in sunlight.

"No," she said. "You are."

LATER, AS LAURA took a quick shower in his bathroom, Mark sat at his kitchen breakfast bar, worrying. How could he have been so reckless? Coming inside her like that? No protection? He never did that. He'd never been swept up in a moment like that, so out of his senses that he'd barreled on despite all logic.

Yet it had felt so damn good, so incredible, he hadn't wanted to stop. He knew that. He'd made the decision then and there to keep on going. He was as much to blame as her. He'd tried to withdraw, but he hadn't tried that hard.

What if she were pregnant? But surely she was on the pill. Though he hadn't asked, had he?

And even if she wasn't, what were the odds of a pregnancy after just one time? It had taken Elle months and months to get pregnant with Timothy and they'd done it multiple times.

It only takes once. And even just the tip can do it.

He remembered his Dad's awkward sex talk when he'd been a teenager. He'd taken Mark and Edward out on a fishing trip off the Florida Keys when they were both teenagers. The entire talk had lasted about three minutes, and the upshot of it was that one time could mean a lifetime of paying child support.

But, Dad was wrong about a lot of things. Like Edward being the better son, for one.

Not that he'd ever know. He'd died three years ago believing Edward could walk on water and Mark couldn't get anything right. Now there'd be no way to change his mind.

The shower stopped.

"Mark?" came a hesitant voice from the bathroom. That's when he remembered he'd forgotten to put a towel out for her. In fact, they were all in his dryer.

"One second!" he called. He swung open the utility room and grabbed a fresh towel from the dryer. He opened the bathroom door and saw her peeking out from the fogged glass door of the shower, hair wet, luscious curves only slightly visible through the door. The steam from the hot water hung in the air, heavy and wet. He held the towel in his hands, but suddenly he didn't want to give it to her.

The sight of her, naked in his bathroom, made him stir once more. He wanted her. Again.

"I'll help you," he offered, holding up the towel. She gently stepped out of the shower and he dried her off, laying a kiss on her shoulder. She stood, back facing him as he worked the terry cloth over her body. She groaned a little and leaned into him, pressing her body against his, setting all his nerve endings on edge. He wanted her. Badly. He dipped his head and laid a trail of kisses down her neck.

She turned around then and stood on bare tiptoes, kissing him on the lips. The kiss turned passionate, and the towel dropped away. He pulled her into his arms, all caution long gone. All he knew was that she belonged here, with him, and he wanted to explore every delicious crevice of her body once more.

CHAPTER FIFTEEN

LAURA COULD STILL feel Mark's hands on her, even though she'd long since headed up to her condo to get a fresh set of clothes before dinner. She still remembered the long, deep kiss they'd shared at his front door before she'd ducked out and hurried upstairs.

The whole day felt like a blur, a wonderful, awesome blur. He'd promised to take her out to dinner, and she needed to change. Laura hummed to herself, happier than she'd been... well, since before Dean. She'd almost forgotten what happiness felt like.

She did a little twirl in her condo living room, not caring how silly it looked. She wanted to take advantage of the lightness, of the wonderful feeling of contentedness. She knew how quickly life could take it away. If there was anything she'd learned from the miscarriage, it was to celebrate life's small victories. The big fails were always just around the corner.

Even the distant worry about unprotected sex retreated to the back corners of her mind. The chances of an STD were likely low. She'd been tested after Dean and knew she was clean, and Mark had told her he'd had only one partner since his ex-wife, and he'd used protection. The chances of a pregnancy were even lower than that. *But I'll get condoms*, she promised herself. *Not making that mistake again. Just in case.*

Her cell phone blared on her kitchen counter, announcing her sister calling.

"I've been trying you all day," Maddie scolded when Laura picked up. "Where have you been?"

Laura hated that tone—the motherly, nagging, you-owe-me-an-explanation tone.

"Sailing," Laura replied, almost biting off the word.

"Sailing! Well, isn't that nice. I've been working all day *and* running around the kids in the never-ending mommy shuttle service and..." Maddie began listing all the ways her life was busier and more important than Laura's.

Laura sighed as she listened. She knew that on some level it was just Maddie's way of venting, but she wished she didn't have to make it sound so much like a life competition. Just because Laura didn't have kids and wasn't, right now, employed, didn't mean her life was amazingly easy.

Maddie eventually took a breath and switched subjects. "When are you coming home?"

"I don't know," Laura said, hedging. Now with Mark in the picture, she didn't even want to think about going home. Ever. Not that she should allow herself the luxury of even thinking there might be a future with him. Still, if she went home to California, she'd ensure there never would be one.

"It's not right," Maddie declared. "You. Alone on that island…"

"I'm not alone," Laura said, sounding more defensive than she should, and then immediately regretted making the confession.

"What do you mean? Have you met someone?" Now Maddie's radar was up. She'd pounce on the little detail like a mother hen worried about a wandering chick.

"Well…sort of. I'm helping a man build a boat."

"You're what?"

"Restoring one. He races sailboats. Wants to sail around the world. He might even teach me."

A long pause met her on the other end of the phone. "Let me guess. You're not just helping him. Are you? He's good-looking?"

"Yes." Very.

"And he just happens to have enough cash to sail around the world, and you're just 'helping' him? Helping him what? Take his clothes off?"

"Maddie!"

"I'm just saying. It's one man after another. When are you ever going to get serious? Settle down? First, a married man and now a sailor?"

Laura felt the hard sting of her sister's judgment. Why couldn't Maddie just let her be? Let her live her own life without her running commentary? *You're not our mother*, she wanted to shout. *You don't get to tell me what to do with my life.*

But Maddie wasn't finished. "And you need to stop blowing through your retirement savings. Not to mention, you head to the Caribbean during hurricane season. I mean, are you crazy? If you'd just think for once."

Now Laura's blood was boiling. She was so very tired of Maddie telling her what to do. So done with it.

"Maddie, it's not hurricane season yet, it's…" But her sister didn't give her the chance to explain.

"You need to grow up, Laura. Be an adult."

"I *am* being an adult, Maddie. Just because you're stuck in a…" Laura almost said *loveless marriage*, but she bit her tongue. That was too low a blow, even when prodded.

"Stuck in a what?" Maddie challenged.

"Never mind."

"No. Finish the thought, Laura." Maddie's

voice was taut on the line. Laura squeezed the phone against her ear.

"A marriage to a man who clearly makes you miserable," Laura managed.

"Marriage isn't always fun, Laura. Life isn't always fun. Adults have responsibilities, and not all of us can just run away when things get rough. I've got the kids to think about." Maddie's voice sounded flat.

Anger bubbled in Laura's chest. She was so tired of Maddie wearing responsibility like an albatross around her neck. It was a choice she made every day to subject herself to the misery. Laura had made a different life choice. She didn't want to slog through the bad job and awful relationship she was supposed to just suck up and endure.

"And what are you teaching my niece and nephew, Maddie? That in life, you're stuck with all your past mistakes? That life is supposed to be one miserable slog until death? Well, I'm choosing a different path for me. One that I hope will make me happy." Laura thought of Mark. After all, she never would have met Mark if she hadn't taken the rash step of giving herself a time-out. "I'm not being irresponsible. I'm staying true to me and to what I need."

"I can't believe you just said that to me. After all I've done for you. Since Mom." The hurt in

Maddie's voice was real. Laura hated to hear it, but she couldn't quite bring herself to regret what she'd said.

"I never asked you to do any of that, Maddie. Maybe you need to look after yourself. Stop being the martyr for everyone else. *No one* is asking you to be." Laura wasn't finished, but she heard the click of the line going dead.

Maddie had hung up.

Laura sighed, staring at the phone. She'd never stood up to her sister like that before, never, not once. Ever since they were kids, Maddie always got her way, and Laura always went along. Older sister bossing younger sister around, but Laura was tired of that. This time, she wasn't going to let Maddie rule her life. She was her own person, and she was tired of letting other people tell her what to do.

Maddie had been mad at Laura before, and usually, Laura would call her back, apologize, grovel a little, and Maddie would bestow her forgiveness. *Not this time.* Laura wasn't going to be the first one to blink. She wasn't sorry about telling Maddie to butt out and to maybe stop lording her own unhappiness over everyone else. Nobody was asking her to be unhappy. *That's her choice.*

Laura brushed off her sister's call.

Why think about the future? Live in the moment. Forget about tomorrow.

And right now, the moment called for her to find a dress worthy of a nice dinner out on the island. And for her to make that stop at the convenience store. She'd not let passion rule her tonight.

MARK RANG HER doorbell exactly at seven, wearing khakis and a button-down shirt, looking freshly showered and shaved. He swept his eyes over her outfit—a white linen strapless sundress—and gave a slow nod of approval. She wore a dash of red lipstick and a bit of mascara, and her hair was finger-dried in delicate, easy waves. She'd picked cork wedge sandals and felt a little bit taller, though Mark still towered above her.

"You look gorgeous," he said, his dark eyes lighting up with appreciation.

"Oh, this old thing?" she joked. Laura had gone through literally all the dresses she'd packed: three. Thank goodness she'd thrown this one into her luggage. She almost hadn't brought any, figuring an emotional sabbatical on a faraway island wouldn't afford many fancy eating opportunities. Her mother, however, had always been a stickler for being prepared. *Always pack a dress and a swimsuit*, was her motto. Laura was glad she'd followed her mother's advice, which was almost so ingrained she didn't even think about it.

He opened his arms for a hug, but she went in for a kiss. He tasted like mint and aftershave, and before she knew it, she'd wrapped her arms around the back of his neck, pressing her body against his. He deepened the kiss, taking it to another level and all rational thought drained from her mind.

Eventually, he broke free, panting a little. "Should we stay in and order pizza?"

"Maybe," she agreed, thinking that despite all the work she'd done to get ready, she wouldn't mind slipping out of her dress right now if that meant feeling his bare skin against hers once more.

"No," he said, shaking his head and detangling himself from her embrace. "I promised you a nice dinner, and I don't renege on my promises. Besides, we can save *this*—" He dipped down to kiss the back of her hand "—for dessert."

"Ooh, I love dessert."

Mark barked a laugh. "Oh, I know you do." He grinned. "Shall we?" he asked her, offering his elbow. She slipped her arm through his.

"Ready as I'll ever be," she said. "Where are we going?"

"To the only 'nice' restaurant in town. They even have linen napkins."

Laura laughed a little. She remembered how small Smuggler's Cove was, and the main street was mostly lined with souvenir shops.

It was a quick drive to the only "nice" restaurant in Smuggler's Cove.

"Sorry we don't have more options," he said as he held the restaurant door open for her and she slipped through. "But they have the most amazing conch chowder here. You have to try it."

The hostess seated them in a candlelit corner of the restaurant, which was already mostly full of dressed-up tourists and a few locals. Mark ordered a bottle of house wine from the waiter. After their glasses were filled, Laura offered a toast.

"To my hero, the man who saved me from going overboard," she announced, raising her glass. Mark laughed a little and clinked his glass with hers. She never broke eye contact as she took a sip of the sophisticated red wine.

"Thanks for catching me," she added. "I wasn't sure I wanted to go for a swim."

"Didn't think you did." Mark grinned, showing even, white teeth. God, he had an amazing smile.

"You should smile more often," she said before she had time to think. "It suits you."

"I don't smile very much?"

Laura snorted a laugh. "No. Not much at all. When I first met you, I thought you were the grumpiest man on earth."

"That's because you were telling me I was being too loud and it was too early when it was practically noon."

She chuckled as she shrugged, studying the wine in her glass. "Fair point. Still. You should smile more. You are really…" She was about to say *handsome.*

"I'm really what?" Now he looked a little suspicious. The sun above them hid behind a puffy white cloud. He put his sunglasses up on his head, and now she could see his intelligent dark eyes watching her every move.

"You just look…" *Like you ought to be starring in rom-coms when you smile.* The roguish middle-aged bachelor, hard to tame but worth the time.

"Like what?" He leaned forward.

"Sexy. Damn sexy."

Mark's eyes widened in surprise, and then he threw back his head and laughed.

The waiter came then. Laura ordered salmon,

Mark ordered snapper and both had a cup of conch chowder to start.

"Now, where we were? Let's get back to the part where you were telling me I'm a sex god."

"Sex god?" Even though he *was* that, she might not be willing to admit that to his face.

"I've never heard a woman so thoroughly enjoy herself."

Laura felt her cheeks turn bright pink. "Was I that loud?"

"Louder," he said and grinned. "Good thing I own the first floor."

Laura slapped her palm against her forehead. "Ugh. Sorry. I've been told I can get…loud." It had been Dean's biggest pet peeve, even when they'd managed a tryst in a hotel room. He was always terrified of getting caught, even when they were supposed to be in private.

"Don't apologize," Mark said, eyes sparkling with delight. "I love it."

"You do?" She felt a little shiver of delight run down her spine. She wanted him to love it. *Love her.*

He gave a slow nod.

"Good, because I can't change it." She shrugged. She'd tried, with Dean. But the fact was she couldn't help it. "Dean hated it."

He reached out and grabbed her hand. "Dean

was an idiot," Mark said, clutching her hand. "You're an amazing woman and he was a fool for letting you go."

Laura felt her heart swell. If he kept talking like that, she *would* fall in love. She squeezed his hand back. She stared into his dark eyes and felt she could get lost there. She *wanted* to get lost in them.

"Besides me nearly drowning, how do you feel the boat handled today?" she asked.

"Good," he said. "I'll need to make some minor adjustments, but I think we'll be fine."

"Ready in time for the big race?"

He shrugged. "Not that it matters. Don't have a crew."

"Will you reconsider teaching me?" She knew to tread softly here. She also knew he was still reluctant to bring her on board.

"It's just dangerous."

She squeezed his hand. "I want to do it. Please."

He sighed. "I just don't know. It's just so much responsibility and—"

Laura let out an exasperated sigh. "You sound like my sister."

"Why?"

She filled Mark in on the conversation she'd

had with her sister. About the nagging, about her disapproving of Laura even being here.

"I disagree," Mark said after Laura finished relating the conversation. "I don't think it's irresponsible of you to take a time-out. I think it's actually *responsible*. Sometimes in life, we need to hit the reset button."

"Exactly," Laura exclaimed.

"Even if that costs us or even if it seems silly. My ex, Elle, she should've done that. I told her she should see someone, a therapist maybe, after Timothy was born. She had postpartum depression."

"Oh! I didn't know. That must've been horrible." Laura took a sip of wine. She wondered if she should ask him about what Edward had said about putting her in jail. Was there a reason she didn't know about?

"Terrible. She should've taken some time out for herself. Hit the reset button." Mark looked thoughtful for a moment, as if he was slipping into the past. "Instead, she limped along. So listen to your gut. Do what's right for you. Don't let your sister live your life. Only you can do that."

Laura raised her chin, feeling defiant. He *got* her. Her own sister didn't get it, but this man, this grumpy sailor, got it. "I will. Thanks, Mark. You're a good man."

"Only when I'm sleeping," he joked, and she laughed.

Laura felt buoyant for the first time in a long time. Mark really understood her. Maybe they might even be more than just a fling.

She shook her head.

No. That was cart-before-the-horse thinking. No need to get ahead of herself. They weren't going to be a thing. She wasn't going to let her overactive imagination plan out a happily-ever-after that wasn't there yet. *And after my big speech about guys falling in love first. Looks like I'm proving myself wrong.*

"Penny for your thoughts?" Mark asked.

"Just happy that you don't think I'm crazy for cashing in a 401(k)," she said and left it at that.

Just then, the waiter put their food down in front of them, and the two began to dig in. The meal was amazing. Laura had never had salmon that flaky, that tender and delicious. She was so engrossed in the meal that it took her a second to notice that Mark wasn't eating. In fact, he was staring over her shoulder at the front door of the restaurant.

Laura craned to look and saw his brother,

Edward, standing there, holding hands with a woman—tall, leggy, blonde and gorgeous.

Her stomach tightened. Could that woman be…?

"Mark?" Laura asked, questioning, even as she felt a little prick of dread at the pit of her stomach.

"That's Edward and Elle," he said, frowning. "My ex-wife."

CHAPTER SIXTEEN

MARK WAS BEGINNING to hate this small island. It seemed he could never get away from his brother or his ex, and now here they were at the only nice restaurant on the strip. This was why he'd become a hermit, he remembered, why he took all his meals on the couch in his living room. But with Laura, he'd decided to take the risk. Now, he was regretting it. Of course he'd run into *them*. The island was microscopic, the restaurants few.

Edward, the smug jerk, looked just as smug as he had at the bar. *Elle*. Mark hadn't seen her for months, he realized. She looked just as beautiful as ever, blond hair bleached by the sun, blue eyes soft as she glanced around the restaurant. But her belly was growing full with the baby, and he couldn't help but notice that she was showing much more now than the last time he'd seen her.

Seeing her belly made his temper flare. How could she so easily move on? How could she have another child when Timothy was barely gone? Children weren't like dogs. You couldn't just replace one with another. Plus, what was to guarantee Elle wouldn't make the same mistakes with this one? Had she really gotten her life together that fast? He doubted it.

He felt like he might choke on the bitterness. Mark watched Laura stare at the couple and wondered what she was thinking. It better not be thoughts of his brother. Even the thought of him hitting on her at the bar made his stomach tighten.

They hadn't seen them yet. Mark and Laura were tucked away in a darker corner of the restaurant. Mark noticed that Edward was holding Elle's hand, and the two of them looked cozy. He felt the knee-jerk jealousy, even though he was long past caring who Elle slept with.

Truth was, the day she'd let their boy walk into the ocean, part of him had just disconnected. Yes, it had hurt him when she'd turned to his brother for comfort, but it hurt more that Edward had offered it. Edward was supposed to be his brother, his blood. Still, he didn't much need it in his face.

Elle glanced up and met his gaze. She looked startled, as if she'd forgotten he lived on the island, too. Maybe he'd been a hermit too long. Elle clutched Edward's arm and that's when he glanced up, a frown crossing his face. Mark felt his shoulders tense as Edward saw them, too. The couple hesitated at the hostess stand.

"I didn't know…" Laura began. "I didn't know she was…pregnant." She looked visibly pained. It was one of the reasons he hadn't mentioned it to her. He knew how the thought of other pregnancies made her sad. He didn't want her to be sad about Elle's—that should be a burden he alone carried.

"Yeah." Mark stared at the tablecloth.

"Should we go?" Laura asked, not looking over her shoulder at the couple as she carefully watched his face. He could feel her eyes on him.

"No. We stay." Mark was tired of hiding. He reached out and took Laura's hand, squeezing it gently. He refused to care what they would do. He glanced at Laura instead. She looked uneasy.

"You sure?"

"We haven't even finished our main course." Mark took another bite to show how determined he was to hold his ground. He grinned at Laura, and she tentatively smiled back. That's when he saw Edward and Elle turn and leave the restaurant, Elle practically pulling him out the door.

"They're going," he said and then exhaled a sigh of relief. The muscles in his shoulders relaxed, and he realized he'd tensed up, readying for a fight.

Laura swiveled in her seat, watching Elle as

she ducked out of the restaurant. The couple was visible through the big glass window facing the parking lot.

"She's really pretty," she murmured, almost to herself.

"Yes," Mark admitted. "But she's not pretty to me anymore." Not since Timothy. Not since Edward. Not since she decided to become a mother again.

"I don't know what I expected... I..." Laura faltered.

Was she intimidated by Elle? Most women were, Mark realized. It was why she generally got the cold shoulder when most women met her. She was gorgeous, tall and thin, and it came as a surprise to no one that in her younger days she used to model. When they'd been married, she'd even mugged for the camera. He'd thought it was adorable until he realized her self-absorption with her looks and herself in general meant little room for him...or Timothy. When she'd retreated away from them so she could take her pills.

"You're a million times more beautiful than she is," Mark said and squeezed Laura's hand once more. She glanced up at him, surprised.

"No, I'm not."

"You are to me," he said.

She sent him a hesitant smile, unsure of the compliment, but in his mind, he spoke the truth.

Laura was shorter, true, and a brunette, but the spark in her green eyes, her beautiful fair skin, well, it put Elle's freckles to shame. Besides, it was what was inside a woman that made her pretty. Mark was certain of that.

"It's true," he added.

She blushed a little. "Would you like dessert?" she asked him.

He grinned at her. "The kind of dessert I want isn't on this menu." She laughed a little, and the tension was broken.

After he paid for dinner and drove her back to the condo, he kissed her good-night outside her condo door. He wanted her—badly—but he didn't want to make any assumptions. He would let her set the pace.

But she deepened the kiss and grabbed his shirtfront with both hands, practically dragging him into her condo. In a tornado of flying clothes, they made it to her bedroom, and they sank down on her palm-tree bedspread, neither one able to get enough of the other, their mouths hungry for one another.

"God, Laura," he breathed, not sure if he'd ever felt this passionate about anyone, not even Elle. He wanted to be inside this woman *now*.

He flipped her over so she was on top, her thick dark bob swinging forward as she straddled him. She broke the kiss and sat up and he felt her delicious weight against him. He hardened beneath her pelvis as she moved slowly against him. She grinned, a look of mischief in her green eyes.

"Someone's eager," she said.

"You have no idea," he murmured, feeling his whole body on fire for her.

She laughed deep in her throat, and he felt the reverberations all the way in his stomach. God, she was the sexiest woman on earth. He had no desire for anyone else in that moment. All he wanted was her.

He remembered her last time—wet, soft and eager and how she'd moaned beneath him, her faced flushed with pleasure as he brought her to climax. He wanted badly to do that again, to see her overtaken by ecstasy.

She put both hands on his chest. "But first, we need to talk."

"Now?" It seemed the worst possible time to talk.

She reached behind her and grabbed the small plastic bag on her nightstand. "We should be using one of these." She pulled a condom package from the bag.

Condoms. Of course. He should've thought of that. He should've. So why hadn't he? Part of him knew why. He wanted to feel her bare once more. She'd been so delicious, so amazingly wet.

But condoms. That's what they should be using.

Even though, wasn't the horse already out of the barn? He pushed the thought away. No. Condoms were the right thing to do.

"Yes. Of course." It was the safe, rational thing to do. They should've done this the first time.

"I mean, I hate these, just so you know, but we really need to…"

"I get it." Mark wiggled out of his pants. She took the condom expertly in her hands and then slid it down the length of him. He groaned beneath her touch. Condoms wouldn't be so bad, after all, he thought, as she lifted up her dress and pulled it over her head.

He admired her lacy bra and she slipped it off, exposing two perfect breasts. He cupped them in his hands, admiring their weight as she arched her back, pushing herself into him. She straddled him then, and he was once more inside her.

After that, he didn't give the condom another thought.

AFTERWARD, AS THEY both lay spent and sweaty in each other's arms, Laura grew quiet.

"What's on your mind?" he asked as he traced her bare shoulder with his finger.

Laura hesitated, and he could feel her reluctance as she rested her head on his chest.

"Edward told me…that you had Elle arrested."

"What?" Mark felt his blood pressure rise as his hand stopped, mid-caress. "What did he say exactly?"

Laura lifted her head and met his gaze, the look in her eyes uncertain. "That you had her arrested for neglect. Because of Timothy…"

Mark shut his eyes. He couldn't deny it, but it's not how Edward framed it, he was sure.

"It's not what you think," he said, rolling away from her. He sat up and swung his feet over the side of the bed, keeping his back to her. "I'm sure Edward painted me as a monster going after a grieving mother." Mark felt his shoulders tighten once more. He knew the story Edward told. He told it all over the island, which was why Mark had so few friends. No one bothered to ask him his side of the story. Now here was Laura, ready to jump right in with the pitchfork crowd. Why did that hurt so much?

"What happened?" she asked, moving to him, putting her arms around him from behind. "Can you tell me? I'm not saying I believe Edward. All I'm saying is he said some bad things."

Mark nodded, weighing whether or not he even wanted to try to defend himself. After all, what was the use? Most of the island had judged him and found him guilty.

"Mark. Please. I want to know."

Mark sighed. He thought about the little detail Edward left out. About Elle. He still felt strangely protective of the woman, even though everyone on the island thought he had been determined to see her behind bars. That wasn't it at all.

"It's not really my story to tell."

"You're not going to tell me?"

Mark hesitated and turned to face her. He had a hard time telling those green eyes no.

Laura lay back on the bed, pulling the covers up over her bare breasts. "You were the one who told me that it didn't matter what secrets I told you, remember? I'm leaving in a couple of weeks? I told you what not a single soul other than my sister and my ex know about me, and now you're not wanting to spill any beans? Seriously?"

He guessed she had a point there. Who was Laura going to tell? And besides, Elle wasn't his problem anymore.

"Elle had—or, hell, probably still has—a prescription drug problem."

Laura grew silent. "What?"

"On the island, prescriptions aren't as regulated as they are on the mainland," he admitted. "It's easier to get things. Things to make you sleep. Make you stay awake or things that just make you feel…better."

Laura listened to him, rapt. "I'm sorry. I didn't know."

Mark lay back down next to her and stared at the ceiling. "No one did. Not even Edward. Although, I bet he does now." Mark sighed, rolling over to face her.

"But she's pregnant." Laura sucked in a breath.

"And I hope she's quit the pills. For now, at least."

"But she took them. When she was with you."

He nodded.

"We'd been fighting about how many pills she took. She needed one every night to go to sleep, and then she needed one every morning to wake up, and then she'd take a different one in the middle of the day when she was feeling bored or unhappy or whatever it was." Mark so vividly remembered those days. How she'd be so slow to get up, so sluggish. How she wouldn't hear Timothy cry in the middle of the night.

"What about Timothy?"

"She said she did it because Timothy made her so tired, that she needed a boost to keep up with him. She didn't take all that readily to motherhood. She was depressed after he was born, and it never really lifted."

"Postpartum depression. And she used the drugs to cope."

He nodded. He took a deep breath. This next part of the story was the hardest. "I thought she was doing better, I really did," he said. This was the excuse he always told himself. The one that made it okay that he'd left her alone that morning. "Just the week before she told me she was clean. She'd thrown all the pills away with me watching, and I thought she was done with them. But she wasn't." He sucked in a deep breath. "I had to go to work, and I left her, and she said she'd be fine. That she'd take Timothy to the beach, and they'd have a nice day of it." Mark clenched his jaw, and it was almost as if his body didn't want him to get the words out. "But I shouldn't have left them. She hadn't thrown them all away. She took a pill that morning. She was groggy and in a hurry and she took a sleep pill instead of an upper pill. And that's why she fell asleep on the beach that day."

Laura looked at him, every bit of her face registering shock.

"I didn't want her arrested. I wanted to get

her into a treatment program. But maybe I wasn't very nice about it. Maybe I was angry, too, that she'd lied to me about being off the pills. So, yeah, I asked my friend to arrest her. I thought she'd...get help."

Tears rimmed her eyes. He was amazed how much she was affected by the story.

"Oh, Mark. I'm...so very sorry." She reached for him and he moved into her arms. She held him tightly.

"It's not your fault."

"No, it isn't, but it's terrible, and you shouldn't have to have gone through that. I can't believe Edward let the island believe you wanted to lock up your grieving wife for no reason."

Mark shrugged. "I'm sure it's what Elle told him, and I'm sure it's what she told herself because the truth is probably too painful."

Laura cradled his head against her chest. "You lost your boy and your wife all at once."

Mark nodded into her. "But things weren't right with Elle for a long time before that. The pills—well, I don't even remember the woman I married, to be honest. She was long gone."

Laura bit her lip. "I just...I just think you deserve so much better than that."

Mark lifted his head and met her gaze, and for once in a very long time, felt heard. He felt understood. When could he say that? Even

Dave deserted him in his time of need. And his brother had done worse than that. But Laura, she understood.

For the first time, he felt a little bit of hope. Maybe he shouldn't give up on everything just yet. Maybe Laura was right. Maybe he could still win the race.

"You really want to learn to sail? To race?" he asked.

Her eyes lit up. She nodded fiercely.

"Then what have we got to lose? Lessons start tomorrow, first thing."

CHAPTER SEVENTEEN

LAURA WOKE UP bright and early, ready to learn how to sail. She rolled over, expecting to find Mark there, but his side of the bed was empty. Where had he gone?

She pulled herself from bed, realizing she was still naked from the night before. Her muscles felt deliciously sore from all the exercise. She'd never tried so many positions in one night. Mark was adventurous, and she'd never felt as wanted or as sexy with any other man. She pulled the top sheet from her bed and wrapped it around her.

"Mark?" she called but heard no answer from her condo. He wasn't in the kitchen or bathroom. Where was he? She glanced around for a note but found none. Her phone was also void of messages from him. Her dreamy mood from the night began to evaporate. *Maybe he went to get coffee. Or breakfast. Or...maybe he just ran out on me.*

The thought jarred her. Had the condoms pushed him away? She thought back about falling asleep in his arms the night before. Things had seemed fine then. So what had happened? *No. Don't panic. Maybe he went downstairs.*

Laura pulled on some clothes, slapped on a baseball cap and headed downstairs to his condo. She knocked on the door but got no answer. Then when she glanced in the parking lot, she saw his truck was gone.

He could still be getting breakfast, she thought hopefully. Even though the small little ball of dread in the pit of her stomach told her otherwise.

She hated this. The insecurities that bubbled up in her when she least expected it. There was always that little voice in her head that told her she wasn't good enough, that men wouldn't stay, that she wasn't worth the effort. The same little voice told her *I told you so* when Dean went back to his wife.

Now it told her that Mark had tired of her, that he'd sneaked out because he hadn't wanted to hurt her feelings or because he was scared to tell her that he didn't really care that much about her, after all.

She hated that she couldn't stop the wheels in her mind from turning, but the more she tried, the louder her insecurities became. She told herself she just needed to get busy. Maybe she'd clean her condo, put her hands to work, and then when Mark resurfaced, she'd figure out what was going on.

Still, a nagging doubt lingered.

Where was he?

MARK RANG GARRETT'S doorbell several times in a row. He'd gotten his friend's text message that morning. Come over. Urgent.

Usually, Mark never heard from Garrett, Dave's brother. He hadn't even talked to him since before Dave had broken the news he was bailing on helping him restore the *Timothy*.

When Mark had asked Garrett what it was about, he'd simply responded, The race.

Garrett, a bachelor, opened the door to Mark.

"Good. It's you. Come in." Garrett was a younger, leaner version of his brother, Dave, with sandy blond hair and clear blue eyes. Garrett was five years younger than Dave and almost as good a sailor. He held open his front door and gestured for Mark to come in.

"I was surprised to hear from you," Mark admitted as he walked across the threshold into a small condo overlooking the ocean. "I assumed you were in Dave's camp and wanted nothing to do with me."

"Look, first off, man, I want to tell you that Dave bailing, that was his idea, not mine."

Garrett's condo was decorated with surfboards hanging on the wall—boards that Garrett sometimes used—as well as brightly colored upholstered furniture and a big round leather ottoman in the middle of his living room. But it was a signature bachelor's pad. The condo was a mess, with empty pizza boxes lying on the kitchen counter and dirty clothes on the floor.

"I heard about Katie, so I get it." Mark stepped over a pair of dirty board shorts to get closer to the kitchen. "So what did you want to talk to me about?"

"Okay, so…just that I'm not bailing. I'm not with Dave on this. I want to sail for you."

"What?" Mark couldn't hide his surprise. "But why not with Dave and Edward?"

"Because I know they've treated you badly. And I don't think it's right. We promised to sail with you first." Garrett narrowed his eyes. "Anyway, the point is, we promised you. We should stay with you. That's what I told Dave."

"But won't he need you? To race for Tanner?"

"Edward's got other friends."

Edward had plenty of sailing buddies. Dave might be the best, and Garrett the second best on the island, but there'd be plenty of others Edward could call on. Tanner Boating had a loyal sailor following, even if that following didn't extend to Mark these days.

"You'd really do that for me?"

"Yeah, and I've got a third and fourth, but we still need a fifth. But might be hard to find one, this close to race time," Garrett said.

"I have a fifth. But she's a novice. Are you up for helping her learn?"

Garrett shrugged. "I'm game if you are."

WHEN MARK GOT back to the condos with Garrett in tow, he found Laura furiously vacuuming her condo. She cut the switch and glanced up, seemingly surprised to see them.

"Who's your friend?" Laura asked, a bit cool.

"Our third sailor, and he's going to bring two more soon," Mark announced proudly. Laura stood there, apparently still unsure. He got the feeling he'd done something wrong, but he didn't know what it was. "Garrett, this is Laura. Laura, Garrett. You still up for sailing?"

Laura hesitated a beat, which wasn't lost on Mark. Yesterday, she was so excited about sailing she could barely contain herself, and today she was a little lukewarm. "Uh. Sure. Yeah." Laura gave Garrett a weak smile. "You're Dave's brother."

"Yes, that's right. But don't hold me to anything that jerk does." Garrett shook Laura's hand as she laughed a little. Mark could see whatever tension was in the room loosen a bit.

"I dragged this guy outta bed this morning to tell him I'd join your crew, if he'll let me."

Laura suddenly looked happy. "Oh! So that's where you went!"

"Sorry. Uh, yeah, I went to Garrett's." Mark fidgeted. He guessed he should've left a note. Now he realized why she was miffed. He'd up and left her in an empty condo. *Nice move, Casanova.* But she was focused on Garrett.

"Did Mark warn you I know nothing about sailing?" she asked.

"He might have mentioned that."

"Think you guys can teach me?"

"It depends," Garrett said. "How badly do you want it?"

AFTER SIX WEEKS on the boat, every day, day in and day out, Laura was beginning to think that maybe she'd signed up for too much. Her arms ached, her hands felt raw and her back muscles screamed for mercy. Maybe she'd been too quick to assume she could do this, even as Garrett and Mark tried to patiently teach her the ropes—literally. Garrett's sailing friends, Tim and Gretchen, also helped, rounding out their crew of five.

Still, she hadn't fallen overboard or let a line go this time, and she was slowly but surely starting to feel more comfortable on board. At least she'd learned all the jargon and could follow orders, which was more than her first day. And her base tan had settled in, so no more burns and no more peeling, even though she still religiously slathered on sunscreen.

She'd overstayed her initial trip, but instead of extending her condo rental, Mark had asked her to stay with him. It had been a delicious six weeks, passing in a blur, and she'd had the time of her life. They spent every day, shoulder to shoulder, on the open water.

Laura hadn't even cared about cashing in another small 401(k). She'd worry about getting a job, about going back to reality, after the race. She both looked forward to the race, for Mark's sake, but also dreaded it because it would mean facing up to the problems she'd been avoiding.

She'd have to make a decision soon—in the next week or so—when she planned to leave. Staying would mean taking more money out of savings. She hadn't planned on draining all her retirement savings, but maybe she'd have to. Yet, the idea of going back to San Francisco made her feel weak-kneed. She wasn't ready.

And then there was another nagging little problem.

She was late. Laura tried not to think about it too hard. After all, her period was never regular, not for as long as she could remember. She'd skip them all the time with no consequences. She hadn't even known she was pregnant until week seven, only because a missed period was never cause for alarm.

This time, it was most likely just another skipped period, or maybe her body had not quite gotten back to normal after the miscarriage. Laura couldn't even wrap her mind around the possibility that she might be pregnant. After that ill-advised first night, she and Mark had been religiously using condoms, and while she knew it was technically possible to get pregnant from one time, she felt her body, *her defective body*, certainly couldn't do that.

She ignored the tenderness in her breasts, the dragging feelings of fatigue she felt every night. *It's just all the sailing, all the physical work*, she told herself. Just like she told herself that her appetite, which never seemed to be satisfied, was just the sailing. That's all it was.

Laura didn't let her mind go there. She couldn't. Not yet.

She thought of this as she hung on to the bow of the boat. Her empty stomach rumbled. She'd just eaten a granola bar but couldn't seem to stay full. She sat at the stern of the boat.

"You are really getting good at this," Mark commented, bringing her to the present. She almost jumped.

"You think so?" she asked.

"I know so," Garrett yelled from the bow.

Tim and Gretchen stayed silent, but she knew they also agreed. They'd been more than encouraging these last weeks.

Laura laughed. Maybe she could really help. Maybe they could win the race in four days.

Suddenly, she felt a surge of nausea that seemed to come out of nowhere. What the— She didn't get seasick. But she was feeling a little woozy. The boat kicked up under a sudden wave.

"Whoa," she said, feeling dizzy as she clung to the boat. Mark reached out and clutched her elbow.

"You okay?" Mark asked, concerned.

"I…I think so." She smiled weakly, but she felt like hurling off the back of the boat. *Just don't throw up*, she told herself. "I'm just feeling a little nauseous."

"Seasickness?" he asked, looking sympathetic. "Happens to the best of us."

"Uh…yeah." Laura was beginning to think it wasn't seasickness. All the clues added up. Could she be pregnant? God, she couldn't be. Could she?

The thought sent another white-hot wave of nausea through her. *Hold it together*, she told herself. She glanced at the horizon and saw dark clouds headed their way. A storm?

"We'd better head in before that hits," Mark said, and Garrett, Tim and Gretchen agreed. Laura glanced at the storm rolling in behind them as they turned the sailboat back to shore. The sun hung low in the horizon, so darkness would be coming soon as well.

"Is it a bad one?" Laura asked, feeling a little nervous as she remembered hurricane season approaching. The winds picked up, making it harder to hear. Her nausea retreated a little as adrenaline spiked.

"The radio says it could be," Gretchen yelled over the gale.

In no time, the boat made it back to the marina.

"We might just have a shot at this thing," Garrett said, sounding amazed as they pulled into their slot at the dock.

"You think so?" Laura asked, sweaty from her time in the sun and working the lines.

"You are a fast learner. We might do this. Really." Garrett grinned and gave her shoulder a squeeze. "Never saw a woman so determined to sail."

"Well, I want Mark to win." She glanced at Mark as he secured the boat to the dock.

"You care for him, don't you?" Garrett asked

suddenly. Laura stared at Mark, who was too far away to hear the conversation. She just nodded once. The nausea had gone almost as quickly as it had come. Maybe she'd imagined it.

"I thought so. I've got an eye for these things." Garrett grabbed a line and hopped off to help secure the sailboat.

THAT EVENING, AFTER a quick dinner at the Rusted Anchor, Mark walked with Laura down Smuggler's Cove, through a busy crowd of tourists. In fact, so many strangers crowded into the tiny port that there was barely room for cars to drive. The jewelry and souvenir shops were packed, and all the restaurants had long waits, even though the sky was crowded with angry storm clouds, ready to burst. The sun dipped below the horizon, not that anyone could tell with the darkening storm rolling in from the sea.

Mark glanced at the clouds and felt glad they'd turned in when they did. Being on the water with that kind of storm was never fun. A few light raindrops hit the sidewalk in front of them, leaving dark circles.

"Where did all these people come from?" Laura asked. "I didn't think that many people lived on St. Anthony's."

"They don't." Mark felt a surge of annoyance as a man nudged his shoulder without looking up. "They're on the cruise ships. The last one of the season." The two tried to navigate through a packed crosswalk in the middle of town, even as the rain started to come a bit harder. Still a sprinkle, but held the promise of more to come.

"Why?"

Mark shrugged. "Hurricanes. The cruise ships will be headed up to Alaska or wherever it is they go. Not a good idea to have a big boat out in the sea when the storms hit."

Laura frowned, looking worried. "How often do hurricanes hit?"

"Not often. But sometimes. We had a big one about ten years ago. Lots of flooding, a bit of damage. The Rusted Anchor survived, but some of the shops on the strip here had to be rebuilt."

Laura held Mark's hand a little tighter as a family with four kids surged past them, all wearing neon-colored baseball caps and shirts advertising other Caribbean islands.

"Anyone hurt?" she asked.

"No, thank goodness. And the tourists came back right away, so that was good. The winds blew pretty fierce then."

"You stayed?" Laura asked, amazed. "Why didn't you leave? Did you not have warning?"

"No, we did." Mark remembered that time. It had been rough for those who chose to stay on the island. Many evacuated under orders by local police, but Mark had stayed. He'd boarded up his windows and he'd waited it out. He had just gotten Tanner Boating off the ground then, and he'd be damned if he'd let the winds rip apart his boats while he was safely snuggled somewhere in Florida.

"I had just started Tanner Boating. I wasn't married then, so why not?"

"You could've been killed." She sounded so concerned. He kind of liked that.

"I wasn't." He pulled Laura close, putting his arm around her shoulders. "I'm hard to kill," he joked, and then instantly felt an inward cringe as he remembered trying to walk into the ocean just weeks ago. Too hard to kill, probably. He couldn't even manage to do it himself.

He shook off the morbid thoughts, and that's when he realized that since he'd been with Laura, he hadn't really thought of killing himself or of sailing off to sea and never coming back. He knew on some level that was a fantasy. He doubted he could actually pull it off. Like the last time he tried and his body took over. He knew it was just his way of not thinking about the future without Timothy.

But the romanticism of leaving this world, of returning to Timothy beneath the waves, had faded to the back of his mind. When had that happened? he wondered. Instead, he found himself just looking forward to seeing Laura every day, with her beautiful smile and bright green eyes.

"You've changed my life for the better," he told her, pulling her close. "You might have even saved...my life."

"Saved your life!" she cried. "I doubt that."

How little she knew.

"Laura," he said, stopping her in the street, crowds of tourists streaming by them. He wanted badly to tell her how much she'd grown to mean to him in such a short time, how she had changed him irrevocably.

"Yes?"

"I..."

Her eyes looked so hopeful then. Was he going to tell her he loved her? Did he? How could he love her? They'd only just met. And he still planned to sail around the world or die in the attempt, didn't he? Had his feelings about that really changed so much? Would it be fair to her to declare his love and then leave her?

"I am grateful for you. More grateful than you'll ever know," he managed, and even though the sentiment was real, the fact that he didn't say *I love you* made him feel like he'd chickened out.

She smiled. "Aw, well, I'm grateful for you, too. You've really helped me see my problems differently, and made this…time-out I gave myself well worth it."

"It *is* worth it," Mark said. "I would've never met you if you hadn't given yourself a time-out."

Laura slipped her hand in his and they continued walking down the street. All the while, Mark wished he'd said more but was afraid to. Afraid of what it would mean if he actually said *I love you* out loud. He wondered if she felt the same or if, like she'd said, men fall in love sooner. Harder.

She glanced up at him and he smiled down at her, giving her hand a little squeeze. For now, they had the race to focus on. He could worry about his feelings—and hers—later.

The sky really opened up just as they got to the end of the storefronts and to his truck parked on the street. They ran the last few steps and Laura hopped in the cab as the rain started to flow.

"Wow, that came fast," she said, shaking raindrops from her hair as Mark slid into the cab and turned the ignition.

"Better get used to it," he said. "Hurricane season brings the rainy season, too. And with climate change…well, it seems that the season starts earlier and the storms are worse. Bigger.

We'll have lots more of this, maybe even more than sunshine."

"Great. What about race day?"

"It's been clear almost 70 percent of the time somehow. The organizers keep threatening to change the date, but so far, nobody wants to mess with tradition." Mark steered the truck down the lane and onto the narrow two-lane highway, the rain pelting down now. He squinted through the window as his headlights barely made a dent in the sudden downpour. His windshield wipers batted back and forth urgently but hardly made a dent.

"How can you even see?" Laura asked, her hands gripping the handle hanging above her window.

"I can't, really."

"And there aren't any lights on this highway." Laura seemed worried.

"Calling it a highway is a stretch," Mark said. "St. Anthony's has always been a little rustic, and a little off the beaten path, until the cruise ships found us anyway. We don't need no stinkin' highways." He grinned and Laura laughed a little.

Ahead, oncoming headlights flashed through the torrential rain and Mark heard Laura suck in her breath.

"Look out," she murmured, even as the oncoming car seemed to recognize it was coming into their lane and swerved back. Mark adjusted the course of the truck, too, just to be safe, and the oncoming car sped on by, safely back in his lane.

"We'll be home soon," Mark promised her, hoping the rain would let up. The cliffside highway had been known to become a little unstable after serious rains, but he wasn't about to tell Laura that. She was anxious enough as it was. One year, after the rainy season, a stretch of the outer part of the road fell into the ocean. Luckily, no one was hurt, and they fixed it quickly, but that was on his mind as Mark steered the truck around a tight bend.

Just a little farther, he thought, and then they'd be safe at home.

"You really think I'm ready?" Laura asked, sounding unsure. "For the race, I mean."

Mark wasn't certain, but he also knew that really didn't matter. They were going to try their best. That's all they could do. "Well, you're going to race whether you're ready or not, so I guess we'll find out on race day."

"Not exactly an inspiring talk, Mr. Grumpy Pants," Laura joked.

"I just call 'em like I see 'em," he said. "And given how little you knew about sailing even a week ago, I'd say you're amazingly ready."

"You do?"

Mark nodded, keeping his attention focused on the road ahead. How could he explain to her that working with her on the boat felt like they were engaged in a kind of waltz, that they worked together as well on the boat as they did in the bedroom. Reading each other's minds, instinctively knowing where to put their bodies. Garrett was almost unnecessary. The two worked together like they had one mind.

"We're a good team," he said. "I mean, a really good team. Elle and I could never...I mean, we could never sail. We tried, but she never listened to me, and her instincts were all wrong."

"Really?" Laura perked up at this.

"It's true." He risked a glance at her and saw her beam from the compliment. "You're like no other woman I've ever met."

Laura reached over and covered his hand, which was resting on the gearshift.

"You're like no man I've ever met, either."

"That's a good thing, isn't it?" he joked, and Laura laughed. Then, Laura spotted a drugstore on the corner.

"Hey, can we stop?" She pointed through the windshield.

Mark pulled into the small parking lot. "Sure. Want me to come in?"

"No. I just wanna grab something really

quick. Women's stuff." She gave him a peck on the cheek and opened her door.

"Take my coat to keep you dry," he said, handing her his rain slicker. She took it, held it over her head like a tent and ran into the store.

LAURA STEPPED INTO the small, brightly lit drugstore, biting her lower lip. She was going to get a pregnancy test. All the symptoms, the missed period…she owed it to herself to take it. Put the unease to rest. She was 99 percent sure she wasn't pregnant. One night? She doubted it could happen.

She grabbed a pregnancy test and then a box of tampons. Wishful thinking? Maybe, but if she wasn't pregnant, it meant that she would get her period eventually. Besides, the tampons in the opaque bag would neatly hide the pregnancy test box.

She checked out under the watchful eye of the clerk, feeling the heat rise in her face. Laura would find a way to take this…later. When Mark was sleeping, maybe.

She ran back through the rain to his truck.

"Want to come to my place for a drink?" he asked.

"Only if we do more than drink," she teased as they pulled off the highway onto the exit leading to their condo building. As he steered into the parking lot, he squeezed her hand a little tighter. He pulled into a parking space and cut the engine.

Together, they ran to the shelter of the patio overhang, giggling as Mark pulled her into his arms and kissed her. Rain ran down the storm gutters in rivulets, splashing on the ground near them as they stayed dry beneath the overhang. The kiss turned more passionate as he opened his mouth, his tongue flicked hers, soft and inviting. They kissed for who knows how long, the rain pelting down in the dark around them. Eventually, Mark pulled away.

"Why don't we just skip that drink?" he offered.

Laura, feeling her heart hammering in her chest, her hands still wrapped around the drugstore bag, just nodded.

"The way you look right now, you're so beautiful," he said. "Makes me want to kiss you again."

"Then do it," she murmured.

CHAPTER EIGHTEEN

THE RAIN SCOURED the island for two straight days, turning some of the roads into streams as the deluge continued. Tourists stayed inside, and Mark and Laura found themselves land-locked, unable to take the boat out for a sail. Laura actually didn't mind. The two hibernated inside, cooking simple meals and just relaxing together.

But it was hard not to think about the future, about when the rain let up, about the impend-ing race. Then there was what could happen after the race. What if they did win and Mark sailed around the world without her? What if they lost? Would that mean she could some-how keep Mark? But how? Relocate to St. An-thony's? How would she earn a living?

Worse, she hadn't had a chance to discreetly take the pregnancy test. Mark was with her all the time, even in the shower. The unused test sat hidden beneath some of her clothes in one of his drawers. She'd need to do it. Soon. She'd had one chance in the bathroom but she chickened out at the last minute. Laura had to find the resolve to do it.

The more time passed, the more she told herself it couldn't be possible that she was pregnant, despite the fact that her period never arrived. And she wasn't sure how she felt about it. She wanted a baby more than anything, but would a pregnancy scare Mark? And what would she do if she was pregnant and had another miscarriage? The thought made her want to curl up in a fetal position. Laura wasn't sure she'd ever be ready to survive another blow like that one. Could she risk it?

It seemed easier not to know. She knew she needed to take the test. Put to rest the nagging doubt. Yet part of her didn't want to. Didn't want to face the reality.

The same part that ran away to St. Anthony's. It's what her sister, Maddie, would've told her. *Time to be an adult.*

"Penny for your thoughts?" Mark asked as he stirred the spaghetti sauce on the stove. He'd opened a jar and then added a few ingredients of his own—sautéed onions and peppers and some ground beef—and now he dipped a wooden spoon in and gave it a little taste.

"Just thinking about the future," she admitted, not yet ready to tell Mark about her missed period. She needed to take the test, figure this out once and for all.

"That's dangerous," he said, and she felt a little flutter of nerves in her stomach. *Don't be that girl*, she told herself, *the one clamoring for clarification, for commitment. Just live in the moment. Just...be.*

"Wondering what happens if we don't win the race," she managed.

Mark held out a spoonful of spaghetti sauce for her to taste. She took it, the sweet, savory flavors hitting her tongue in the perfect combination. "Mmm," she said. "Delicious." Her stomach grumbled a little, eager for more. She seemed not to be able to get full these days. Her appetite had more than made a comeback, and her once-loose shorts were getting tight again. But she'd worry about that later. Right now, she was *in the moment* with Mark, here in his kitchen, feeling...happy.

"We'll do fine, whether we win or lose," he said.

"But your dream—sailing around the world. I want that for you." Laura wanted it more than anything, even if it meant being separated from him. If it helped him honor his son, then she wanted it. If there was something she could do, something for her baby who'd never been born, she would, too.

Mark frowned, lost in thought. "Look, Laura, are you sure you want to do this?" He stopped stirring and looked at her.

"Of course I do."

"It can get dangerous. Things happen in races. Sometimes, boats run into each other. Boats stall. Sailors get thrown overboard. Sometimes it can get dangerous." Mark studied her. "Once, a few years ago, someone fell overboard and because it was so close to the other boats, he got knocked unconscious by another one behind his. Drowned. It was a freak accident, but still. Sometimes things happen."

Laura wasn't deterred. "I don't care."

"Tomorrow it will be *far* more stressful than it has been so far," Mark warned her. "Not nearly as relaxed as it's been in practice."

"I figured."

"Sometimes things get intense," Mark said. "Are you ready for that?"

"Definitely," she said, thinking about how much she'd enjoyed putting her hands to work since she'd been on the island and how much sailing had been a part of that. She loved helping to steer the boat and feeling like she was part of something bigger than herself. It wasn't just being on a racing team. It was also being out in nature, on the water and in the wind and sun.

He grinned, stirring the pot once more and looking thoughtful. "We make such a good team."

He'd mentioned this before, but something about his tone took Laura by surprise. *Team* almost sounded like...couple. She tried not to let her thoughts go there. That was a black hole of insecurity waiting for her.

"We do, don't we?" she said, keeping her voice light. She turned away from him and glanced at the television in his living room, running on mute. The local news had a story about the flooding in nearby Smuggler's Cove. Laura hoped everyone was okay.

"I really am amazed how quickly you picked up the sailing," Mark said. "It takes people months, even years, to learn what you've done in such a short time."

Laura shrugged. "You're a good teacher," she said simply, even as she kept her attention on the television. "You think the rain will stop by tomorrow for the race?"

"The forecast says it will, and there might be a hurricane forming out there, but if it does, everyone says it'll miss us," Mark said. "I've been monitoring the weather."

"Looks like someone up there is looking after you," she said.

Mark hesitated as he stirred. He smacked the

spoon on the side of the pot. "You know it's okay if we don't win," he said, not meeting her gaze.

"No!" Laura squeezed his arm. "Don't say that. We can win. Garrett thinks so, right? So do Gretchen and Tim. Don't start planning for defeat. That's what my mom used to say. When she cheered my sister and me on in little league soccer." Laura remembered those days so vividly. Her mom so loud on the sidelines, jumping out of her folding lawn chair so much she wondered why she even brought it to the games.

Thinking about her mom and Maddie made Laura remember the spat she'd had with her sister. She still hadn't heard from Maddie. No texts, no calls, no emails. Laura wasn't going to be the one to apologize first. Not this time. Even though, at moments like these, she was sorely tempted. But the fact was, Laura still didn't think she'd done anything wrong. It was time her sister learned to respect her boundaries.

"Must've been a great woman," he said. "I'm sorry she passed."

"She was very unhappy and I hope she's found the peace she was looking for." Laura hugged herself. "Maddie never forgave Mom. Not really, for taking her own life. I get that. I'm mad at her, too."

"She shouldn't have left you." Mark hit the

pot with the spoon too hard, and a bit of sauce splattered on the countertop. Laura grabbed a towel and sopped it up. She wondered where the sudden show of emotion came from. "I don't like the idea of her leaving you…alone."

"Well, I had Dad. And Maddie. And I was grown, but I guess, I mean, we still need our parents, even when we're grown. But yeah, I get what you mean." Did he care? Was that why he seemed so angry on her behalf?

Laura stirred the boiling pot of spaghetti, and scooped up a limp noodle. She blew on it and then tasted it. Perfect.

"Pasta's ready," she said. She grabbed pot holders and gingerly took the oversize pot to the stove, where she dumped the pasta into a metal sieve in the sink. Pretty soon, they'd dished out plates and sat to eat at the breakfast bar, sitting shoulder to shoulder. Even a day in had made both of them ravenous, probably because they'd spent most of it out of their clothes.

Laura found she'd devoured half the plate before she even took her first breath.

"Boy, you were hungry," Mark said, not even a quarter of the way into his own meal. "You clearly worked up an appetite today."

Mark wiggled his eyebrows, and his reference to their naked wrestling was clear. She felt her face grow hot. "That I did," she said and giggled.

As they dug deeper into their meal, Mark grew serious.

"So how are you feeling about tomorrow?"

"Good. Why?" Laura spooled pasta around her fork and sent a big bite into her mouth.

Mark pushed spaghetti around on his plate. "I just want you to know that the race tomorrow, it can get intense. But even if we don't win—hell, even if we don't finish—it's okay."

"But what about the prize money? What about you sailing around the world?" Laura was down to her last couple of bites. She had inhaled her food. Normally, she never ate this fast.

"I've been thinking lately that maybe I should think about other options," Mark admitted.

It was the first Laura had heard of this. "Why? I thought you wanted to see the world. Be closer to Timothy."

"That's not the only reason why." Mark's shoulders stiffened and she could feel the tension in the moment. He put down his fork.

What wasn't he telling her?

He took a deep breath and turned to face her. He took her hands. "When I first decided to try for the prize money, yes, I wanted to get away and I wanted to sail off to a faraway place and be on the water, where I think Timothy's spirit is." He took a deep breath, his dark eyes troubled as they met hers. "But I'll admit to you that part of me hoped I wouldn't come back."

"What do you mean?" Laura frowned. "You'd settle somewhere else? A different country?"

Mark shook his head slowly. "No." He took another breath. "It's dangerous in some parts of the world, you know. Storms come out of nowhere. Sailboats get lost at sea all the time."

Suddenly, Laura's heart rate sped up. She squeezed his hands. "So you mean you wanted to sink the ship? On purpose?" The weight of the revelation hit her and she leaned against the kitchen counter for support. Was Mark suicidal? She thought about that day at the beach, when he'd gone under and hadn't come back up right away.

"I don't know exactly," he admitted. "All I know is that since Timothy died, I haven't found much of a reason to get out of bed in the morning. And I liked the idea of trying to go out in a blaze of glory."

"But..." Laura was still processing this. Was he still considering suicide? "Are you serious about this? I mean, really serious? Or is it just a passing thought?"

Mark dropped her hands and then let out a long breath. "I've tried to drown myself," he said, not meeting her gaze as he studied the wooden spoon sitting on the counter.

"When?" Laura felt like her heart almost stopped. Her appetite suddenly fled as she studied his profile.

He sighed. "That day. On the beach. When I went for a swim and you were there."

Laura hugged herself, not knowing what to say. "I knew something was wrong that day. How you just walked out there. How you stayed under so long."

He nodded. "But I couldn't do it. My reflexes took over...and..." He held out his hands, palms up.

"I'm glad you failed," she said.

He nodded. "Me, too."

She glanced at him, realizing maybe for the first time just how wounded they both were, how much healing they both still had to do. And then she remembered the pregnancy test. She ought to take it. She needed to take it. But first, she needed to know how Mark was.

"Do you..." She almost didn't want the answer to this question. She almost didn't want to know, but she had to ask it. "Do you still want to..." She couldn't bring herself to say the word *die*. The idea of him killing himself made her feel panicky. He couldn't do that. He couldn't leave her. He couldn't do what her own mother did to her—abandon her and leave her wondering if there was something she could've done to save him. Left wondering if it was all her fault.

Mark moved his bar stool closer to hers, so their legs were touching.

"No," he said. "I mean, I'm not sure."

Not sure. The words hit her like a punch to the stomach. All the air left her lungs.

"Before you came into my life, I had a plan," he admitted. "I knew exactly what I was going to do. I was going to race, win the money, sail around the world and then when that was over, I'd either figure out how to put this all behind more or just…not come back. But, you…you changed all that."

Laura glanced up at him, saw the earnestness in his dark brown eyes. He took her hand.

"I used to wake up in the morning and just think about the boat. The boat and Timothy and nothing else." He reached for her hand and linked his in hers. "But now…"

She studied their interlaced fingers, her heart pounding in her chest like she'd just run a marathon. She had no idea she'd had this effect on him.

"But now, I think of you when I wake up. I think of the boat and Timothy…later." He moved closer to her. "Laura, you changed me. You have." He put his arms around her and she moved into his embrace. The truth was he'd affected her, too. He'd given her a reason to hope again.

"You changed me, too." Laura knew what it felt like to be hopeless. "I came to this island not knowing what I'd find. I ran away from my problems, and in doing so, I found you. You gave me a purpose. You helped me see how my life *could* go on." Laura clung to him. She felt a tear slip down her cheek. "You can't leave me. You're not allowed to die."

Mark chuckled. "I'm not?"

"No. Because then *I'd* be suicidal and you'd have my blood on your hands."

"Well, I can't have that." They held each other a long while. Then Laura pulled away. For the first time, she felt she had the courage to actually take the pregnancy test. She was able now to see the result, no matter what it might be.

"I need to go to the bathroom," she said, sliding off her bar stool.

"Sure. I'll get started on these dishes," he said, gathering up their dinner plates and hopping off his stool.

Laura went to the bedroom, grabbed the pregnancy test from its hiding spot in her drawer and went to the bathroom. She listened as Mark moved around the kitchen, the sound of the tap running and dishes clanking together. It was now or never.

She ducked into the bathroom, locked the door and readied the test. Her heart beat quickly as she finished, put it on the counter and waited. She'd flush the toilet in a second. She glanced at the window. *What do I want?* She didn't even know. She couldn't imagine being pregnant, but if she was…did that mean she'd have a second chance to be a mother?

She felt a jumble of emotions—panic, hope, stress.

Laura eyed the test with some trepidation, waiting for the window to change with her result. She bit her bottom lip as the letters started to materialize.

Pregnant.

CHAPTER NINETEEN

LAURA WAS…PREGNANT. *Oh, God.* She felt both overjoyed and horrified all at once. She'd have to tell Mark…but how could she? *Hey, by the way, I know you want to sail around the world in honor of your son and you might be just getting over serious thoughts of suicide, but what do you think of being a dad…again?*

A knock on the door made her jump.

That's when she realized the sound of the kitchen tap running had disappeared. He must've finished the dishes. How long had she been in here staring at the pregnancy test?

"Everything okay in there?" Mark's voice came from the other side of the door.

Um, no, everything is not okay. I'm going to have your baby.

If my body can actually carry that baby to term.

Hastily, Laura flushed the toilet. "Uh, yeah. Coming!" Her mouth was suddenly dry.

Laura couldn't imagine telling him the news. How could she? Theirs was not supposed to be a long-term thing. They'd both signed on for something short-term. This changed all those rules.

And what if he *was* excited about the prospect of being a dad again…and what if she miscarried the baby? Could she really risk getting Mark's hopes up when she knew her body was faulty, that she couldn't manage her last pregnancy?

Laura stuffed the test back into the box and then hid it at the very back of his bathroom cabinet, behind the plunger. She'd retrieve it later. Right now, she had to hide the evidence. Deal with it later.

"Coming," she said. She opened the door and Mark was there, a puzzled look on his face.

"Everything okay?"

She nodded. "Just a little upset stomach. Probably nerves. About the race tomorrow." She laughed uneasily.

Every fiber of her being wanted to tell him, and yet…she couldn't. Not now.

Not to mention, if she told him, there was no way he'd let her sail tomorrow. He'd step out of the race, and who knew if that would even ensure she'd carry to term? She might lose the baby anyway. There was no way she'd let him give up on sailing for Timothy.

"No need to be nervous about tomorrow. You

don't have anything to worry about," he said and took her into his arms.

She so hoped he was right.

MARK TOSSED AND turned most of the night, worrying about the race the next day. Was he doing the right thing? Allowing her to race? Was she ready?

Races could get dangerous. Accidents happened all the time.

And what if they did win? He wasn't even sure what his goals were anymore. Laura had changed them all. In his arms, Laura slept fitfully. She was worried about the race, too. Not that he could blame her. It wouldn't be an easy thing. To race or to win.

Eventually, the alarm sounded with Mark not sure he'd gotten much sleep at all.

"Time to get up," he said, nuzzling the top of her head. Laura yawned and sat up, looking every bit as beautiful as an actress ready for her close-up. Her pink cheeks and pink lips invited his kisses. She looked amazing, even without makeup. Her natural beauty drew him to her. He dipped down and kissed her on the lips.

"Morning, gorgeous," he said, and she smiled. "Ready to race?"

"I hope so."

Mark flipped on the morning news as he

brewed them a pot of coffee. Then a loud alert blared as an emergency announcement popped up on the screen.

"What's that?" Laura asked, poking her head out of the bedroom as she pulled on a clean shirt.

"No," Mark said as the words flashed across the screen. "No. Can't be." He only caught a few words, but they made his blood run cold: *hurricane headed to St. Anthony's*.

"Wait. Mark. Turn up the sound."

Mark reached for the remote and clicked up the volume.

The weather forecaster, a petite brunette in a blue dress, stood before a map of the Caribbean. "Here you see Hurricane Jimmy is forming off to sea, but it's now changed its course. We thought it was headed north, but now, see, it's turned south. It could make landfall as soon as tomorrow."

"Mark." Laura stood next to him and squeezed his arm. "I thought the storm was supposed to miss us."

"Apparently, it slowed, changed direction and got bigger instead." Mark frowned. "They'll have to postpone the race." He turned up the volume a few more notches.

The forecaster looked solemn. "We're forecasting winds over a hundred miles an hour.

We're advising all residents to leave the island or to take precautions. Board up your homes, make sure you have gas for your generators. This could be a big one. It's picking up speed and St. Anthony's might be the first island hit."

Mark sank into the couch, still staring at the screen, feeling all the blood drain out of his face.

"The race," he murmured. And just like that, his phone lit up with an announcement from the race organizers. Race postponed. Of course. They couldn't very well race in a hurricane.

"What about the *Timothy*?" Laura asked, voice full of concern.

"We'll have to hope it's not as bad as the fore-casters are saying." Mark stood. "But we need to get you off this island."

"Me? You mean us." Laura crossed her arms across her chest and jutted out her chin in a way that told Mark she was going to make this difficult.

Mark shook his head. "You're going. I'm staying."

"Nope. You come with me, or I'm staying."

"Laura." Mark sighed. He hated being right. "This isn't actually a choice I'm giving you."

"Last time I checked, you were not, techni-cally, the boss of me." Laura's chin rose a few notches higher. Mark knew her well enough to know that meant difficult just got impossible.

Mark's phone rang and he dug it out of his pocket. "Garrett," he said.

"You see this? I can't believe that storm turned into a hurricane. What the hell?"

"And it decided to come early," Mark said.

"Climate change, man," Garrett lamented. "More storms and sooner. Do you need my help with the boat? There's a flight in two hours to inland Florida, but I can stay if you need."

"No. Go ahead. Get on out of here, man. Get safe. I can take care of the *Timothy*."

"Okay." Garrett breathed a sigh of relief on the phone. "You and Laura going to get out, too? Last flight is at ten tonight, I think."

"Laura will be on it," Mark said, staring at the obstinate woman standing in his living room. She shook her head in a warning. "Even if I have to throw her over my shoulder and carry her there."

This time, Laura shook her head harder, mouthing, *No way*.

Garrett laughed. "You know women don't go for that caveman stuff, right?"

"So I've heard. Okay, man. You stay safe."

"I'll be praying for you," Garrett promised on the phone.

"Pray for the boat," Mark corrected. "I'll be fine."

He ended the call and turned to study Laura. "Pack up your stuff," he said. "We're getting you off this island."

"Let me help you with the boat. Then you can join me. On a plane."

Mark sighed. He knew that it was a losing battle. If he protested, they'd waste more time arguing about who would be on the plane, and they didn't have much time. The hurricane was coming and coming fast.

"Come on, then," he said. "Let's go to the marina and make sure the boat's secure."

CROWDS OF CARS and people swarmed the marina, making it a chaotic mess as folks tried to secure their boats. Some people loaded them up on trailers to haul away to shelters inland, while others just lashed them tightly to their moorings in the dock. Laura watched as Mark set about doubling the knots and making sure the sail of the boat was lashed tightly to the jib and then set about securing it to the trailer at the back of his boat.

"Where are we taking it?" Laura nodded at the trailers lined up to haul boats away from the sea. Mark frowned at the line of trucks hauling trailers.

"We're going to take our chances and store it not too far from here," Mark said. "Garrett told me of a place."

Laura supposed that made sense. "What do you need me to do?"

"Tie more knots," he said as he furiously secured the sail.

After about two hours, they'd finished securing the boat in the large storage facility a mile in from shore. Sirens sounded, alerting the folks the hurricane was on its way.

"Time to get you to the airport," Mark said.

"Only if you're coming with me." She wasn't going to leave him.

"Laura." Mark sighed. "I love your loyalty. It's one of the many, many things I love about you."

The words hung there. *Love?* Did he say he loved things about her?

"But you're going to get on that plane whether I'm on it or not." Mark helped Laura off the boat, offering her a steady hand to the dock.

Laura clambered onto the wooden slats and shook her head. "No. That's not how this works."

"What's this?"

"Us. It's now how *we* work. And by the way, there are plenty of things I love about you, too."

"Really? Like?"

"Like I will tell you on the plane."

Mark laughed a little, showing his even, white teeth. He grinned and put his hands on his hips, leaning over her small frame. Laura had to crane her neck to look at him, the dark clouds past his head threatening rain and worse, a storm that could rip this island apart.

"You drive a hard bargain," he said.

"I know," she answered. "So what are we going to do? Are *we* going to stay? Or are *we* going to get on the plane?"

"There's a *we* now, is there?" he asked, cocking one eyebrow. "I thought we were a temporary thing."

Laura shrugged. "I'm not talking about the future. I'm talking about right now. The us of right now. And we're partners and partners don't split up or abandon one another. Real partners stick together."

A QUICK CHECK of all the flights on the island found them all booked. Laura and Mark tried standby as well, but as the day went on, it became clear they might not be able to make it off the island. No matter how hard they tried.

"If you hadn't helped me with the boat, you would've gotten on a flight," Mark said, frowning as they reluctantly left the airport.

Laura dashed out after Mark as they headed for his pickup. There was no reason to stay at the airport. Now they only had a very little bit of time to get the condo ready for the impending storm.

"You don't know that," Laura said. She slid into the cab of his pickup truck and shut the door, shaking off the rain from her poncho. Laura thought about the tiny baby in her belly. Was she putting them both at risk by staying? But she didn't have a choice now. No flights out, and no boats could go out in that choppy sea.

"I do. It's my fault."

"It doesn't matter," Laura said, grabbing his hand. "We're together. That's what counts."

Mark pulled Laura in his arms and she went, feeling his warm arms encircle her. She craned her neck to meet his gaze as he dipped down to kiss her. His lips felt warm on hers, sending a little rush of want down her spine. He pulled back and studied her face for a minute. He stroked her cheek.

"God, I *love* you," he said, and Laura froze. "You do?"

"Hell, yes, I do. I love you, Laura."

Laura felt her heart speed up as the realization hit her that she felt the same way.

"I love you, too," she said, and Mark pulled her into his arms and squeezed her so tightly she almost couldn't breathe. For a fleeting second, she thought of the baby inside her. "Can't—"

"Breathe? You need to breathe?" Mark let her go and she took in a breath. He started up his pickup and drove them to the store to get supplies.

"Kind of important, don't you think? But then again, I guess since we're waiting out a hurricane, we're going to live dangerously."

"Well, I think you need a new nickname. Instead of Miss Noise Pollution, I think I might start calling you Miss Dangerously. That has a nice ring to it."

Laura grinned. "Is it dangerous to fall in love with you?"

Mark grabbed her hand and kissed it even as he kept his eyes on the road. "All my exes say yes."

She laughed a little as Mark pulled into a store parking lot. "Just how many exes do you have?"

"A thousand, give or take a hundred," he teased. "If we're going to do something so fool-hardy as to stay on this island, then we're going to need to board up our windows, get some food and batteries and hope we're not making the mistake of our lives."

"If it is, it'll be the last mistake we ever have to worry about," Laura said and Mark threw back his head and laughed. The ominous skies above them began to leak rain.

Mark checked the sky through the windshield of his truck. "We'd better get moving," he said. "Storm's coming fast."

CHAPTER TWENTY

THE RAIN PELTED Mark's shoulders as he hammered in the last piece of plywood across his patio doors. Now all of his windows were covered and secured as best he could make them. The winds were already starting to pick up.

He didn't like the idea of potentially risking Laura's safety, but then they didn't have a choice. He'd waited out other hurricanes before, and he hoped this one would be like the others—all bluster, no real damage. The admission that he loved her came as easily as breathing at this point. It was just such a simple and uncompromised truth. They belonged together, hurricane or no.

He dropped the hammer back into his toolbox and then walked back around to the front door of his condo. As he walked through the door, shaking raindrops off his blue slicker, he found her humming in the kitchen, making sandwiches.

"I thought you might like a snack," she said. She deftly sliced a turkey sandwich in half.

"We just ate!" he cried, surprised, since they'd only had lunch an hour ago.

Laura shrugged one shoulder. "I guess I'm just extra hungry today," she said.

He took the sandwich anyway and managed a bite. "At this rate," he mumbled through chomping, "we might run through our supplies before the hurricane even hits."

Laura laughed and playfully slapped his arm. "We have enough food here to last a week," she reminded him. "Besides, seeing you work so hard was enough to make me hungry."

They'd hit the grocery store, which already had pretty thin pickings as everyone on the island had the same idea. But combining what they grabbed there and the food they already had meant they were more than set for a long haul if the hurricane knocked out power or flooded the island.

Flooding, Mark knew, was the real danger. The high winds could certainly take off a roof or two, but the island had already suffered its fair share of rain. The extra deluge from the hurricane could wash out roads or cause landslides, making getting around the small island more than difficult.

Laura dug into her sandwich with gusto, making Mark laugh.

"You're acting like you haven't eaten in

days," he said and moved closer to her, putting his hand on the small of her back. He loved touching her. How soft and small she was, how delicate. She leaned into his touch, even as she mumbled something that sounded like delight as she ate three more bites in succession. The moans of satisfaction made Mark think of other sounds she made—in bed, and he suddenly wished snack time was over.

"You want to put that down for one minute?" he asked her, tugging her by the waist to him. "I don't mind kissing turkey sandwich, but…" He grinned.

She finished her last bite and tilted her head up, and he kissed her, gently at first, but then she deepened the kiss, drawing him closer.

Dramatic music from the TV broke them from their kiss as news of the storm scrolled across the screen.

"This just in. Hurricane Jimmy has been downgraded from a Category Four to a Category Three storm," the newscaster said. "Residents are still advised to take cover, but for now, it looks like the island will be spared the big storm predicted."

"That's good news," Laura said, glancing at Mark.

"The best," he agreed and pulled Laura closer once more. They kissed again, their passion turning hotter. "I think we should take this to the bedroom," he murmured in her ear, and she nodded enthusiastically. He led her by the hand into the darkened room.

The wind howled outside, but he suddenly didn't care. All he wanted to do was trace the lines of her body with his fingers and be inside her once more. The need to feel her, to take her, was suddenly so urgent he began tugging off her clothes, impatient to feel her skin on his.

Outside, the tropical storm closed in on the island, whipping palm leaves, but here, inside, the noise only felt like a proper soundtrack for their lips meeting in a roar of need.

God, he wanted her. He wanted her now. He wanted her forever. Had it ever been like this with anyone else? He couldn't remember a time when he felt so desperate for someone, so blindly needing their touch.

Laura met his lips and his tongue with a ferocity that continued to surprise him as he pushed her gently down on the bed. She wiggled away from him, climbing on top, as she straddled him in a way that made all his senses come alive. Soon, she'd undone his damp shorts and shoved them down past his ankles. Then, she gently took off her own T-shirt, revealing full breasts in a lacey bra.

He cupped her, feeling her delicious weight

in his hands. Had she…gotten bigger? Fuller? It seemed so. He reached behind her back and undid the bra strap, and she came tumbling out, beautiful.

He took one of her nipples in his mouth and sucked, and she groaned for him, making his whole body come alive. He let it go and took the other one, and she pressed against him, and all he could feel was her heat and want. Mark came alive, growing stiff as her mouth found his, and their tongues competed in an ancient dance.

She pushed her own bottoms off, and then it was just them, skin on skin. He could feel her delicious wetness. God, he wanted her. Wanted her more than he'd ever wanted anything he could remember in his life. He belonged in her. She moved against him, teasing him, and now it was his turn to moan as he felt her silky wetness.

Then he remembered condoms. How had he almost forgotten again? He reached backward to the drawer on the nightstand where he'd put them, but she reached for his wrist.

"No," she said, shaking her head. "No, we don't need them."

"We don't?" he asked, puzzled. "But…" *Pregnancy*, he thought distantly, and then the thought evaporated as she moved him inside her. All rational thought disintegrated in his mind like shells pulverized into sand by the endless lash-ing of the waves. She felt so amazing, so deliciously wet, he didn't want a barrier any more than she did. She seemed so sure, so confident. His mind thought of a million reasons she could be so sure, but in the end, it was the all-consuming desire that made the decision for him. All he wanted was to get deeper inside her, and he did. Thrust after delicious thrust.

She cried out almost instantly, a high-pitched come. He decided he'd make this last, make her scream in delight. He wanted to feel her bare, as long as he could. Mark felt at last he'd finally found home, here in this woman. This was where he belonged.

Finally, when he felt he could hold back no longer, he flipped her over, stomach down on the bed, and began his own journey to quench his need as he took her, harder and faster. God, so good. Then, at the very end, he remembered—no condoms. He withdrew before he came, spilling himself across the small of her back.

The come was so hard, so fast, he'd almost not had time to withdraw, but now he felt at least he hadn't put her in danger of a pregnancy. They couldn't repeat the mistakes of that first night, which had been reckless. Irresponsible. No matter how much she believed she might not carry a baby to term, Mark knew how biology worked.

Laura lay still and quiet as he gently cleaned

her back with his own dirty T-shirt, and then he rolled her up in his arms, spooning her from behind. The wind rattled the boards on the windows, but here, holding her, he felt safe.

"You could've come inside me," she murmured into his arms.

He squeezed her tighter. "I know, but…we should be careful." He thought about after that first time, so hot with passion, how neither one of them had been thinking clearly. He'd never acted so rashly his whole life, and he didn't plan on repeating the same mistake.

Laura, back to him, traced the line of his forearm with a delicate finger. "You're afraid of a pregnancy."

"Well…" Of course he was. "Yes," he admitted.

"You don't want any more children?" The question came out sounding small, a whisper almost. He knew what children meant to her, and how she said she was worried she might be getting too old to have them or that her body didn't know how to have them at all. He knew he had to tread carefully here. But he had needs, too. He had wants. And he had fears.

"No," Mark admitted. "After Timothy died, well, all my hopes for children died with him. I'm not going to be like Elle. Trying to replace one baby with another, or so I assume. Somehow, it just...disrespects Timothy's memory. I'm not going to do that to Timothy."

Mark couldn't imagine having another child, if he were honest with himself. Would that make him love Timothy less? Or even worse, forget him? He couldn't take that risk.

"I told myself I wouldn't have more," Mark said. "Not ever."

"Never?" Laura asked.

"Never," Mark echoed, remembering the day he stood at Timothy's small grave in the city cemetery on the far side of the island. He'd promised his small gravestone that he'd name a boat after him and sail around the world. That he'd never be replaced in his heart, no matter what happened. The more he thought about the possibility of having a baby, the more he worried that he could break his promise to Timothy. And Mark's memories were the only thing Timothy had. If he forgot Timothy, it would be as if that amazing little boy never existed.

"More kids aren't in the plan," Mark said. "After Timothy died, some well-meaning relatives like my mother-in-law told me I'd have more children and that everything would be okay. But I knew more kids wouldn't make everything okay."

"I remember my sister telling me that after

my miscarriage. It stings." Laura sounded sad, hollow even.

"Yeah. It does. Because loving a new child seems like it takes love away from Timothy." He sighed and took a deep breath, his chest pressing against Laura's bare back. "I don't want another baby. I want Timothy. I want him back, but since I can't have him, then I'm just going to honor his memory."

"But...Timothy would want you to be happy," Laura argued, flipping around to look at him.

"My job is to remember him. To focus on him. I'm the only one who can. Elle isn't... I mean her memory is foggy at best with all the pills, and now that she'll have a new baby, she'll forget him all the sooner. I'm all that Timothy has."

"Mark." Laura said his name like a sigh, sadness lingering in the single syllable. "So that's the reason you won't..."

She didn't have to say *come inside me*. Mark knew what she meant.

"The first time was a crazy accident," Mark said. "It can't happen again."

"Oh." Laura sighed, and he got the feeling there was more she wanted to say. But he also knew that he wasn't in the mood to hear it.

Yes, he loved her, and he wanted to make her happy. Yet things with them were far from settled. The race, then his plans to sail around the world…was he ready to invite her into that? He wasn't sure. Hell, he didn't even know if he *wanted* to sail around the world now. Laura had turned everything in his life upside down, and he didn't know what to do, but he knew that some part of him, a big part, liked it. But, having children? That was something he couldn't even begin to think about. Not now. Not when he still felt like his heart needed to grieve.

"But…" Laura tried once more.

"Let's not talk about it," Mark said, squeezing Laura tightly to him. She fell silent then, and he hugged her to him as his eyelids grew heavy and he drifted off into a dreamless sleep.

LAURA LAY AGAINST MARK, wide-awake, her mind going a million miles a minute. He didn't want children. Not now…not ever. *Oops, too late*, she thought bitterly. She gingerly touched her abdomen. She could almost imagine a little tickle inside her, the baby growing at a rapid rate. A girl? A boy? Who knew? Mark didn't want a baby. Just like Dean didn't want a baby… at least, not hers.

The sadness hit her harder than the high winds outside. How could she possibly tell Mark now that he would be a father? She'd heard the pain in his voice, the determination as well. Laura felt like the baby was a second chance, a way of starting over, a miracle really. If she could hold on to the baby, that is. But she'd do her best.

Except Mark didn't want any part of it. He only wanted to be a father to a boy who'd died, not one who might live.

Laura felt a mix of emotions, each one hitting her in waves. Anger, of course—why couldn't he see that starting anew, having another baby, wouldn't tarnish Timothy's memory, not in the least? Fear—if Mark knew about her pregnancy, would he ask her to end it? Like Dean? She loved Mark, and if he told her to end the pregnancy, she knew she couldn't. Wouldn't. She'd leave the island without him and have her baby in San Francisco. Alone.

Outside, the wind howled, ripping shingles off the condo roof and battering the walls even as her own thoughts swirled in her head. No matter how she imagined it, telling Mark now about the baby would be the worst possible thing she could do.

CHAPTER TWENTY-ONE

THE STORM ROARED OUTSIDE, and the two of them watched news reports until the power blinked out.

"This happens even in a bad thunderstorm," Mark assured her. "We'll be okay."

He had brought in the generator from his workshop, and they used it to power a hot plate and their phones, scanning news as they could. In a day, the storm moved through, leaving just a light rain. Eventually, even that stopped as Mark and Laura went out to inspect the damage. Palm leaves were scattered across the beach, lawn furniture was upturned in the sand and a few windows were broken in some of the condos on the second floor.

"It did some damage," Laura said, glancing at the debris on the beach as she grabbed a broom to sweep up the glinting glass shards that had toppled down to Mark's patio. Together, they'd both taken off the boards off his patio door so they could once again move in and out easily. She cleaned and Mark went to inspect his workshop, which amazingly had stayed intact, not a board out of place. The news said the entire island would be out of power for at least another day or two but that the damage from the storm could've been far worse. Still, some islanders had lost their homes, crushed under the wind or flooded in the rains.

As she swept up the last of the glass into a dustpan and dumped it in the garbage can, Mark nodded at her. "We should go check on *Timothy*," he said.

It took her a second to realize he was talking about the boat and not the boy. She nodded silently as her phone pinged.

"What is it?" Mark asked.

"Text from my sister. She's worried about me."

"So you two are talking again?" he asked.

Laura shrugged. "Sort of." She showed him the text message feed, which was curt and to the point, asking only about whether or not she was okay. "There's no apology in it, though."

"At least she cares if you live or die," Mark pointed out. "That's probably more than I could say for Edward."

MARK WAITED IMPATIENTLY in the slow line of traffic as cars and trucks flooded into the marina's nearby storage facility with ship owners coming to assess the damage. With dread, he realized that half the roof of the building had caved in. Once parked, Mark jumped out of his truck, barely waiting for Laura as she followed him out.

Edward and Dave were there, and Mark realized they'd all picked the same storage facility. They were inspecting the *Tanner*, which looked to be in tip-top shape or at least with just minor damage. Mark pushed past them without a hello. He didn't have time this morning to pretend he was glad to see them. All he could think about was the boat that bore his son's name. *Please let him be okay.*

Mark ran past two sailboats sitting on a rack, and felt a sinking pit in his stomach as he marched through debris from the roof. Above him, he saw blue sky and clouds where a roof should've been. *Timothy* had to be okay. He just had to be. He skidded around the corner and jogged between boat owners, not able to see *Timothy's* mast in the distance and suddenly feeling panicked. Where was he? Where... Mark turned the corner, moving past a crowd standing by a different boat and saw *Timothy*.

He skidded to a stop, his heart pounding.

For a full second, he couldn't process what he saw. The boat was still upright, yes, but part of the roof had fallen on it. Something was wrong.

Very wrong. The mast, a huge piece of tall timber, was broken in half like an upside down V, lying limp and useless across the side of the boat, the lines, loose and lying on the ground.

In that second, Mark felt all his hopes dashed. *Timothy* wouldn't sail in the race. He might not sail at all.

"Oh…Mark." Laura was by his side then, clutching his arm, but he couldn't feel anything. His face had gone numb, so had his arms and legs. *Timothy* wouldn't sail. Couldn't sail.

"Tough break," came a familiar voice— Edward's—behind him.

Mark whirled, and seeing his older brother, he felt the undeniable urge to punch him in his smug face. "Go to hell," Mark murmured instead.

"Mark," Laura began, but then he shrugged off her touch as well. He couldn't talk to her, either, couldn't talk to anyone; the disappointment was so thick, so horrible, all he could do was retreat back to his truck. He could hear Laura running after him, calling his name, but all he wanted was to be alone. His whole future died with that boat.

MARK WOULDN'T TALK to Laura the whole way back to the condo. Laura watched him, clutching the steering wheel, glancing out dead-eyed at the road, not knowing what to say. *Sorry* just didn't seem to cover the staggering loss. They hit traffic ahead, the tiny road covered in water as cars crept over low-lying curves.

"Can it be fixed?" Laura asked, voice soft.

Mark remained silent for a long second and Laura thought he might not answer her. Then he spoke, still not looking at her.

"There's no way a new mast could come in time for the race, even if they postponed it a week," Mark said. "Even if I could locate one, I'd need special equipment and many hands to put it in place."

Laura nodded. "Maybe we could…try."

Mark slowed the truck, as traffic up ahead of them ground to a stop while a small SUV crossed the water. He glanced at her.

"It's over, Laura," he said, grabbing her hand. "Nothing we can do now."

Laura, however, wasn't ready to give up. Not yet. She knew what she could do.

WHILE MARK TOOK a shower, Laura borrowed his truck keys and set out for Tanner Boating. She'd called their main office on the way to check that they were still open post tropical storm, and a harried-sounding assistant assured her they were. Edward might not be there, but it was worth a shot. She'd go to his office first, then back to the marina and then, if she couldn't find him at either place, she'd try stalking him at the Rusted Anchor. Maybe even try to find out where he lived. There weren't that many residential neighborhoods on this island.

Laura didn't know what she'd tell Edward once she found him, but she knew she had to try to solicit his help. Mark would never do it, but Edward owed Mark in Laura's mind. Edward had taken his friends and his wife, and now, in his time of need, Mark needed him, whether he'd ask for that help or not. She'd told Mark she was going to the drugstore—a lie, though it would keep his suspicions at bay for a while.

Laura still couldn't believe the devastation from the storm. Even though it had been downgraded from a hurricane, everywhere she looked she could see its imprint, from the flooded streets to the downed palm trees and the damaged roofs. Mark's boat wasn't the only one damaged, either.

She had to cross several flooded intersections to make it to Tanner Boating and sent up a small prayer of thanks that Mark's truck sat so high off the ground. Laura carefully drove through each, all the while too aware how just a little bit of water—half the tire wells—could sweep a car off the ground and into the torrent. She clutched the steering wheel as she drove through the brown water and made it to the other side.

She pulled into the near-empty parking lot of Tanner Boating, half of the lot beneath murky floodwater, and found a dry spot near the door. The shipbuilding company had a huge warehouse and sat facing the sea. Laura glanced at the sparkling blue-green water, the sun shining brightly in the crystal-blue sky, and thought how odd that just a day ago the island was battered by hundred-mile-an-hour winds. Now it was right back to paradise.

Laura took a deep breath as she strode to the front door. She swung it open and saw a frazzled woman in her twenties answering phones. Right next to her was Edward, wearing the same cargo shorts and T-shirt she'd seen him in on the dock earlier that day.

"Laura," he said, surprised. "What can I do for you?"

"That's what I wanted to talk to you about," she said. "Is there a place we can—"

"My office," Edward said, moving from behind the desk. He led her down the hallway to a corner office with large windows overlooking the sparkling blue-green bay.

"How did this survive the storm?" Laura asked, amazed. So much glass, all facing the sea.

"I've got automated shutters." Edward grabbed

the remote on his desk and hit a button. Metal shutters began to extend from either side to cover the windows and block the sun. He reversed them quickly and then motioned for her to take a seat in front of his large, oak desk. He perched on the corner, one leg up, the other straight and holding his weight.

Laura was struck by how similar the brothers were physically—the same muscular and lean body types, same brown hair.

"What can I do for you, Laura?"

"You saw Mark's boat." She was going to be as direct as possible. No need to beat around the bush. "He needs your help to fix it."

Edward quirked a surprised eyebrow. "Really? Did he send you to ask me?" Edward crossed his muscled, tanned arms over his chest.

"No," Laura said, quickly shaking her head. "He doesn't know I'm here."

Edward threw back his head and laughed. "Well, he'll be pretty pissed when he finds out. You know we're not on the best of terms."

"I know, but his boat is badly damaged, and you can help him. You owe him that much."

Edward's eyes narrowed. "I *owe* him? What about what he did to Elle? Getting her arrested? And then he nearly ran our business into the ground, Laura. He should've taken the time off, but instead, he came in here angry and irrational and insulted most of our suppliers. He nearly lost us our biggest contract. Then, when I ask him to take time off, he tells me to go jump in the ocean, and I'm forced to push him out. Where in that do I owe him anything?"

Laura could see Edward's face flush a bit, his temper rising.

"He owes you, too. I'm not saying it's one-sided," Laura explained, holding up her hands and trying to be a peacemaker. She sighed. This wasn't going as well as she'd hoped. She needed to regroup and hit him from a different angle. "I didn't mean to make you angry. Look, you guys are brothers. You founded this amazing company together. You've been through…well, everything."

Edward slipped off the front of his desk and moved away from her, staring out at the sea and putting his back to her. Laura stood, hoping to make her point.

"You are brothers, and no matter what happens, no matter what fights, when bad things happen, brothers need to help one another. It's what they do. You can go back to being furious at each other after the *Timothy* is saved."

Laura suddenly thought of her sister and their petty argument. She hadn't talked to her since that explosive phone call.

Edward stood silently, his back to her.

"I have a sister, and we're barely talking right now. But if a storm had destroyed the only thing she thought might be worth living for, I'd go help her save it. Tomorrow."

Laura knew that was true. She might have differences with Maddie, but that didn't change the fact that they were blood. She also knew Maddie would probably show up in her time of need, even if she'd spend the next twenty years rubbing it in her face.

Edward let out a long sigh and shot her a short glance over his shoulder. "He probably won't even accept my help. Even if I tried."

"Leave that to me," she said, hoping she could find a way to convince Mark to let his anger go.

Bzzzt. Bzzzt.

The next morning, Mark woke up to the sound of a loud buzz saw.

What on earth?

He sat up, glanced next to him and noticed that Laura was gone from bed.

"Laura?" he called to his condo but got no response. Was she in the bathroom maybe?

Bzzzt. Bzzzzzt. Bzzzzzzt. There went that awful saw again. He glanced at the clock and saw it was six thirty.

Who was working this early?

He fell back into his pillow and groaned.

Where was the racket even coming from? It sounded like his living room, for goodness' sake. Who was working this early?

He thought it might be someone making repairs to another condo, but why with a saw? Hammer, okay. But saw?

He sat up and rubbed his face, running his hands through his disheveled dark hair. There was no sleeping through that noise. He pulled himself from bed, wearing just a pair of gym shorts. He snagged a shirt and tugged it over his head and headed out his patio door.

He realized the noise was coming from his lit workshop.

Who the hell was in his workshop?

He padded over, wishing he'd had the foresight to bring a baseball bat. Looting was always a problem after bad weather but, he reasoned, what thief would *use* the tools he planned to steal?

Mark swung around the corner and that's when he saw *Timothy* back on the working blocks and Laura standing in front of the boat. What the—

But she wasn't the one with the saw. That was Edward, who happened to be on the deck, working to removing what was left of the broken mast.

"Hey!" Mark called. "What the hell are you doing?"

Edward stopped his work, cut the loud saw and raised the protective goggles on top of his head. "Too loud for you?" he asked.

Laura turned and rushed to him, putting her hands on his chest. "Before you say a word, I asked Edward to be here. He is going to help you fix this boat. You're going to put aside your petty differences because right now, you both *need* each other, and if a hurricane can't help you bury the hatchet, then I don't know what will."

"Technically, tropical storm," Edward corrected.

Mark glanced at Laura and then at Edward, feeling numb. What was happening? Edward... helping?

"You can hate me again after I finish helping you restore this old heap," Edward said, throwing a bit of sawed-off mast down to the heap of discarded splintered pieces.

"No. You. Me. The beach. Now," Mark ground out, not sure if he was going to talk to his brother or punch him in the face.

"You want to fight? Fine, let's fight." Edward threw down his work gloves and stalked out to the open beach. Mark followed him, his hands balled into fists.

"No. Please. Mark!" Laura ran after him, grabbing his shirt.

"You stay here." Mark's voice was low and dangerous.

"Let me help," Laura pleaded, tugging on his T-shirt. "Let's talk about this."

"No." Mark whirled, feeling the venom all but choke him. He no longer knew who made him more upset. Why did Laura think all problems were solvable? Why did she think they could all get along? "You've done enough."

"I was just trying to help. I was just trying to—"

"Well, don't, okay? Stop meddling in things that aren't your business." Mark bit off the words, but they still found their mark. Each syllable landed against her like a blow, and she looked like he'd slapped her.

He felt a momentary surge of guilt then. He was being harsh, mean even, and he didn't like it. Mark knew she meant well, but he was also tired of her trying to fix everything. Some things just remained broken, and that's how life was.

He glanced at his brother stalking far out to the beach. When he looked back at Laura, he saw her eyes glisten with hurt. But he didn't have time to apologize. Besides, she needed to learn to stop meddling.

He stalked away from her, not bothering to look back.

CHAPTER TWENTY-TWO

LAURA RAN BACK into the condo, slamming the patio door shut behind her. Tears streamed down her face as she hugged herself. Was she being oversensitive? Was it the pregnancy hormones? Or had Mark been a total jerk? She was just trying to help.

She felt as though she was right back in the relationship with Dean, when he'd shut her out and given her the cold shoulder. That look in Mark's eyes, the coldness, it made her believe they might be over.

She was just trying to help. Just trying to help Mark overcome his stupid pride. Edward was willing to help, and she knew that they had history, but the fact was the *Timothy* would never sail if they didn't get it fixed, and Edward was the only man on the island who could get the job done.

What was she even doing here? This wasn't her fight. All she'd tried to do was help Mark fulfill his dreams of sailing around the world, but what about her hopes? What about her dreams? Did Mark even care about those?

She couldn't even tell him about the baby in her belly. She thought about breaking the news now and hearing him tell her the baby was just one more way she was meddling. The thoughts felt like tiny pricks of a needle. Stabs of sharp, thin pain.

She could leave. She could head to the airport right now. But first, she'd wait. See if the brothers killed each other. If they started throwing punches, someone would need to call the police.

Laura went back out on the patio, determined to watch.

EDWARD STALKED DOWN about twenty feet along the beach and then turned to face Mark. He glowered at him, every ounce of muscle in his body tense. Mark knew that look, the one Edward saved for moments he was particularly pissed, like when they were kids and Mark scuffed Edward's new baseball glove. Edward had always been high-strung, hard to manage, demanding. Why their father loved him better was beyond Mark. When Mark looked at his brother, he just saw someone who spent his life spoiled, with everything, including affection, handed to him on a silver platter. What Mark never understood was why, when Edward had so much, he still felt the need to take from him. Over and over again.

"You're going to hit me? Then go on, hit me. I was just trying to *help you*," Edward began.

"I told you that I never want your help." Mark's jaw clenched.

"Well, tell your girlfriend that because she's the one who came pleading to me."

Mark flinched. He hated the idea of Laura asking Edward for anything. "She doesn't know you like I know you."

"How long are you going to be mad at me?" Edward asked, throwing up his hands. "It's not my fault you had Elle arrested, and then I helped her, and she fell in love with me. That's not my fault."

"She was my wife."

"You didn't treat her like your wife. You shut her out. You blamed her for Timothy's death." Edward strode forward, and poked him in the chest.

Mark felt the guilt blossom there. He did blame his ex-wife for Timothy's death. If she hadn't taken those pills, she would've been more awake, more aware, and she'd never have let Timothy walk into the ocean that day. "She wasn't watching him," he said. "She had taken those pills. Did you know about that? The pill problem?"

Edward went silent for a minute. "Yeah, I know. She told me."

This surprised Mark.

"Taking those pills was a mistake that she beats herself up for every single day," Edward said. "She punished herself enough. She didn't need you to try to get her arrested." His eyes flashed with anger.

"I wanted to get her *help*. That's all."

"Really? Was that all? You weren't trying to punish her?"

Mark hesitated. Was he? Maybe a small part of him was. "She sure did get pregnant again in a hurry. She sure doesn't mind replacing Timothy with a new model."

Edward let out an exasperated sigh. He backed away from Mark, turning his back on him and angrily running his hands through his hair.

"Before the pregnancy, did you know that Elle tried to kill herself?"

That stopped Mark cold. "No. How?"

"Those pills you like to lord over her head. She took a whole bottle of them."

Mark felt stunned. He'd never heard this. He'd never even realized Elle had been so affected. She just seemed to be the one who had everything together...who bounced back when he didn't.

"I made her throw them up, and then I rushed her to the ER," Edward said. "*I* did that. And then she started seeing a counselor and she got better and she kicked those pills. Did you know that? Kicked them cold."

Mark shook his head. "I didn't know."

"Why would you know? You haven't cared about anyone since Timothy died except yourself. You let Elle twist in the wind for this."

Mark glanced down at his bare feet. He supposed he had. He was having trouble focusing. "But you slept with her. When we were still married. She was *my* wife."

"She was mourning. I was, too. He was my nephew. We didn't plan it, Mark. It wasn't a grand scheme. She needed comfort. That's all. I'm sorry for that. I should never have done it. But I wasn't thinking straight, and I'm sorry. I am."

Mark felt a bit of his chest loosen. Here was the apology he'd been waiting for so long.

"You were supposed to be there for me. That was the worst time of my life."

Edward looked guilty as he glanced out over the water. "I know. I'm sorry." He turned back to Mark. "It might not mean much, but I'm here now. I want to help you. I know what this race means to you. Let me help you race in it." He kicked some sand by his toe. "I know I wasn't there for you before, but let me be there for you now."

Mark looked at the sand by his feet. He realized in that moment he didn't have much choice. After all, if he wanted to sail the *Timothy* in that race, his brother would be the only one who could help him.

Edward took a step closer. "We don't have to be friends, okay? And after I help you with this, you can go back to hating me just like before. Just let me do this. Please."

Part of Mark wanted to fight, but then he realized that all the fight had drained out of him the minute that storm had wrecked the *Timothy*. Maybe he could stomach Edward being here, for now. Suddenly, he realized that some things were more important than grudges. Like winning that race. Like racing the *Timothy*.

Mark nodded. "Fine," he said.

The two brothers walked back to the patio, where Laura was waiting for them, arms crossed.

"Have you two made up?" she asked, her eyes still a little red from tears.

"Sort of." He wasn't sure he was ready to fully forgive his brother just yet. But, he supposed, letting him work on the *Timothy* was a start. "And...I'm sorry," he murmured. "For what I said to you."

"Good. You should be." Laura sniffed.

Mark grabbed hold of her and pulled her into a hug. He inhaled traces of her lavender-scented shampoo. She melted into him a little, leaning her head against his chest.

"I was grumpy. Not used to be woken up so *rudely*," he joked, referencing the very first time they met.

Laura chuckled into his shirt.

"Okay, Mr. Noise Pollution," she joked, and then he knew she'd forgiven him. Mostly. In that moment, he felt for the first time since the storm that everything might really work out.

In a week, the *Timothy* was as good as new. With Edward's help and Tanner Boating supplies, a new mast had soon replaced the old one, and now he was ready to sail. The race was postponed so that racers could get their bearings and get back to the island if they'd evacuated for the storm, not to mention, it gave time for the floodwaters to recede.

Laura had to cash in a bit more of her 401(k) to stay, and even as she did, she worried about the future. Her waistline was growing a bit, as far as she could tell, and the morning sickness just kept getting worse. In fact, they should call it *morning, noon and night* sickness, because it wasn't just when she woke up.

"Are you sick again?" Mark asked, knocking on the bathroom door after a particularly strong-smelling calamari Mark brought home from a local restaurant made her sprint to the bathroom. They'd finished taking down all the boards over the windows and now the condo was full of sunlight once more, but the warm light didn't help her upset stomach.

"I'm fine," she said, running the water loudly. "Nothing to worry about."

"But it's been going on all week," he cried, knocking harder. "You sure you don't need help?"

"Fine," she called. Laura wondered how long she'd be able to keep up this charade. He'd find out soon, she just knew it. First, she'd been able to claim seasickness when they'd taken the *Timothy* out for a test run. Then she said it might be food poisoning, but now, he was going to get suspicious.

She splashed cold water on her face and willed her body to get it together. *No more hurling, little one*, she scolded her own belly. She looked down at her shorts, unbuttoned at the waist because her waistline had grown too much.

Despite the fact that she couldn't keep much down, she'd still managed to gain a little weight, her shorts becoming tighter. Soon, she'd really have to think about finding a doctor and having a checkup. She'd called her old ob-gyn and had her call in prenatal vitamins to the local pharmacy. Laura had also promised to get checked out as soon as she could.

"Laura?" Mark knocked again. "You okay?"

She opened the bathroom. "Fine," she said, brightly. "Just…leftover stomach bug, I think."

"It's gone on for too long, though," Mark said, forehead wrinkled in concern.

Laura shrugged.

"You should go see a doctor."

"No! No, I'll be fine. Really. I'm feeling better already." She wasn't, but Mark didn't need to know that. "Let me eat some crackers and see if that helps. Then, we can talk about strategy for the race."

Laura knew talking about the race would refocus Mark's attention for the next several hours. Then he wouldn't be thinking about her upset stomach.

I should tell him. I should just admit that I'm pregnant, right here and tell him. Then what? He already said he didn't want kids. Not after Timothy. He had no interest in starting another family. Laura couldn't imagine seeing disappointment on his face. Not again. Not like Dean. If she saw that, it would break her heart, and she wasn't ready for it. Might never be ready for it.

"Edward had a good idea, actually," Mark

began. The brothers had bonded over repairing the boat. They might not be best buddies exactly, but they did talk, and for that Laura was grateful. Laura listened to Mark talk about race strategies and thought of her own sister. She would reach out to her.

"Want a beer?" Mark asked suddenly and she started, realizing he'd long since finished his story about Edward and she hadn't exactly been listening.

"Uh. Thanks but…no. Still not 100 percent." She grinned sheepishly. How long would she be able to hide the morning sickness? He was already getting suspicious and now she was suddenly giving up alcohol? She needed advice. She needed…her sister. "I think I'm going to call Maddie."

"Really? That's great. You should." Mark grinned. "It's about time you guys make up."

Only I'll be the one to apologize—again.

"I've got to run out to get some resin for the boat, but I'll be back," Mark said. "Want me to get you something for your stomach?"

"Uh…no, I'll be fine." *I hope.*

"You sure?"

Laura nodded. Mark grabbed his keys and left, leaving her on the couch. She watched him go, admiring the broadness of his shoulders and his long, lean step. He made her heart beat a little bit faster. She wondered if she were going to have a boy and if he'd look as handsome as his father one day.

She stared at her phone. What were the chances Maddie would even pick up?

Laura dialed her number and her sister answered on the second ring.

"God, Laura. Are you okay? I only got the text from you since the hurricane and I've been worried sick."

"You have?" Maddie's text messages sure didn't give the impression she was losing sleep over the bad weather on the island. They'd been terse and to the point.

"Absolutely! I was about to board a plane and come see you, but flights are outrageous and—"

"I'm fine, Maddie. The storm wasn't that crazy, and I was here with Mark and—"

"Mark is the sailor?"

"Yes."

Silence filled the line. Laura could tell there was still tension between them, about what had been said and not said the last time they talked. Laura had promised herself not to be the one to apologize this time, and yet, seeing Edward and Mark feud and then make up had left her feeling like maybe she ought to extend an olive branch.

"Maddie, I'm sorry I hurt your feelings." There, that was true enough. She wasn't sorry for what she'd said, exactly. All of it was absolutely true. But she was sorry if it made Maddie upset.

Maddie sighed. "I know. I'm sorry, too. It's hard for me to say, but you're an adult and you should make your own decisions. I know you hate it when I tell you what to do, but it's only because I love you. I care about what happens to you, and I don't want you to be hurt." Maddie let out a deep breath. "After your miscarriage, I know you were so heartbroken. When I saw you in that hospital, I thought I might even lose you and…and I just couldn't stand that thought. Not…after Mom."

Tears welled up in Laura's eyes as she clutched the phone harder. "I'm sorry, Maddie."

"I'm sorry, too. I just want you to take care of yourself, okay? You're not supposed to go first. I am. Why are we talking so much about death anyway?" Maddie complained. They laughed a little together, as they both choked back tears.

"You started it," Laura teased and Maddie chuckled once more.

"That I did." Maddie let out a long sigh. "Are you okay? I mean, really okay? This…sailor. He's being good to you?"

Now, the tears welled up in Laura's eyes once more. "He's being wonderful." *That's not the problem.*

"So why do you sound so sad?"

Laura walked out on Mark's patio and slumped into a deck chair. She stared out to the ocean, watching the waves roll in on the pristine sandy beach. She was in paradise, she was pregnant and she was finally starting to believe that maybe, just maybe, she'd been forgiven for her past sins, and yet, somehow she was still not happy.

She hated to admit to her sister that she was pregnant. She knew Maddie would get on her high horse and talk about how she was being irresponsible again and about how she needed to be more of an adult. But at the same time, Laura had been bottling up this secret for so long, she didn't know how much longer she could keep the news to herself.

"Well…will you promise not to scold me? Promise not to say *I told you so*?"

Maddie sighed, already seeming to try not too hard to hide the *what-now* tone. "Of course."

"We had one time when we—didn't use protection. Maddie…" Laura sucked in a deep breath. "I'm pregnant."

The confession was met with a long pause on the other end of the line. Laura's stomach clenched. Would the lecture begin now? Would Maddie tell her all the ways she was messing up her life? Again?

"Oh, Laura. I'm so happy for you. A baby is what you've always wanted. How far along?"

"Nine or ten weeks. I think." Laura felt stunned. Her sister was actually happy for her? This might be a first. "But…I thought you'd be mad. I'm not married and haven't been dating Mark that long and—"

"Do you love him?" Maddie interrupted.

"Yes." Laura had no doubts about that.

"Does he love you?"

She swallowed hard. "Yes, I think so."

"Then what's the problem? Get married. Start a family. This is great news!" Laura could feel Maddie beaming through the phone. "I told you that you'd get pregnant again. Didn't I tell you that this would happen?"

"Hey—I said no I-told-you-so's."

Maddie laughed a little.

"But there's another problem," Laura said. "I haven't told him. About the baby."

Now Maddie made a sound of exasperation. "What? Why not?"

"First of all, I don't even know if I can carry a baby to term. I might lose this one, too."

Maddie sniffed. "So, you're just going to wait until the delivery to tell him? He *might* notice before then."

"And he lost a son and told me he doesn't want more children."

"So? He might change his mind once he knows he's going to have one," Maddie said matter-of-factly. She had an answer for everything. She always had.

"It's not that simple."

"Tell me why it's not." Laura could almost envision Maddie standing with her hands on her hips, daring her to try.

"It's just…he plans to win this sailing race and then sail around the world. It's not like he can do that if he's got a wife and new baby." This was the hard truth that Laura didn't even like admitting to herself.

"He doesn't want commitment, then," Maddie said.

"I don't think so." Laura bit her lip. She didn't know where he stood, actually. She wasn't sure.

"You have to change his mind." Maddie made it sound so easy, like all Laura had to do was snap her fingers and it would be done.

"How am I supposed to do that?"

"Use your wiles. Women have been doing that since the beginning of time."

Laura rubbed her stomach even as a seagull swooped down and landed on the roof of Mark's workshop. It stared at her with beady eyes.

"You make it sound like all I need to do is throw on some sexy lingerie, and he'll ask me to marry him."

"Might not be a bad plan," Maddie joked.

"Thanks. You're a *huge* help." Laura rolled her eyes.

"That's what I'm here for," Maddie said. "But seriously, Laura. Talk to him. You've got to at least try."

Laura heard Mark arriving back home then and quickly wrapped up her call with Maddie. Her heart sped up a little. She knew she had to talk to Mark, but how would she even tell him?

Mark came into the condo and unloaded a few bags of groceries.

"Got you some of this," he said, holding up a pink bottle. "Might help your stomach."

"Oh, thanks." It was sweet of him to try, but she knew it wouldn't help. "Mark…" she began. Then he glanced at her with his loving dark eyes.

"Yes?"

"There's something I need to tell you."

CHAPTER TWENTY-THREE

MARK WAITED FOR Laura to finish her thought. She seemed anxious all of a sudden, nervous even as she fidgeted with the hem of her T-shirt. What was the big news? Mark felt his muscles tense. Was she telling him she was leaving?

He knew at some point, she'd have to go home, and with the rescheduled race in just a couple of days, he knew it shouldn't be that much longer before she'd break the news to him. How much longer could she live on savings? She'd now moved into his condo, giving up the rent on hers, but still. She'd have to think about her financial future soon. But he wasn't ready to hear it. He might never be ready.

"Is it bad news?"

She hesitated. "It might be."

"Then, why not tell me while we walk," he said, not quite sure he wanted to hear bad news. Not yet. Not when the race was in front of them, not when it was such a gorgeous day outside.

She nodded, and when he took her hand, she let him as they walked outside into the bright sunshine. Mark kicked off his flip-flops, and since Laura was already barefoot, they proceeded to the warm sandy beach.

The ocean ran up on the beach, leaving a trail of sudsy white water. Their feet sank in the wet sand, leaving footprints behind them. Mark held Laura's hand, feeling her soft, delicate skin, thinking not for the first time how well they fit together in all ways. He never would've thought there'd be a woman out there so perfectly made for him, but Laura was it. Suddenly, he badly didn't want to hear her news. Her news that she'd be leaving him.

She didn't seem to want to tell him what was on her mind, either.

"It's beautiful, isn't it?" he asked her, staring at the sea. She nodded.

"What's it like? On the wide-open ocean?"

Mark glanced at her. "Like you're the only person on earth. Like everyone and everything has fallen away and it's just you and the water. Sometimes, it feels like… I don't know. This is going to sound silly."

"What?"

"That you're closer to God."

Laura squeezed his hand. "That's not silly." She glanced up at him and her bright green eyes caught the sun, bringing out the gold flecks in them. Her cheeks glowed. In fact, her whole face glowed. How was it possible she got prettier every day? He bent down and kissed her then, lightly on the lips.

"I love you," he said.

"I love you, too," she replied and she leaned into him. He put his arm around her shoulders and they both looked out at the sea. It went on farther than the eye could see.

"In a couple of days, we'll be racing on that," she said.

"Yes." *And afterward, you'll leave me.* But why was he feeling sad? Wasn't he planning to leave her first and sail around the world? But... then again, why couldn't she come along?

The idea popped into his head and he felt like smacking himself. Why hadn't he just thought of an easy solution?

"Laura, there's something I want to talk about with you, too," he said, hoping to cut off her bad news.

She pulled away from his side. "Yes?"

"You know that all I've ever wanted to do since Timothy died was sail around the world. I even...I even wasn't sure I wanted to come back."

She nodded, shading her eyes from the sun. Suddenly, Mark's palms started to sweat. What if she said no?

"But now, I think I want that trip to be different. I don't want it to just be me and Timothy's ghost."

Laura froze, staring at him.

"Would you…consider coming with me? Just you and me? A year on a boat?" Hope swelled in his chest as he looked at her. *Say yes*, he willed her. *Say yes*. "If we win, the winnings will pay for it. If they don't, I can somehow support us. You won't have to worry about a thing."

Laura looked surprised, then happy and then, inexplicably, sad.

"Mark. I wish I could…"

Suddenly, the hope that had been growing in his chest felt flattened like a delicate daisy crushed beneath a steel-toed work boot. He almost didn't want to hear what came next. Whatever it was would just be an excuse to cover up the fact that she didn't care about him as much as he cared about her. A commitment of a year seemed too much, he saw with perfect clarity. She wasn't ready to give him a year.

"Never mind," Mark said quickly. "It was a dumb idea."

"No, it's not a dumb idea…it's—"

"I mean, it should just be me alone out there anyway. I shouldn't be celebrating Timothy's death with a romantic cruise. What was I thinking?" He shook his head. He saw a glimpse of hurt cross her face. "This is why I should just be alone. Why I'm the last person on earth to try to settle down with."

"Mark, that's not—"

But Mark couldn't let her explain. Wouldn't. He didn't want to hear the platitudes, the excuses. He was broken, and she saw that, and she didn't want to be with him, not in the way he wanted to be with her.

"You don't have to tell me anything. I get it." He swiped his hand through his unruly hair. "It's a good thing I'm never going to be a father again. I mean, I'm a mess." He had hoped the joke would lighten the mood, but for some reason, Laura's face darkened.

"Never be a father again? You're sure?"

"Positive. I'm one walking screwup. And the last thing anybody needs is for me screwing up someone else's life."

The words seemed to hit Laura like a punch, but he wasn't sure why. Why was she taking his self-bashing so personally? The warm Caribbean water pooled around their toes, but he hardly felt it. Somehow, he felt like their conversation was like quicksand—the more they fought, the deeper and more stuck they got.

"What did you want to talk to me about?"

"Nothing," Laura said, curt, her feelings somehow hurt, though he didn't understand why. She was the one who'd rejected him, not the other way around. Why was she upset?

"You sure?"

"Positive." She crossed her arms angrily across her chest and stared out to the ocean. He knew that look and there'd be no talking to her now. Whatever it was she wanted to tell him would have to wait, he thought.

THE DAY OF the race, Mark woke on the couch feeling stiff. Since their disagreement on the beach, Laura had been cold and distant. He'd offered to sleep on the couch and she'd let him, and he was beginning to wonder what he'd said that was so bad. So offensive. *She* was the one who'd rejected him. So why was she acting like he'd rained on her parade?

They went about making breakfast silently, Laura calmly eating a cup of yogurt but not saying much to him. She'd been cold but polite, not ignoring him exactly, but not loving on him, either. Mark felt frustrated. He didn't want their romance to end like this. He could only think it was because he'd mentioned he'd thought about suicide. That's the only sticking point he could see.

"Time to go," Mark said and Laura just nodded, a distant, empty look on her face. He hated that look. He wanted to grab her by the shoul-

ders and pull her into his arms and kiss the life
out of her and make her *his* again, but he didn't
know how. He felt like he should apologize for
something, but he had no idea what. Why was
she angry after turning him down? Should he
never have asked her to sail with him?

They drove in mostly silence to the dock,
with Laura staring quietly out the window,
hands in her lap. He wanted to know what she
was thinking, but at the same time, he didn't
know how to ask. When they arrived, the parking lot was already crowded as he steered his
truck into one of the few remaining spaces.

Sunshine greeted them outside as they made
their way to the marina, where overnight, dozens of sailboats had loaded in for the start of
the race.

Mark stood on the dock, checking out the
competition, the marina crowded with sailboats
as far as he could see. Beside him, Laura stood
solemnly, dressed and ready for a day of racing. Garrett was already on board, getting the
sailboat ready.

Mark recognized the faster boats: the *Jetstream*, *St. Claire*, *Ciao Bella* and, of course,
Tanner. He squinted but didn't see Dave or any
of his crew. He wondered if Edward would be
sailing today. The thought made his stomach
tighten. *Even if I don't win, let me beat Edward.*

Crowds of onlookers lined the marina, snaking up around the tall dunes near the beach. They were dotted with folding chairs and people making a day of it, watching the race while picnicking with their families. More onlookers sat in spectator boats, bobbing out in the sea. Thankfully, all the cruise ships were out to sea, and the sea was clear and calm. The swells weren't too high yet, though the forecast said they could get as high as six feet. Mark hoped for Laura's sake that the seas remained calm.

"You ready?" Mark asked her as he helped her aboard the sailboat.

"As ready as I'll ever be," she said, still a little listlessly and not looking him in the eye. He hated that so much had gone wrong between them and he had no idea how to fix it.

She climbed aboard, her knees immediately adjusting to the sway of the boat beneath her. She inhaled the fresh sea air and greeted Garrett with a grin. Mark so admired her grit and determination. Few men or women he knew would be willing to take on such a challenge.

"Ahoy," Garrett said with a wave. "You ready for the big time, kid?"

"I hope so," Laura said and giggled nervously. Mark couldn't help but notice how much friendlier she was with Garrett and felt a flash of envy.

"You're going to be great. Don't sweat it," Mark said, fully confident in her abilities, though she barely acknowledged the compliment. Mark pulled himself up on the boat, watching as she took up her position on the stern.

Tim and Gretchen loaded in just after Mark, greeting everyone with hugs, and then got busy stowing their gear.

"So who's the fastest competition?" Laura asked Garrett, surveying the other boats.

"*Tanner*, you know," Mark interrupted, not giving Garrett a chance to answer as he nodded in the direction of his brother's boat. "But probably the next fastest are *Ciao Bella* there—" he pointed to the white boat with the tall black-and-blue sail "—and *St. Claire* there, with the red stripe across the white sail? And, probably *Jetstream* at the far end, the one with the bifurcated red-and-blue sail."

"Ah," Laura said, nodding, as she shaded her eyes from the sun.

"You've got be careful about *Ciao Bella*," Garrett warned. "They cut corners when they sail and are always looking for a way in. They hit a boat last year, in one of the few collisions in race history. They had to be rescued by another competitor."

"That doesn't sound good." Laura squinted.

"You sure you want to do this?" Mark asked her. She was so sullen, he wondered if her heart was really in this. A race was no place to be if her mind was elsewhere. "I mean, race. It's hard work, and...these guys take it seriously. It could be dangerous and you'll need to focus."

Laura raised her chin, defiant. "I'm sure," she said.

"Well, then, let's get to work," Gretchen said and grinned, as Mark assigned her to work on the rigging. Mark looked over and saw Dave's boat, emblazoned with the name *Tanner* across the back. It was a majestic boat, slightly bigger than the *Timothy*.

Dave looked the part of the impressive captain, but Mark would always bet on himself over Dave. Dave always stuck to sailing by the book. The man never took risks, never put himself out there. That meant that if he got the lead early, he was likely to hold it. His motto was always steady wins the race. It explained another reason why Dave picked racing the *Tanner* over racing *Timothy*, Mark realized. Dave always played it safe. He should've known.

Mark, on the other hand, took risks. Sometimes, they didn't always pay off. More times than he'd like to admit, he'd been too aggressive at the starting line and got pushed over early—

watching the fleet sail away from him while he turned back to do his penalty maneuver.

"You think we got an icicle's chance in hell?" Garrett asked him in a low murmur as Mark checked the boat's engine, preparing to take them out to the race starting point.

"Maybe slightly better than that," Mark said. "Who knows? How lucky is your brother feeling today?"

"With his wife?" Garrett rolled his eyes. "I think she picked out his underwear this morning. I'm sure she picked the lucky ones."

At that, Mark threw back his head and laughed and the tightness in his chest lifted. Laura might be angry with him for a reason he didn't understand, but he was about to sail, and he couldn't feel bad about that. The horn sounded, announcing for all racers to take their marks.

Soon after that, they were underway, headed out to sea to the buoy marker for the starting line. They joined the dozens of boats lined up in a row, ready to take on the rest. White sails dotted the horizon, each stretching to different heights. They'd have at least two hours of racing before the winner crossed the finish line.

Laura looked nervous. Mark gave her a thumbs-up sign and she returned it with an uneasy smile as she put on her sports sunglasses.

Mark was proud of the boat they'd restored. The *Timothy* looked ready to compete. It was all he could hope for. He only wished Laura was in a mood to celebrate this with him. He still wished Laura would sail with him, actually, for the year. It hurt him that she didn't want to go.

As the boats began to leave the marina, he took in the majestic sight of all the differently colored hulls surrounding them.

The race committee sounded the horn for their starting sequence. Five minutes before the gun, he felt his chest swell with excitement. They were going to do this!

He glanced at Laura and felt so very grateful for her. She made him a better person. For the last year, he hadn't been able to imagine a future, and now he could actually imagine living past tomorrow, past the race, past sailing off into the sunset. He could actually imagine a future life. It was just too bad Laura didn't want to share that future with him.

As he watched her look out to the horizon, he realized he wanted her in his life. That when he thought of *future*, he thought of her. It was that simple. Why didn't she want that as well?

Mark managed to take his place between *Tanner* and *Ciao Bella* with *St. Claire* on the other side. His boat, on the leeward side of *Ciao Bella* meant he had the right of way, but the boat with the black-and-blue spinnaker didn't move to the start, effectively blocking *Timothy*'s right of way.

"Head up! Head up!" Garret shouted at the crew, though they didn't hear him over the wind. "We have the right to head-to-wind!"

Mark frowned. He knew *Ciao Bella* played dirty, and it was already starting with cutting in at the starting line. Tim and Gretchen had noticed, too.

Laura glanced back from her post, worry wrinkling her forehead. "They're going to regret that," Mark said.

As the boats jockeyed to get into the best positions on the line possible, the race committee sounded the gun, announcing the start. Mark, Garrett, Tim, Gretchen and Laura jumped into action as they trimmed the sails and caught the wind, taking off from the start ahead of *Ciao Bella*.

But *St. Claire*, a boat made up of an all-woman crew, matched them nearly gust for gust as the boats took the lead, with *Ciao Bella* and *Tanner* close behind.

They continued to sail close-hauled, the fastest point of sail, keeping their eyes on the windward mark in the distance. The wind showed no signs of letting up as the *Timothy* cut through the water, sending up cool sea spray into Mark's face. This was where he was born to be, he thought.

Yet as they caught sight of the first mark rounding, the *Tanner* gained on them as Dave expertly steered their boat up wind. His crew, including Edward, worked furiously on the lines to keep the sail full.

"Dammit," Mark cursed, as the *Tanner* pulled ahead, as did the *St. Claire* and the *Jetstream*. The *Ciao Bella* slashed windward at a sharp angle to try to beat *Tanner* to the inside position on the turn, but that put the *Ciao Bella* right in their path.

"Helms a lee!" he cried to Garrett and Laura, who worked furiously to trim the sail as Mark tacked the boat. Now the *Timothy* might end up wrecked, too. They caught the wind and lurched hard, sending Laura somehow off her feet. For a heart-stopping second, he couldn't see where she went. *Please, God*, he sent up a prayer, *let it not be overboard.*

CHAPTER TWENTY-FOUR

LAURA FELT HERSELF free-falling. All she knew was that one second, it looked like they might hit the *Ciao Bella*, and the next, she'd lost her grip as the boat lurched. In a harried moment, she didn't know where she'd land, the deck or the sea.

Then suddenly, she hit the wood floorboards, skidding on her side and belly toward the bow. She curled up, instinctively trying to protect herself as she fought against physics and clung to the boat. *The baby*, was her first thought as she curled inward, everything in her wanting to protect her midsection.

Please, don't let this hurt the baby.

Then she slid into the bow, her head knocking into the interior, making her see stars and stunning her for a second.

"Laura!" she heard someone shout. Mark?

Her head rang but she shook off her dizziness. It was all she could do to hold on and not let go.

Then came another thought. *Do not fall over-*

*board. In the middle of a sea of racing sailboats
that won't be able to stop.* She remembered the
story Mark had told her about the sailor who'd
fallen overboard and gotten knocked unconscious by the other boats nearby.

Hang on, she willed herself as she clutched to
the small metal loop on the bow. Then slowly,
as the boat settled down, moving less at an
angle, she managed to right herself, letting out
a long slow breath of relief.

"Laura!" Mark was suddenly at her side, lifting her up. But who was steering? In a panic,
she glanced at the boat's wheel and saw Garret
there, a determined look on his face.

Her ears still rang a bit as she glanced at
Mark.

"Are you all right?" he asked, his face twisted
in concern.

"I am. I'm fine." She rubbed the back of her
head where she could feel a goose egg rising.
"At least I don't see two of you."

"Want to stop?"

"No." She stood up. Her knees felt slightly
wobbly, even as she fought against the boat's
deck, but she still didn't want to stop. She
wouldn't be the reason Mark quit the race. "I'm
okay. Really."

"Mark!" Garrett shouted, glancing backward.
Two other sailboats raced past them, as the *Tim-*

othy dropped in the standings. The *Ciao Bella's* rash move had put it in second place. Dave was fighting her off but not doing a great job of it. The *St. Claire* and the *Jetstream* battled it out for the lead ahead of even the *Tanner*. Soon, the *Ciao Bella* would catch them.

"Let's do this," Laura said.

Mark nodded. "Okay." He directed her back to her post and then he took the wheel from Garrett. He nodded at Gretchen and Tim.

"Let's get the spinnaker up!" he said. And the five of them worked furiously to get the boat back on course, as they focused on gaining on the *Tanner*. The *St. Claire* fell back two boat-lengths as the *Tanner* passed it and then the *Timothy* did, too. Laura could see the female sailors on that boat furiously working together to keep the boat competitive.

Then the wind kicked up and they sailed on, nudging forward, and Mark managed to inch the boat ahead, surfing on the waves as they headed downwind. Soon the inches grew into feet as the *Timothy* knocked out its first competitor. But they had one more lap to go. And the *Tanner*, *Ciao Bella* and *Jetstream* were still ahead of them.

She told herself that she would just live in the moment and that she'd think about what happened to her and the baby later. That for now, she'd just focus on the time they had and on the wind in the sails. How she wished she could sail around the world with Mark. But when a baby arrived in seven months, then what? They couldn't have a newborn on a boat. And even worse, Mark had made it clear he didn't want children. Not in seven months, not ever.

She focused on the other boats and all their colorful spinnakers, as they sailed down the race course together.

"I'll never get tired of this," Mark shouted and Laura nodded. She could see why he loved racing so much—the thrill, the amazing expanse of water and being part of a floating city, the sea dotted with these majestic boats. The only blemishes on the day were the dark storm clouds hanging out to the west, out to sea. They were far enough away not to be a concern, and the weather report had said rain wasn't supposed to hit until later that evening.

Ahead, the *Jetstream*, the *Ciao Bella* and the *Tanner* jostled for positions. Mark inched closer to the *Jetstream*, alongside its huge red-and-blue spinnaker, looking tall and menacing as they tried to move forward. The *Jetstream* wouldn't be an easy boat to catch, but they'd have to do it.

Laura tried to focus on her task at hand, trimming the sail, but then she thought about her fall and the baby.

Is the baby okay? She hoped so. But there was hardly any time to think about it. The race continued as the bow slashed through the water, the spray dotting her legs. The sun beamed down and Laura focused all her attention on the boat. The *Timothy* had to win.

It seemed like just a few minutes, but Laura realized more than an hour had passed as they worked their way around the course. Soon came the last rounding, a big neon yellow buoy, and the homestretch. Right before the turn, they managed to inch past the *Jetstream*, the sail sinking a bit as it just narrowly lost wind.

Now it was a race of just the top three: the *Ciao Bella*, *Tanner* and *Timothy*. But it looked as if there was no way the *Timothy* would ever catch either boat. They were too far ahead.

Laura glanced at Mark, and his face told her everything. There wasn't enough time to make up the difference. Not enough time, not enough wind. They were almost certainly going to come in third.

They could see the finish line, and Laura felt her stomach tense. How could they ever make up that distance? It seemed impossible.

Meanwhile, the *Ciao Bella* had spent the entire race using aggressive and risky tactics, and now as they barreled down on the *Tanner*, it looked like they had a serious chance to win.

The crews had one more chance—the final tack to the finish line. As they headed into the tack, the two boats ahead of them clustered together, while the *Timothy* lagged behind half a boat length. Then, hoping to make their move, the *Ciao Bella* headed up hard, trying to inch out the *Tanner*, but it also put the *Ciao Bella* right in their path.

Mark shouted, "Look out!"

And Laura realized that they needed to maneuver away, or they'd hit the stern of the *Ciao Bella*.

"Trim!" Garret called and they worked hard to take the boat up, barely making it away from the *Ciao Bella*, but with the *Timothy* out of the way, it meant that the *Ciao Bella* was heading on a collision course straight for the *Tanner*. And Laura noticed, Dave wasn't going to get out of the way.

"They're going to hit," Garrett shouted, and Laura realized he was right. The *Ciao Bella* wasn't going to make that angle on the turn. They were going to ram right into the *Tanner*.

Laura could see Dave struggling to avoid it, but there wasn't going to be a way out.

Laura watched helplessly as the boats converged, each one trying to steer clear of the other. Dave, smartly, whipped leeward, trying to get parallel to the *Ciao Bella*. For a second, it looked like he might make it. Then they heard the earsplitting crunch as the *Ciao Bella* slid into the *Tanner*, the boats scraping across each other's hulls. The impact sent the boats slipping toward the *Timothy*.

Were they next?

"Come about!" Mark shouted, and they all worked furiously, trimming hard to tack the *Timothy*. Amazingly, they managed to avoid smashing into the other two boats, still tangled together in the water and veering off course. They'd never make it to the finish line now. Laura glanced backward. The next closest boat was at least ten boat lengths away.

Mark flashed Laura a smile. "We're going to win this," he said as the *Timothy* soared past, the only leader now for a quarter mile. They churned on to the finishing line buoy, where one of the race administrative boats waited, officials' cameras pointed at the water.

Mark, Laura and the rest of the crew fell silent as they focused on making it the last few meters. Only when the bow slipped past the buoy did the whole boat erupt in cheers.

"We did it!" Laura shouted, still not quite believing it was true. They had won! A hundred thousand dollars!

Garrett took the wheel as they eased their sails to slow down. Mark scooped up Laura from behind and she giggled. When he set her down on the rocking deck of the boat, she whirled and kissed him and didn't even care when her hat flew off, sailing over the deck and into the water.

"Another one gone," she breathed as she pulled away from him.

"I'll buy you a hundred more," Mark promised. His face shone with happiness. "We did it," he said, and he only had eyes for her as he held her close. Tears slid down her cheeks. She was so very happy—for him. But also she couldn't help but feel a pang of sadness. *He'll be leaving me. Maybe these are pregnancy hormones at work*, she thought as she swiped away her tears.

"Hey, what about me?" Garrett shouted from the stern. "Do I get a hug?"

Laura and Mark laughed and folded Garrett in. Gretchen and Tim joined in, shouting. Other sailboats whizzed past them, crossing the line in a parade of colored sails.

A high-pitched whistle sounded, and Mark glanced up. Laura followed his gaze, and the team stopped celebrating long enough to glance at the two boats lagging behind them. Other boats passed right by.

"That doesn't look good," Garrett said.

The *Tanner* was listing badly. So was the *Ciao Bella*.

"Are they okay?" Laura asked.

Mark frowned. "I don't know." As the other boats finished the race and then sailed easily back toward shore, nobody seemed to pay the crash much mind.

"Will someone help them?"

"There's supposed to be a crash boat." Mark grabbed the radio near the ship's wheel. The radio crackled to life as he called in to the race committee.

"The crash boat is dealing with another incident on the race course," a voice told Mark over the CB. "Near the windward mark. Two boats got tangled up and it's a huge mess."

Laura squinted but she couldn't see the windward mark, as it was too far around the bend of the island. Mark shaded his eyes from the sun and glanced at the sailboats streaming in and then out at the *Tanner*, which was now listing even worse. Would the boat even stay afloat much longer? Even worse, the dark clouds rolling in from the west seemed to be moving faster than she first thought.

The radio crackled to life again, this time, it instructed all boats to head back inland to avoid the storm sitting on the horizon.

"With all the boats headed in, and the storm, there's no way the *Tanner* gets help." Mark slammed the radio back on its cradle.

"We've got to go help them." Garrett peered at the troubled boat as his brother struggled to keep the boat from sinking.

Mark nodded. "We have to," he agreed. "Let's go."

He returned to the ship's wheel and Garrett moved to adjust the jib. Laura steadied herself as they whipped the boat around, careful to avoid the incoming boats, the wind in their face as they tried to maneuver their boat.

They managed to get alongside the *Tanner*, as the *Jetstream* circled back to the *Ciao Bella* to help that crew. They busied themselves hooking up the *Ciao Bella* for a tow.

The *Tanner* wasn't going to do so well. That boat was sinking and sinking fast. In fact, Dave and Edward and the third crewman jumped in the water, swimming for the *Timothy*. The boat was sinking so fast half the mast was underwater. The three swam for the *Timothy*.

Garrett and Mark helped them climb up the back of the boat, and the three crew members sat, dripping.

"Thanks, man," Dave said and clearly meant it.

Edward said nothing, just stared at his sunken boat. "That was my best boat," Edward mumbled, shaking his head. The *Ciao Bella* moved past, towed by the *Jetstream*. "Thanks a lot, assholes!" Edward yelled, even as the boats slipped past. He glanced at Mark. "Took you long enough."

Mark sent him a wry grin. "Had to win the race first."

"You only won because we got sidelined, brother." Edward quirked an eyebrow.

"What was that you always say? 'A win is a win'?" Mark clapped his brother hard on the back and Edward let out a reluctant chuckle.

"What are we sitting around for?" Dave asked. "Let's get back to the marina so we can hand this loser his trophy."

Everyone laughed at that as they steered toward the marina. Laura stood near Mark at the wheel, watching the shore grow closer.

"Glad you two have made up," Laura said. Mark pulled her into his arms and she went, hugging him freely for the first time in days. Maybe their argument was finally over. He hoped so. Maybe he could still convince her to sail around the world with him. There might still be a chance.

"I'm feeling…light-headed," Laura said all at once.

Next to him, she seemed to stagger a bit on her feet. Then her eyes rolled back in her head and she fainted.

CHAPTER TWENTY-FIVE

LAURA CAME TO at the docks with a circle of concerned faces around her.

"Are you all right?" Mark asked, his face crumpling in relief. What had happened? The race, yes…they won! And then the boat rescue and somewhere along the way, she'd lost it.

Laura sat up, but then her vision filled with stars. "Oh, boy," she said, holding her head.

"Here, have some water," Garrett said, offering her a water bottle. She took a deep swig of the cold liquid and smiled gratefully at her shipmate.

"Thanks."

"You gave us a scare," Edward said. "Fainted dead away on the boat right when we were about to dock."

"I know winning is stressful, but sheesh," Dave echoed.

"I'm okay, really. Probably just an empty stomach," Laura lied. The last time she'd been pregnant she'd gotten light-headed spells, too. Her mother had them as well. Maddie said their dad used to call their mom London Bridge because she always fell down. If she had any doubt about the pregnancy test results, those were long gone now.

"Then let's get you something to eat," Mark said.

Laura's stomach, empty and roiling, wasn't so sure that was a good idea, but now she'd have to try.

Mark helped her to her feet and she stood, a little unsteady. He held her tightly by the arm. "I've got you," he promised.

They all walked to the Rusted Anchor, where the race judges had gathered. Garrett went to talk to the officials and sign the finishing papers for the *Timothy*, and Mark steered her to one of the few open booths in the back. Most of the bar was filled with race spectators.

Edward glanced at his phone. "Elle wants to join us. Is that okay?" He glanced at Mark. Laura felt her stomach tighten. What would he say?

Mark glanced at Laura. "Is that all right with you?" he asked her.

She nodded. It might be awkward, but at some point, they would all have to start acting like a family. Elle was pregnant with Mark's niece or nephew, and that child shouldn't suffer for the mistakes his or her parents made.

"Okay, then," Mark told Edward. Then, he studied Laura. "You want a beer?" he asked her.

Did she. But she couldn't. "Uh…no. No, thanks."

"Come on! We're celebrating," Edward pushed. "And who knows when *this* loser will ever win anything again?"

Laura laughed a little at the joke. "I think I'll just start with water, if that's okay. Because… my empty stomach."

Edward eyed her, and she almost wondered if he suspected her condition. She hoped not.

"The lady fainted, so let's not give her another reason to get light-headed," Dave interrupted. And Laura was suddenly grateful.

"Water it is," Mark said. "But beers to follow."

Laura rubbed her forehead. She felt the start of a headache, and the worry about her fall on the boat never quite left her. While her shorts were tight, her stomach was largely flat. She'd heard from her sister that later in the pregnancy the regular kicking of the baby helped calm new mom nerves, but now, she had no idea how the little one inside her was faring. Was she…or he…okay?

Mark went to the bar to get beers for the table and a water for her, and she watched him go. *I need to tell him.* But how?

He returned to the table, slid the water in front of her and beers in front of the other men and Gretchen. Laura took a sip of water and then Edward's phone lit up. He answered in the noisy bar, moving away from the table so he could hear.

"Are you okay?" Gretchen asked, concerned. "Did you hit your head…when you fell on the boat?"

"Just a little bit. But, don't worry. I don't think the fainting had anything to do with that."

"Maybe you should see somebody," Mark said. "Like a doctor. First the stomach bug and then the fainting…" Mark took a long sip of beer.

"I'm fine." *I know exactly what's wrong with me.* When would he start to suspect? Yet he seemed stubbornly blind to her symptoms.

Edward came back to the table, face white. "Guys, Elle's labor started. Her friend is already driving her to the hospital."

Mark slowly put down the beer. "We'll drive you to the hospital," he said.

"I can do it," Edward said.

"No, man. You'll be liable to hit a tree. Let us drive you."

"You sure?" Edward looked anxious as he glanced at Garrett.

"Hell, we'll all go," Garrett said.

MARK SAT WITH Laura in the waiting room of the small island hospital, holding her hand.

"If you'd told me a month ago I'd be waiting at the hospital for my ex-wife to deliver my brother's baby, I would've told you that you were nuts," Mark said, shaking his head.

Laura laughed a little and leaned into him. She loved the feel of his strong shoulder beneath her cheek. She wanted that feeling to last forever but wondered if it would.

"Stranger things have happened," she said. "But I'm glad for the baby's sake that you two have made up. It's important for kids to have extended family."

"I'm not sure we're exactly friends again. It's a lot to process."

Laura rubbed his arm. "I know. But I'm proud of you. Proud that you let him help us and that you're here. Supporting him."

"I still don't know what I'm doing here really."

"Being an adult. Being a bigger person,"

Laura said. She squeezed his arm. "You're amazing, you know that?"

Mark brightened. "For nearly getting you thrown overboard on the ship? Hardly!"

"It was an accident," Laura said.

"How's your head?" he asked, leaning over and gently probing the back of her hair. He touched the goose egg and she flinched a little.

"Ouch."

"Sorry." He withdrew his hand and then gazed at her a moment. "You sure that bump isn't more serious? You fainted on the dock and—"

"It's not the bump," she said quickly. *At least not that bump.* She fought herself once more. Why couldn't she just *tell* him?

"Okay." Mark let it go. He held her hand, studying her fingers, and then he gently brought it to his lips and kissed her knuckles. The gentle touch sent a shiver down her spine. How she loved him. How she loved how he touched her, bringing every nerve ending in her body alive. "Have you thought about my offer? To go sailing?"

"Mark." *Not now,* she thought. They couldn't talk about this now.

"We won the money, and I can support us on the boat. And I know you said you didn't want to go, and I can't really blame you since you almost got thrown overboard, but would you at least think about it?" Mark looked so hopeful then. How could she dash his hopes?

"But…" Yet, it was all so hopeless.

"I know you want to go back to San Francisco. I know that's your plan."

"I don't know what my plans are," she confessed. "I have no job. I…" *I'm about to be a single mom.*

"Then it's the perfect time to sail around the world with me. Come on. Say you'll consider it." He studied her a moment. "Are you worried about me? About what I said?"

Laura frowned. "About not coming back?"

Mark nodded. "You don't have to be. I realize now that with you in my life, everything has changed. I've got so much to live for now. You've made me see that, Laura. I'm not going to make this a one-way trip. I promise. But if you come with me, it'll be a trip of a lifetime."

It would. Laura had no doubt.

"Mark, I just…" *I can't because I'm pregnant.* Why couldn't she say those words? Yet, every time she tried, they stuck in her throat. All she had to do was admit the real problem and then he'd understand. Laura glanced at him once more. She had to find the courage to tell him. She just had to...

"Mark?" Edward was standing in front of them. Laura cursed his rotten timing. Mark turned. "It's a girl," he told them both.

Laura jumped up and hugged Edward. "Oh, I'm so glad." She gave him a huge hug. Edward, surprised, hugged her back. Mark stood, too, and gave his hand for a shake. Edward looked at it, touched. He took it and slowly shook his brother's hand.

"Congratulations," Mark said.

"Thanks, man. You don't know what this means. Thank you." Edward grinned. He looked at Mark. "Uh, Elle wants to...she wants to talk to you."

Mark frowned. "About what?"

"I'm not sure. But she asked for you."

Mark glanced at Laura, who didn't know what to say. She felt a bit of jealousy in her stomach, but knew she should fight it off. Reluctantly, Mark nodded and then walked down the corridor toward Elle's room. Edward glanced at Laura, studying her a beat.

"Mind if I sit?" he said, and when she shrugged, he plunked down into the seat next to her.

"How is Elle doing? And the baby?" she asked.

"Fine. They're both fine and healthy. Baby is

eight pounds, one ounce. And she's got strong lungs—used them right out of the gate."

Laura smiled. For the first time in a long time, she realized, news about a baby didn't make her want to cry. Maybe it was because she knew she was carrying one inside her. The hope had already started to take root.

"When are you going to tell him?" Edward asked her, his sharp eyes missing nothing.

Laura turned abruptly. "What do you mean?"

"You know what I mean." He stared at her for a long beat, his meaning clear. Somehow, he knew about the pregnancy.

"How'd you guess?"

"Well, I didn't know for sure until just now."

Laura's mouth dropped open. "You tricked me."

"Of course, I did. Didn't Mark warn you I was the bad brother?" Edward chuckled. "Besides, I already suspected. Elle had all those same symptoms—nausea, fainting. I wasn't quite sure until you ordered water at the bar, but then, I was pretty confident."

Laura's shoulders slumped. "Mark doesn't want to be a father. How can I tell him?"

Edward nodded. "Mark's stubborn all right, but eventually he always sees reason."

Laura shook her head. "What if he doesn't,

though? He wants to sail around the world. He thinks a baby will dishonor Timothy's memory. How can I disappoint him like this? He's worked so hard for so long, and against all odds we actually *won* the damn race, and now I'm going to tell him he can't go?"

Edward laughed. "I think he'd rather be a father than not."

"No. He thinks it betrays Timothy. He's sure of it." Laura sighed. "And we've only been dating a short while, and now a baby? I mean, it's crazy. It will never work."

Edward quirked an eyebrow. "Love isn't a straight line," he said. "Sometimes we find it in the most unexpected places." Edward paused. "Says the brother who fell in love with his sister-in-law."

Laura couldn't help but laugh. "That's a terrible example."

"I know." Edward shrugged. He patted her on the knee. "Still, you need to tell him. He has a right to know."

Laura nodded. "I know he does. I just... I need to tell him in my own time."

"Just make sure that's *before* he starts sailing around the world." Mark shrugged. "He'll probably want to sail to Bora Bora soon. That's the next big sailing race."

"Then I still have some time," Laura pointed out.

"You do," Mark agreed. "But not much." He stared at her. "What's it going to take to convince you to talk to him?"

A miracle, she thought.

MARK WALKED INTO his ex-wife's hospital room and felt an overwhelming sense of déjà vu. In a room just like this a few years ago, he'd met his son for the first time. He'd seen the doctors clean him and wrap him in a blue blanket and hand him to Elle. Elle had smiled then and he'd hugged her and his son together. That had been one of the happiest days of his life. Now, as he stood at the foot of her hospital bed, he felt like an intruder while she cooed to the baby wrapped in the pink blanket in her arms.

She glanced up at him, looking a little startled.

"You wanted to see me?" he asked. "Edward said—"

"Yes. I did." Elle looked down at her baby once more. The silence felt awkward. Mark remembered why, too. The last time he'd been alone with Elle was more than a year ago, when she'd stood in his living room with a packed bag and told him she was leaving him for Edward. Then his whole world caved in. It felt like yesterday and it felt like a lifetime ago at the same time.

"I...I wanted to thank you, for...bringing Edward to the hospital."

"Sure."

Elle glanced at him, and he had the feeling she wanted to say more, but he had no idea what she had in mind. They used to be so close, he could read her mind, but now this woman who'd once been his wife was a black box to him. He couldn't guess what she was thinking.

"Mark, I know this is hard for you, but..." Emotions strangled Elle's voice as she paused a minute. "I am so sorry. About Timothy. I think about him every day. And...my daughter is not a replacement for him."

The admission hit Mark like a ton of bricks. She did still care. He could see that in her tear-filled eyes.

"I'd do anything to go back to that day," she said. "I want you to know that. I know how badly I messed up, and I'll live with that guilt forever. And I've cut out all the pills. All of them. I just...I just wanted to tell you that."

Mark nodded. The admission didn't make his grief any less, but somehow it did loosen up the hardness in his heart he'd built up against her. She'd had a problem, and he knew she had. Maybe he shared some of the blame, too, for leaving her alone with Timothy when he knew she wasn't 100 percent, when he knew she might slip.

"We both made mistakes," he admitted.

She smiled. "Want to hold Emma?"

Mark glanced at the tiny baby swaddled in a pink flannel blanket. He felt his heart open a little bit. "Sure," he said and reached for the tiny bundle. She was fast asleep, poor thing, as he held the little baby in his arms.

"She's got your nose," he told Elle, who smiled. "Thank you for letting me hold her."

"Of course," Elle said. "She's your niece."

The craziness of that fact had only just begun to set in. Mark held the baby for a second longer and then handed her back to her mother. It was all so much to take in—the baby, Elle, Edward. He was on the path to forgiveness, but he also knew there'd be some bumps in the road before he found his destination.

"I'll go tell Edward it's his turn to hold the baby," Mark said.

"Wait, Mark," she called. "I just want you to know. There's enough love in your heart for more than just Timothy. Love isn't finite, and the heart is a big place."

He ducked out of the hospital room feeling a little bit lighter but also a little bit sadder. There was no doubt that a chapter in his life—the chapter with Elle—was absolutely done. If there'd been any doubts, today quashed them.

Then he turned the corner and he saw Edward standing close to Laura, nearly toe to toe, and he was *holding both her hands*.

Mark froze. *What the...?*

Edward was leaning over, whispering something in her ear. His body was entirely too close, and then, he met her gaze, put both hands on her cheeks and leaned forward and gently laid a kiss on her forehead.

It was tender, and he lingered, and then Mark's whole vision went red.

What the hell was going on?

But then Mark knew exactly what was going on. Edward was being Edward.

He was stealing away something that wasn't his.

But why wasn't Laura resisting him? Why wasn't she putting him off?

No, she wasn't fighting him. She wasn't telling him to go to hell. As he watched, he saw her smile up at him tenderly. Surely, he was imagining it all. And yet, that sparkle in her eye, that gratitude. It was the same look she'd given

Mark so many times before. He knew her so well, and he knew, beyond a shadow of a doubt, there was a little conspiracy between them.

He felt his blood run cold. He'd been here before. With Elle. He felt that same pit in his stomach he had the day she'd told him she was leaving him, the same feeling of having the wind knocked out of him.

No. Not again. Never again. Mark would see to that once and for all.

CHAPTER TWENTY-SIX

EDWARD HAD JUST told her to stay strong for the baby and had kissed her forehead when Mark appeared beside them.

"What's going on?" he asked—half growled really. Laura hadn't seen him approach, and she jumped, a little startled, and of course pulled away from Edward, feeling off balance. Had Mark heard the word *baby*? Did he know what they were talking about? She had to wonder. It made her fidget and feel guilty.

"We were just talking," Edward said, wary.

"It didn't *look* like talking." Mark's dark eyes flashed with anger. He was furious. But why was he so mad?

"Mark, what's wrong?"

"He's what's wrong." Mark nodded at Edward. "Elle just gave birth to your baby and you're hitting on *my* girlfriend."

"Mark, he wasn't hitting on me," Laura tried to explain.

"Really? Why did he kiss you?"

"On the forehead," Laura said. Like a brother.

"What were you two talking about?"

Now that was a tough question to answer. Laura glanced at Edward, worried, but that split second was enough for Mark to jump to all the wrong conclusions. "Right." Mark turned to leave, and Laura popped up, grabbing his elbow. He whirled.

"Leave me alone," he growled.

"There's no flirting," Edward said. "We were just talking. I swear."

"Don't swear to me. You were always a liar." Mark put his hands on his head and spun around, as if the enormity of the situation was just too much for him to speak. "I never should've let you back in my life. Never."

"Man, calm down," Edward said. "You really have no idea what you're talking about here—"

"I know what I saw." Mark turned to Laura. "Is this why you didn't want to come sail around the world with me? Because it would take you too far from him?"

"No," Laura sputtered. How could he think that? "Of course not."

"How long has this been going on?" Mark demanded, and now Laura realized there was no talking to him. He'd gone to an irrational place. A place of deep hurt and betrayal.

"There's nothing going on," she said, trying to be calm.

"Really? So he just decided to help rebuild the *Timothy* just because?"

"Yes, actually," Edward said, staring at his brother evenly. But there was no convincing Mark of that.

"Mark, just sit down, and we can talk," Laura began.

Mark shook his head.

"Mark—"

"I thought you were different, Laura. You're just like Elle."

"How can you say that to me?" Laura couldn't believe what she was hearing. How could Mark be so ready to give up on her, on them?

"You're making a mistake," Edward told him.

That was enough to drive him out of the hospital. Laura watched as he stalked out the sliding doors and into the parking lot. In that instant, her whole world changed.

She and her baby deserved someone who didn't spook so easily, someone who didn't automatically believe the worst about her.

That was the worst truth to bear.

"Are you going to go after him?" Edward asked.

Laura shook her head.

"If he'd walk out on me just like that, then I don't want him staying around just for a baby." Her voice sounded cold and hard even in her own ears. But she had a baby to think about now. If Mark wasn't ready or capable of rising to the occasion, then she'd have to do this alone.

MARK SPENT THE night on the *Timothy*, beneath decks. The gentle list of the boat should've been calming, but instead, he lay awake on his bunk, staring at the ceiling, the very ceiling that Laura and he had painted just weeks ago. And now here he was alone. He couldn't help but think about how crazy it was that in such a short time he'd fallen head over heels in love with her enough that she could hurt him this badly.

Why didn't she fight him off? That's what he wanted to know. Why didn't she fight harder? Why did she give up on him so easily? Why did she allow Edward so close to her? Especially when she knew how he'd hurt Mark in the past. She knew his history and yet, she still did this.

That's what really hurt. He'd finally opened himself up to someone after over a year of heartbreak and grief, and this is how he was repaid. Maybe being vulnerable in the first place had been a mistake. Why had he seen fit to trust a perfect stranger?

Because she was kind and loving and she cared.

At least, that's what he'd thought. Now, he wasn't so sure. He knew when a woman tried to hide something, and Laura was hiding something all right. Her affection for Edward.

He was going to focus on his plan. Get on his boat, sail around the world. None of that had changed. Yet the idea of doing it without Laura made him feel hollow inside. This wasn't grief—it was something even more devastating. His heart was broken.

The irony was he didn't think after Elle and Timothy that his heart could ever be broken again. Yet here he was, feeling like his heart had been ripped out of his chest.

In his mind, he just kept coming back to the guilty look on Laura's face. He could read her like a book, and she had been lying to him.

That was the part that he couldn't stand.

How much of it had been a lie? He could run himself in circles wondering. He'd never know. He knew he wouldn't be able to sleep tonight, but tomorrow, he had a change of clothes on the boat, and he'd figure out something. Maybe he'd hide out for a day or two and then go back to get stuff from his condo? Maybe Laura would come here and they'd talk.

As soon as the thought popped into his head he crushed it. Why would she come here? He'd been awful to her, and she didn't love him anyway. No one who really loved him could've been hanging on to his brother like that, letting him hold her hands. And…Edward. Mark had been the fool to ever trust him. Why had he let Laura talk him into letting Edward back into his life? He knew better.

Tomorrow, he'd get the things he needed from his condo and set sail.

LAURA CRIED INTO Mark's pillow that night, not sure why the tears wouldn't stop. She ought to be angry with Mark, angry for him thinking so little of her, for him throwing a fit when he should've been understanding.

You could fix this in a single sentence. Just tell him what you and Edward were really talking about. Then he'd know.

Maybe she should. She'd been putting this off for too long, and for what? So Mark could make up stories about why she was whispering to his brother? Then again, did Mark deserve to know? He'd acted so irrationally, and he'd assumed the worst of her when she'd done nothing but help him since she first arrived on the island.

Laura sat up in bed and swiped the tears from her eyes. When was she ever going to find someone as loyal to her as she was to them?

She half expected Mark to come home sometime, but the later the hour got, the more she realized he wasn't coming in. Where was he?

It was nearly two in the morning now, and he wasn't answering his texts, which was even more infuriating, and she'd called twice, but her call had gone straight to voice mail.

Even if I wanted to tell him I was pregnant, how could I if he's not answering his phone? Text message? Hi, honey, I'm not cheating. I'm pregnant. And that makes you an asshole.

She was almost tempted. She should. It would serve him right.

Laura sniffed and then sat up in bed. She needed another trip to the bathroom. Was pregnancy bladder starting already? She hurried to the bathroom. It was only when she pulled down her pajama bottoms that she saw it.

Blood.

No. God, no. It was happening. Right here.

Suddenly, she was sucked back into her last pregnancy. She'd had spotting at first. The doctor said it could be normal—as long as it stopped and no cramps began. But it didn't stop, and then the cramps started, and then the blood just came and came. Eventually, she had to go to the hospital.

Laura remembered that horrible day like it happened yesterday. The cramps were intense, and when she went to the hospital, doctors diagnosed her with a rare condition, which led to trouble stopping the bleeding. She had immediate surgery, but she nearly lost her ability to have children at all.

She remembered the shock of it all—the doctor telling her she needed surgery, the definite loss of her baby and her hope. The orderlies rolling her down the hospital with the glaring flourescent lights sweeping by as she stared up at them wondering whether she was going to live or die.

Then she woke up to her sister by her bedside, her sister, full of so many questions. *When were you going to tell me you were pregnant? I didn't even know you were dating anyone. Laura, what's going on?*

And then, on the worst day of her life, she had to admit to her sister everything: the affair, the accidental pregnancy, the miscarriage.

That same day, the surgeon informed her she might never be able to bear children again. That she probably had less than a 50 percent chance.

Laura laughed to herself. Less than 50 percent, and here she was, carrying Mark's baby. At least, she hoped she was.

Dear Lord, please look after this baby.

Yet, as she glanced at the quarter-sized drop of blood, she felt dizzy.

She felt like hyperventilating. Then she remembered—the fall on the boat. It had to be the fall. She was losing the baby. All her worst fears were coming true. She felt the bitter truth of that hit her like a rock slide. *I'm never going to be a mother. I'm never going to hold my baby in my arms.*

She swiped a tear from her cheek. Laura still had the on-call number for her ob-gyn. She glanced at her watch and realized with the time change, it wouldn't be that late there. She dialed Dr. Pamela Goodwin's answering service quickly, wondering if her or her partner would be "on call" for off hours. In just twenty minutes, her doctor had called her back.

"Laura? What's wrong?"

In a blubber of tears, Laura explained about the spotting. She could barely get the words out.

"Okay, deep breaths," Dr. Goodwin said on the line. "Do you have any cramping?"

"No," Laura admitted, inwardly trying to feel out what was happening in her body. No cramps, no tightness, nothing. In fact, she wouldn't have even known about the blood if she hadn't needed to use the bathroom.

"Okay, that's good. It might be nothing." Her doctor sounded hopeful.

"Or it might be something." Laura's mind instantly went to all the worst-case scenarios. She was doomed. Her pregnancy was over. The surgeon had been right to warn her she might never have a baby.

"I know this seems bad," Dr. Goodwin said. "I can't do anything for you while you're in St. Anthony's. Is there a doctor you can see there? Someone at the emergency room?"

Laura remembered Elle's ob-gyn. "Maybe."

"Why don't you see if you can get in? Just given your history, we don't want to take any chances."

Laura remembered being rushed into surgery.

"No, we don't." She hung up and called a cab. She hesitated, wondering if she ought to call Mark as well. This was not the way she wanted to tell him the news. She called his phone and got voice mail instantly. His battery was dead or his phone was turned off. Either way, she wasn't getting through.

Annoyance burned in her. He was off nursing hurt feelings while she had to deal with this. It hardly seemed fair. *Just one more reason I've got to go it alone*, she thought.

SHE SAT IN the small island emergency room, and since there was only her and a tourist who cut his foot on a shell at the beach that day, she got in to see a doctor fairly quickly. The doctor, a young woman with dark hair, placed a heart rate Doppler device on her belly and the room filled with the sound of the baby's heart.

"Your baby's alive," the doctor declared, and Laura felt a huge relief.

"Oh, thank God," she murmured, sending up another prayer. She felt like crying. Her baby was alive—for now.

"But, did you know about your cervix? It's—"

"Incompetent," she said. "I know." One of many ways her body had failed her during the last pregnancy.

The doctor read her chart and frowned. "And given the fact that the placenta detached during the last pregnancy, I'd say you're better off heading home to the States for further treatment."

"Do you think my baby can survive?" she asked, feeling hope brim in her chest. *Say yes. Please, say yes.*

The woman glanced at her, brow furrowed. "I really don't know. There's a chance, of course, but this isn't my specialty. I think you're probably better off back in San Francisco, where they have equipment they can use to monitor you. You need a specialist's care. Here on the island—" she glanced around the simple exam room and shrugged "—we're limited with what we can do."

In the cab ride on the way back to the condo, Laura pulled up the airline website on her smartphone and managed to get tickets booked on the first morning flight off the island. She had an hour to go home, pack and get to the airport. She tried Mark's cell one last time, but got voice mail again.

With the chances high she might miscarry, she wasn't going to tell him about the baby. And given his behavior in the last twenty-four hours, she wasn't sure he really was the man for her. He'd given up on her so easily, assumed the worst of her without letting her explain. She was angry and hurt, but now she needed to focus all her energy on the baby inside her.

She texted him a quick message.

Going back to San Francisco. It's for the best.

There. She'd said it. She'd given him an out, too, though part of her hoped he'd call her bluff. *This is what you get for falling in love with unavailable men.*

Laura waited, watching her phone for any sign of a response. She got none. She put away her phone. No sense in waiting for Mark. Since the hour was so early, she sent a message to Edward.

Have to fly home. See a doctor.

To her surprise, he texted her back.

Everything okay?

She typed:

What are you doing awake?

I've got a newborn! Not much sleeping happening here.

She laughed a little, then she felt a pang of sadness. What if she never knew what that sleeplessness was like?

Edward texted:

You okay?

No. Might miscarry. But I have to go to see my doctor in San Francisco.

Anything I can do?

She wished he could help. She wanted to ask him to knock some sense into his brother. Or maybe just get him to turn on his blasted phone. Then again, why tell Mark? On the very off chance he would've been excited about the possibility of a baby, why tell him he never had a shot at having one? It just seemed cruel.

Besides, Laura thought, he'd made his feelings pretty clear about her. He didn't trust her. Thought she was a cheater just because she talked to Edward. If he thought so little of her, why would she want to be with him?

Because you love him, a tiny voice in her head said.

She shook it off. She had to focus. Laura glanced at the phone in front of her. She needed to answer Edward, and there was something he could do for her, she realized.

Just please don't say anything about this to Mark. If I miscarry, there's no need for him to ever know about this.

And that was the truth of it. If she miscarried, she'd never tell Mark. She'd simply fly out of his life forever.

Laura doubted he'd come looking for her. He'd abandoned her at the first sign of trouble, so she knew he wasn't in it for the long haul. She wanted someone who was in the fight with her, every day, who wouldn't run out on her.

And if Mark couldn't be that person, then she'd just find a way to do it alone.

In the meantime, Laura had to get back home, where the doctors could save her baby.

She sent up a silent prayer that she could make it in time. *Please, God. Let this time be different*. Laura covered her still-a flat belly with the palm of her hand. "Hold on, little one," she murmured to her belly. "Hold on."

CHAPTER TWENTY-SEVEN

MARK ARRIVED AT the condo the next morning around noon. He paused at his own front door. What was he going to say to her? He slid his key in the lock and swung open the front door.

"Laura?" he called, but no one answered.

Odd. Where was she?

Granted, it was almost noon. She could be anywhere. Grabbing a sandwich, even, though he hated to imagine her casually eating lunch when he'd spent the whole evening tossing and turning. It was one of the reasons he'd arrived so late. He'd lain awake most of the night, falling asleep only close to dawn.

As he'd tossed and turned, he realized he'd flown off the handle. He knew he'd been in the wrong, but he'd needed some time to calm down and see reason. He'd never given Laura a chance to explain, and he owed her that much.

He also realized that the hurt on her face, the look of surprise, had been real. If there was flirting happening, it was all on his brother's side. The more he thought about it, the truer that seemed. He owed Laura an apology. He hoped she would understand. Mark had thought he'd worked through all the feelings he had about Elle and Edward, but clearly he hadn't. And he'd taken that out on Laura.

She didn't deserve that.

Sunlight blazed on a gorgeous clear ocean outside, if he could be bothered to look, which he couldn't. He had too much on his mind.

He glanced at the bed and noticed it had been slept in. So she had stayed here overnight. Mark poked around the kitchen and found a single coffee mug in the sink. He walked into the bedroom to get his phone charger, when he realized that something was missing. Laura's suitcase. It had been tucked into the corner of the room since she'd moved into his place, and now he could see it was gone.

Mark pushed open the sliding closet door. Her clothes were gone, too. He checked the drawer she'd used. Empty. He ran to the bathroom, even though he knew it would be no different there. Her toiletries were all gone. Her hairdryer packed away.

She'd left him.

He spun around the room, feeling blindsided. She'd *left* him? They'd had one fight. *One*, and she'd packed up? Cut and run? She cared about him so little that she hadn't bothered to stick around and hash it out with him. He thought he knew her, but clearly he didn't if this sent her packing.

Then again, you were a jerk, he thought. *More than that. An asshole.* Maybe he would've run, too. Maybe what he'd done was unforgiveable.

He realized he had no idea where she might have gone. To a hotel? To Edward's house? He cringed at the thought.

Mark's mind spun. He plugged in his phone and sat anxiously while it rebooted.

Maybe she'd left some clue about where she'd gone. He swallowed anxiously, waiting for his phone to come back to life. Hell, she might even be off the island by now. Would she go so far as to get on a plane? Maybe.

Finally, he saw several missed messages and calls. He saw Laura's last text. Going back to San Francisco. It's for the best.

Mark read and reread the text a million times. That was it, then. She was done with him. Could he blame her? He was a wreck. Grieving over his lost son and then triggered by his wife's past infidelity, he probably didn't come off as the most mentally sound guy.

Then again, maybe Laura had never really loved him. *She could've just been using me*, he thought bitterly. Maybe she did sleep with Edward. She'd needed a fling, a rebound, and he—or Edward—had fit the bill. The thought made his stomach turn. He thought they'd been so much more.

Mark called her, but her phone went straight to voice mail. Now she was avoiding his calls. Maybe she'd even blocked him. *It's for the best*, she'd said.

Well, he thought, she'd made her feelings known. He should fight for her, but wasn't she a grown-up? She'd expressed her wishes, and now it was his job to respect them. Isn't that what a gentleman did?

Mark ran his hands through his hair, his brain still feeling foggy from lack of sleep and from the emotional trauma of the last couple of days. He didn't want to believe Laura would give up on them so easily, but the proof was right here on his phone.

He suddenly couldn't get enough air into his lungs. The condo felt tight, oppressive. He walked out on his patio and studied the waves rolling in on the beach, the steady flow of water up on the sand.

Mark didn't know what to do, but all he knew was he needed to get away. Clear his head. Maybe if he gave her some time to calm down, she'd be willing to talk to him once more. Maybe if he got out to sea, where he could think clearly, where he could *breathe*, then he could figure this all out.

Or maybe, a small voice in his head said, *maybe the ocean would decide this all for you.* The dark thought, the one he'd thought of less and less since before Laura came into his life and turned it upside down, resurfaced. One thing he knew for sure. He couldn't stay in his condo. Not now, maybe not ever.

Every single square inch of the place reminded him of her, of the amazing sex they'd had, of the laughs they'd shared, even the meals they'd eaten together. Her ghost walked through the condo and there was only one way to get away from her—the sea.

He went to his closet and pulled out an empty duffel bag and began stuffing it with clothes he'd need for at least a week. He didn't know how long he'd be on that boat, but he figured at least that long. Maybe longer. Hell, maybe all the way around the world. All he knew was that he needed to get away, needed to clear his head, needed to figure out what he was going to do next.

He grabbed his phone and charger off the kitchen counter and tucked it in his bag. He couldn't stay here a minute longer.

He knew he probably couldn't outrun the heartbreak, but he was going to try.

CHAPTER TWENTY-EIGHT

Five months later

"STOP FUSSING OVER ME," Laura declared as she lay in Maddie's queen-size bed in her home in the suburbs of San Francisco. Maddie carried a tray featuring lunch—a grilled cheese sandwich, fresh fruit, a yogurt smoothie and a glass of water. Laura pushed herself upright, moving a pillow behind her head so she'd be propped up.

"This is what *bed rest* means, Laura," Maddie declared as she set the tray on the table she'd put near the bed. "Doctor's orders, remember? You're to stay in bed if you want to take care of that baby inside you."

The baby gave Laura a big kick then as if agreeing with her aunt.

Laura had decided to find out the baby's gender. She thought it might help her focus on keeping her baby *inside* her. "No peeking early," she'd said on more than one occasion to her belly.

Maddie had met her at the airport when she'd flown home and then taken her to the specialists. When it was clear that bed rest would be the only hope to carry the pregnancy to term, Maddie had offered her spare bedroom. Laura had never been more grateful. And Maddie had kept the running editorial largely silent. Laura didn't feel judged.

For the first time with her sister, she felt supported, nurtured. She didn't have a doubt that they both wanted the same thing: the birth of a healthy baby.

The doctors were hopeful that she might be able to carry to term, but that meant complete bed rest and no stress. The no-stress part was the hardest. She'd not heard from Mark except for a couple of calls where he'd hung up and had not left a message. She'd heard from Edward that he'd sailed off to another race, and that cell reception was nonexistent on the boat, but still…his radio silence irked.

She forced herself not to think about it, and yet, every time something happened with the baby—her first kick, her first sonogram picture—she wanted to share it with Mark, but then realized she couldn't.

Laura glanced at the small black-and-white ultrasound photo taped to the bedpost and wondered what Mark would've thought of all this.

Wondered if he'd be excited or angry, picking out baby names or running for the hills. Her money was on running, since that's what he'd ultimately decided to do.

"Did you hear me?" Maddie asked, quietly.

"Sorry...what? I zoned out." Her mind just ran in circles these days like a frozen computer.

Maddie just shook her head knowingly. "I asked if you wanted some extra napkins, but I see you're a million miles away. Everything okay?"

No, everything wasn't okay. She was trapped in bed, desperately holding on to a fragile baby in her belly, and had no idea what she'd do after the baby was born.

"I don't know. I guess."

"You could still tell him," Maddie suggested. "Mark doesn't even know he's going to be a father. He might be here."

"He made his choice," Laura snapped, feeling that old sense of betrayal. "I don't want the baby to change that. He should be here for *me*. I should be enough." Laura sighed. "But nobody thinks I'm enough."

Maddie sat on the side of the bed, near Laura's knees. "You know that's not true. I think you're more than enough sister. I don't think I could handle *more* sister."

Laura laughed ruefully. "You don't count."

"I don't?" Maddie feigned outrage. "I'm taking back this grilled cheese then."

"No!" Laura grabbed a sandwich half and took a big bite. "I'm starving," she mumbled, mouth full.

"I thought so." Maddie chuckled. Then she studied her sister. "You know, you keep talking about how you think you're not good enough for Mark. That that's why you're afraid to tell him. But deep down, I don't think that's why you're so determined to keep this pregnancy a secret."

"I'm determined because what if I lose the baby? Maddie, what's the point of telling him if there's no baby? The doctors said I'm not out of the woods yet." She ate two more bites of sandwich.

"Nope. I don't think it's that, either. I think you're not sure he's going to be a good father." Maddie stared at Laura. "I think this is about you being worried that maybe he's not ready, maybe he's not fit to be a dad or maybe he's just so wrapped up in his son's death that he can't focus on what it means to be a father now."

Laura stopped chewing. Was her sister right? Maybe. She was worried about Mark's commitment—to her and to a baby. She realized her decision not to tell Mark went deeper than she realized. But the bigger the baby grew inside her, the more she began to doubt her original decision.

"Mark has only called a handful of times," Laura pointed out. "And he hasn't even left a message."

"He's at sea, like you said, with no cell phone reception."

"Yes, but why did he leave so quickly? He was sure quick to head out without me. This is what he wanted—living his dream, sailing around the world. It turns out that I wasn't really a part of his future." The sadness of this fact weighed heavily on Laura's shoulders. That was the true heartbreak of it all. Mark had rebounded so easily, and she hadn't.

"You're the one who told him breaking up was for the best."

"He was supposed to fight for me, fight for us," Laura pointed out.

"How's he supposed to know that?" Maddie asked.

"He just is." Laura sighed. He'd just let her go so easily. It was hard to get over, no matter how she tried.

"Maybe you need to ask yourself if you're keeping this from him because you don't think he loves you or because he hasn't proven himself worthy of being the father to your baby."

"He's worthy," Laura said, feeling sure he'd make a wonderful dad. He was patient, loyal and loving. But what about his depression? The fact that he was unnaturally obsessed with death, with meeting Timothy somewhere? A man who was ready to try to drown himself wasn't father material. Those thoughts plagued her.

And as she thought about him being out to sea, she worried that he might not come back.

"You need your rest, and *no stress* remember? Let's try not to think about him," Maddie said. "What will be will be. How about a brownie? Fresh from the oven." Maddie bustled out of the room and returned with a plateful of moist, chocolaty goodness.

"But the caffeine," Laura worried.

"Is barely anything," Maddie said. "Come on, you need this."

Laura did. She was so grateful for her sister in that moment. "You know, I hope I'm half the mom you are. Mom would be so proud of you, Maddie."

Maddie surprised her by getting choked up, her eyes moist with tears. "Thanks, sis." She leaned over and gave Laura a hug. "Now eat that brownie. My orders. It'll make you feel better."

"Yes, ma'am."

MARK STEADIED THE jib on the *Timothy* as he circled into port at Bora Bora. The sail had been long from Hawaii, and a small storm had blown him a little off course, but he'd arrived just a little worse for wear. He'd come for the annual big sailboat race. His boat wouldn't be sailing, but it was one of the biggest sailing events in the Pacific, and anybody who was anybody would be there.

As he docked at a small port, he glanced at the beautiful bay view, and wished that Laura was here with him to see this. It was ironic. The farther he sailed away from her, the more he thought about her. He couldn't shake her, no matter how hard he tried. He'd called, yes, but found he didn't know what to say. Couldn't leave a message and sometimes just called to hear her voice on the recorded message.

He was a mess. He'd thought getting away from everyone and being alone on the sea would help him clear his mind, but instead, all he did was think about Laura—about her bright green eyes, her deep laugh, the way she wrinkled her nose when she concentrated. He missed her gentle touch; he missed the way she rocked her head back and closed her eyes when she came. He missed…everything about her.

He should've thought about her less, but each day, he thought about her more. It had become almost more than he could bear, and yet he was thousands of miles away from San Francisco, moving farther away every day. *So much for out of sight, out of mind*, he thought.

The more he thought about it, the more he couldn't figure out why she'd left so abruptly, why she'd given up. The only answer he could think of was that she'd never loved him in the same way he'd loved her. That was the only explanation.

Mark pulled into a visitor's slot so he could go seek arrangements for renting a slip to keep his boat harbored here.

He grabbed his boat's paperwork and headed to the marina office, where he ran smack-dab into Edward, talking to the clerk.

"What are you doing here?" Mark asked, surprised.

"Looking for you," Edward said. "I took the red-eye flight out, counting on you being here for the race."

"But what about Elle? The baby?"

Edward shook his head. "If you turned on your phone once in a while or answered your radio, I wouldn't have had to leave them."

"I don't understand."

"You will. Let's get a drink. What I need to tell you needs to be told over tequila or, at minimum, beer."

Mark sat across from his brother in the small sailor's bar, waiting expectantly for the big news. Would his brother be telling him that he was leaving Elle for Laura? He surely didn't need to sail halfway around the world to deliver that horrible news. Mark was just fine never knowing that.

"Okay, Laura swore me to secrecy, and I let her have that secrecy for a while, because… well, it's her news to tell."

Mark felt a prickling in his stomach. Nerves? What was he going to say? *Please don't say Laura has cancer.*

"Is Laura okay?"

"She's fine. She's healthy. Laura's pregnant. With your baby."

Suddenly, the rest of the bar and the entire world disappeared. The edges of his vision grew fuzzy. Laura was pregnant? "That can't be."

"It can be, and it is." Edward took a swig of beer.

"But she left me…she said…" Mark's brain felt like mush. It just wasn't working.

"She left you because you were being a tool and told her that there's no way you ever wanted to be a father because it would trash your memories of Timothy," Edward said. "That day at the hospital when you got all bent out of shape, we were talking about her pregnancy. I guessed she was pregnant. She showed all the signs."

Mark felt a punch to the gut. It was true. The nausea. Fainting. Why hadn't he seen it before?

He was going to be a father? The thought wasn't as scary as he'd assumed. He'd always thought he only had room in his heart for Timothy, but maybe he was wrong about that.

Edward was still talking. "And then when you ran off on your boat, she thought you weren't in this thing and that you didn't love her."

"She told me she was done with me."

"And you didn't bother to fight that? Tell her she was wrong? You know women test you. They do it all the time."

Mark never did understand women. Then he remembered the first time Laura was pregnant, the pregnancy had nearly killed her.

"But how is she? Her health—"

"She's on bed rest. It's not going to be an easy pregnancy, and it will definitely not be an easy delivery."

Mark did some quick math. "She's going to be due soon."

"Which is why I had to fly all the way out here after your ungrateful ass," he said, shaking his head and taking a swig. "And believe me, Elle is not happy about me leaving her with that baby all alone. But I couldn't very well let you go on thinking what you were thinking about Laura. Besides, given what she's told me about the pregnancy, she's going to need you there for the delivery."

Mark would leave that very day. He'd have to find someone to take care of the *Timothy*, so he could catch a flight back to the States. He'd retrieve the boat later. He only hoped he wasn't too late.

CHAPTER TWENTY-NINE

LAURA WAS LYING in her sister's guest bed, flipping through job listings on her laptop and wondering who on earth would hire a new mother when she heard a gentle knock on the door.

Maddie poked her head in.

"Someone's here to see you," she said, looking almost excited.

"Who?" Laura asked, confused. None of her friends knew she was back in San Francisco. As far as they all knew, she was still hiding out in the Caribbean. "I'm not dressed." She pulled up her blankets over the pajamas she wore, her normal daily uniform since she'd been on bed rest. Besides, none of her clothes fit her anymore. Her belly was huge.

"I don't think he'll care."

"Laura?" Mark's voice came from over Maddie's shoulder. Her sister swung the door wide, and there stood Mark, baseball cap in his hands and a newly grown beard on his face. "Can I come in?"

Laura felt a rush of emotions—shock, joy,

suspicion. And, of course, panic. There was no keeping the truth from him now. Her stomach was enormous.

"Mark! What are you doing here?"

"I'm here to see you."

He stood uncertainly at the door as Maddie waited, clearly trying to decide whether it was okay if she left the two alone. Laura felt a sharp pang. Mark looked so good. Tanned and wind beaten, but good. All she wanted to do was feel his strong arms around her once more.

"Laura." Mark's eyes filled with tears, and in that second, she was completely undone. She held out her arms to him and he went to them, hugging her tightly.

"I missed you," he murmured into her hair.

"I missed you, too," she admitted, the tears stinging her eyes. He pulled away, sniffling. "How did you know?" she asked him, already suspecting how.

"Edward tracked me down."

"I asked him to keep it secret." Laura distantly felt angry about the betrayal, but at the moment she couldn't focus on that.

"He did for a while, but then he couldn't anymore, and I'm glad he didn't." Mark glanced at her stomach in awe. "Why didn't you tell me? About…this." He put his hand gently on her giant stomach. Even his big hand couldn't quite cover the top. The baby had grown too big. "I would never have sailed off if I'd known."

"I know. But…you said you didn't want children. You didn't want to dishonor Timothy's memory. And then it seemed like you couldn't trust me, either, that maybe you didn't love me like I loved you. And then…you didn't call me."

"You broke up with me. How was I supposed to act? I thought I was respecting your wishes." Mark shook his head. "But believe me, you have to know that I've thought about you every day since you left. I haven't stopped thinking about you. Laura, I love you. So very much. My life without you…it's not what I want. Let's make this work. I love you. I want to spend the rest of my life showing you how much."

Laura felt her heart fill up with love. He loved her, and she believed him. But they had more problems.

"But what about Timothy? What about his memory…you said—"

"I was wrong," Mark interrupted. "I thought I only had room in my heart to love Timothy, but then you came and showed me that I could love him *and* love you." Mark paused, as he put his hand on her leg, his voice choking with emotion. "And now I realize I can love this baby inside you just as much and not love Timothy any less."

Her heart filled with joy. Could this be true? "You want to be a father?"

"I want to be the father of *your* baby. More than anything else in the world. I sailed half-way around the world—without shaving—just to come and tell you that."

Laura chuckled a little. "You do need a shave," she said and ran her hands down his thick, dark beard.

"I know." He grinned.

"But…what about what you said…about me and Edward—"

"I realize how wrong I was. I can't say sorry enough for that. I jumped to conclusions, and the very next day realized I'd been stupid, but then I came back to the condo and you were already gone."

"I nearly miscarried," she said. "It's why I had to leave."

"I know that now. You should've told me, Laura. I wanted to be there for you. No matter what." He grabbed her hand and squeezed it and then kissed the ends of her fingertips. "When I think of all you've gone through—alone—I just feel so sick. I should've been here, looking after you. Making you meals, making sure you were comfortable. I should've been here."

Laura felt joy and guilt all at once. Had she robbed him of the opportunity to care for her?

She'd just never imagined…that he would. She realized in that moment she'd made the same assumptions about him as he'd made about her. She'd assumed he was just like Dean. That he'd run at the first real test. Mark had assumed she'd also fail the first real test of their relationship. In that way, they'd both been blinded by their past experiences.

"I'm sorry. I should have told you. I was just afraid you'd leave." Like Dean.

Mark gripped her hand a little harder. "I'll never leave you," he said. "I promise."

"But you wanted to sail around the world… and there's no way we can do that with a baby."

"No. But what I wanted was to be with you. I don't care if it's on a sailboat or in the suburbs. Laura, I love you." Mark shrugged. "We can sail around the world when our daughter is in college."

"That's a long way away."

He flashed a grin. "I'm a patient man."

"Mark…" It all seemed so overwhelming. He was here, declaring his love. "But how can I know that you're not just here for the baby?"

"Laura, it's you I want. It's always been you. And I'll prove it." Mark rummaged around in his pocket and pulled out a small black velvet box. He got down on one knee at the side of her bed.

Laura felt shock and, more than that, a happiness bubble up inside her. Could this be real?

"Laura, I promise never to doubt your loyalty again. I promise to love and honor you, if you just give me a chance. Would you make me just about the happiest man alive and be my wife?"

Tears streamed down Laura's face and her heart filled with unimaginable joy. "Yes," she cried. Absolutely yes.

Several weeks later

LAURA WOKE IN the middle of the night and instantly knew something was wrong. A sharp pain traveled around the small of her back, squeezing all the muscles of her large belly. She tried to go back to sleep, thinking it might be another Braxton Hicks contraction. But when she was roused a half hour later by another, she knew these contractions weren't fake. Unfortunately she was still three weeks from her due date.

"What's wrong?" Mark was by her side. He'd also moved into Maddie's house temporarily until the pregnancy was over. Maddie had insisted, fearing that moving Laura might prove dangerous. Mark had been scouting out jobs and places to live, but he thought he had at least three more weeks before he really had to have a nursery ready. He realized he was wrong about that.

"I feel a contraction," she said.

"It's too early." Mark frowned, worried.

"I know." Laura grabbed his hand, feeling nerves shoot up and down her spine.

Mark called her doctor's on-call service and in a few minutes received a call back. He told her all the symptoms. Calmly, but deliberately, her doctor let them know it was serious.

"Stay calm, but I'd like to see you in the ER. Just to make sure everything's okay."

Inside, Laura knew everything was definitely not okay. *I've made it this far, but what if I can't make it across the finish line?* It had been such a joy to feel the baby inside her these last few months. The baby kicked hard against her spleen and Laura welcomed the poke. *Hang on, little one. Hang on.*

Mark drove her to the hospital in the dead of night as Laura squeezed her hand.

"It's going to be okay," Mark said.

"How do you know?"

"I don't," Mark said, anxious. "But I can't think about the alternative."

Neither could Laura. She glanced at the diamond engagement ring on her finger and felt a swell of love. Surely their story would end well. Surely God wouldn't see fit to take another baby from her, and yet she felt anxious all the same. What if she lost this baby? Would her relationship with Mark survive?

"Mark…if somehow we lose this baby…" She clutched his free hand.

"We won't," he declared.

"But if we do—"

"Then I'll be here for you. You understand? Then we'll sail around the world together and figure it out."

Laura sent Mark a weak smile. "That's one hell of a plan B."

"I know. Let's hope we never have to use it. This time next week, I want to be elbow deep in dirty diapers."

Laura couldn't help but laugh. "That's so romantic."

"Actually, it is." He grinned. "Hallmark should make a Valentine's card with just that on it."

Laura laughed more. Then another contraction hit and the laugh turned into a grimace.

"Hang on," Mark said, face serious. "I'm driving as fast as I can." He clutched her hand and squeezed. She hoped everything would be all right. But secretly, she worried that something was very, very wrong.

THEY'D GOTTEN TO the ER hours ago, and Laura was hooked up to monitors with doctors rushing in and out of her room, talking amongst themselves. Mark didn't like the baby's heart rate, which seemed slower than it ought to be. He'd remembered that much from Elle's delivery of Timothy. He'd kept his eyes on that monitor above all others, and he'd noticed in the last hour that the baby's heart rate had slowed. He didn't like that. Not one bit.

Laura was already fatigued by the labor pains, and she clearly looked worried. She was three weeks premature, and Mark worried about what that might mean for the baby.

The doctors had been trying to see if they could stop the labor, but everything they tried failed. All the while, the baby seemed to be more and more affected.

"I'm worried," Laura said and reached for Mark's hand.

That's when the doctors came in and told them she needed a C-section. There was no more trying to stop the labor, and the baby was starting to be in distress.

"Are you all right with this?" Mark asked her.

She nodded. "Whatever it takes," she said.

That's when the medical staff got her ready and then wheeled her away to the operating room. Mark was outfitted with scrubs, all the while his heart hammering. *Let her be okay.*

Let the baby be okay, but more than anything, let Laura be okay.

He couldn't imagine his life without her, and he was kicking himself for ever leaving her side. He should've been there for every prenatal doctor's appointment, for every day she was assigned to bed rest. He wanted to spend the rest of their lives making it up to her. Mark was never going to leave her side again.

"Mark," Laura called as the sheeting was put up and the doctors readied themselves.

"I'm here, baby," he called, holding her hand. She looked at him, relieved, as she squeezed his fingers. All too quickly, the doctors went to work, and soon enough, they had the baby, but she wasn't breathing and she looked pale.

"Is she okay? I don't hear crying," she said, worry fraying her voice. Mark frowned, watching the medical professionals work.

"She's in good hands," he said, hoping that was true as he watched the doctor clear the baby's airway. After what seemed like an eternity but was probably only a few seconds, the baby wailed.

"There she is," Mark said, feeling a rush of relief. He glanced at Laura and saw tears stream down her cheeks. The doctor brought her by so Mark and Laura could see the baby, wrapped up in a blanket and crying for all she was worth.

"Hey, little one," Mark said.

"We're so glad to meet you," Laura said and sniffed back tears. "I'm so very glad you hung on."

"Now we're the perfect family," Mark said and leaned down to kiss Laura and then the baby. He'd never felt so happy in well…ever. This was exactly where he needed to be, here by Laura's side, starting this beautiful family with her. He raced forward in his mind to their wedding, the milestones with the baby, maybe even a younger sibling for this beautiful little girl. He stroked Laura's cheek.

"Thank you," he said. "For making me the happiest man on earth. For saving me and giving me a second chance."

"Thank you," she replied. "For saving me right back." He grinned at her and then glanced down at the amazing bundle of joy in his arms. He couldn't wait to get to know this little person and watch her grow, with Laura by his side.

He almost felt as though Timothy, wherever he was, was looking down at them, happy to see his little sister.

EPILOGUE

Three months later

MOVING BOXES LAY strewn around their new house, half unpacked since neither Laura nor Mark had time to properly settle in their new house. Mark was still looking for work, but the race prize money meant he wasn't in as big a hurry to find a job. Plus, their options were wide open. They could move back to the Caribbean; they could settle here. They were leasing their house month-to-month while they decided the future. Laura, for her part, had never been happier.

The baby cried, letting her know she was not in the mood for the nap Laura had planned for her. Laura made her way to the crib and picked up the adorable bundle of joy in the pink onesie.

"Tiffany, what is it?" she cooed in the baby's ear. She felt the heavy weight of sleepless exhaustion, but she'd never been so glad to be so tired. She'd never thought she would ever get to be a mom, and every day felt like a day worth celebrating, even when she was at her most un-showered and exhausted.

"Is she hungry?" Mark popped his head in the nursery, not one minute behind her. His eyes were lined with dark circles, too. He'd gotten as little sleep as she had, insisting on doing the heavy lifting while she recovered from her C-section. He'd been on strict night duty the first six weeks as she recovered from surgery. She smiled at him.

"Maybe." Tiffany's cries softened as Laura cradled the baby against her shoulder. She was just the most perfect little baby, and Laura's heart felt like it would burst every time she glanced at the little girl. "Or maybe she just wanted a snuggle."

"That's exactly what Daddy wants," Mark said and grinned as he moved behind Laura and wrapped his arms around her. "Have I told you today how much I love you?"

"No," she said.

"Daddy's falling down on the job already," Mark told the baby as he gave her tiny nose a playful tap. "I love you. You've changed my life for the better every day."

"You've changed my life," Laura said. "Look at this beautiful baby. I just…never thought this would happen for me. After the miscarriage, I just really never thought this would happen."

Mark laughed ruefully. "You and me both. It's all just…such a miracle." Mark traced Tiffany's cheek with his finger. "Can you believe she's so perfect?"

"Nope. Can't believe it," Laura said and grinned.

"Well, I can. Her mother's absolutely perfect. That's why." Mark hugged Laura again and lay a soft kiss on her cheek.

Tiffany grew quiet in Laura's arms and pretty soon she could feel the deadweight of the baby asleep against her. Softly, she laid the baby in the crib, being extra careful not to rouse her. Amazingly, Tiffany stayed asleep, her tiny little mouth an open *o*.

"She's got your beautiful eyelashes," Mark said.

"And your chin," Laura pointed out.

Mark sneaked his arm around Laura's waist, and then he kissed her neck. "Mmm. You smell like baby powder."

"Sexy, isn't it?" Laura joked as Mark pulled her out of the baby's room and softly shut the door.

"You have no idea," he murmured. "How about I show you how sexy in the bedroom?"

"But the baby…" Laura frowned, worried.

"Is asleep," Mark pointed out, and then he pulled Laura into his arms and kissed her deeply. His tongue probed hers, and she felt white-hot heat rush through her body.

She didn't know if she'd ever get tired of kissing Mark. They fit together in a way she'd never imagined possible. He deepened the kiss, setting off fireworks in her brain. Suddenly, she forgot all about the baby. In that moment, Laura would do anything he asked. Anything.

"Maybe we can get working on baby number two."

"Mark!" Laura cried, pulling away from him. Everything but that. "You can't be serious. I just had one!"

"All I know is we make the most beautiful babies." He grinned and then pulled her close, dancing her to the bedroom. "Why not make some more? How about four...or five?"

Now, Laura had to laugh. "No way. I don't think I could take it."

"Okay, then. Just three. Three more." He tugged off her shirt and she giggled as it popped over her head.

"You're ridiculous." He kissed her neck and then laid a trail of kisses down to her nursing bra.

"Am I?" he asked as she lifted up his shirt, and she ran her hands down his fit, tanned chest. Then again, with him shirtless in front of her, she couldn't quite manage a coherent thought. He gently laid her down on the bed, kissing her belly, and her mind went blank.

"All I know is, Mrs. Tanner, I want to spend the rest of my life doing just this."

"Me, too," she breathed as the two quietly explored each other. Sleep could come later, Laura thought. All she wanted right now was Mark's touch.

"I love you," she breathed.

"I love you right back," he murmured into her ear.

* * * * *

If you loved
ISLAND OF SECOND CHANCES,
don't miss these wonderful romances
from Cara Lockwood:

SHELTER IN THE TROPICS
THE BIG BREAK
HER HAWAIIAN HOMECOMING

Available now from
Harlequin Superromance!

Get 2 Free Books,
Plus 2 Free Gifts —
just for trying the
Reader Service!

HRLP17R3

Get 2 Free Books,
Plus 2 Free Gifts —
just for trying the
Reader Service!